D0461666

ORPHAN, AGENT, PRIMA, PAWN

ALSO BY ELIZABETH KIEM

Dancer, Daughter, Traitor, Spy
Hider, Seeker, Secret Keeper

ORPHAN AGENT PRIMA PAWN

ELIZABETH KIEM

Published in the United States by Soho Teen
an imprint of
Soho Press, Inc.
853 Broadway
New York, NY 10003

Library of Congress Cataloging-in-Publication Data

Kiem, Elizabeth.
Orphan, agent, prima, pawn / Elizabeth Kiem.

ISBN 978-1-61695-655-4
eISBN 978-1-61695-656-1

1. Ballet dancing—Fiction. 2. Spies—Fiction. 3. Psychic ability—Fiction. 4. KGB—Fiction.
5. Bolshoi Ballet Company—Fiction. 6. Soviet Union—History—1953–1985—Fiction.
PZ7.K54 Or 2017 [Fic]—dc23 2016042099

Interior design by Janine Agro, Soho Press, Inc.

Printed in the United States of America

10 9 8 7 6 5 4 3 2 1

Дяде ТК. Ещё разок.

ORPHAN, AGENT, PRIMA, PAWN

CAST OF CHARACTERS:

Russians use many names. In addition to their first and last names, a "patronymic," derived from the father's name, serves as a sort of middle name. Nicknames, or diminutives, are widely used for friends and relatives. In Soviet times, Russians most often addressed each other using first name and patronymic (Elena Mikhailovna, Natalia Davydovna), or else "Comrade" followed by the surname. Below are some of the names that non-Russian speakers may find unfamiliar.

Svetlana Evgenievna Kravshina (also Sveta)—daughter of Enemies of the People, resident of Orphanage #36, ballerina.

Vera Konstantinovna Kravshina—mother of Svetlana, wife of General Evgeny Kravshin, Enemy of the People.

General Evgeny Kravshin—General under Joseph Stalin, head of Red Army brigade that took Berlin, Enemy of the People.

Marina Viktorovna Dukovskaya (also Marya)—daughter of Svetlana Dukovskaya, former dancer with the Bolshoi Ballet.

Lana Dukovskaya—daughter of Marina Dukovskaya, granddaughter of Svetlana Dukovskaya, former dancer with the Bolshoi Ballet.

Andrei Samoilovich—Sveta's teacher.

Lydia Timofeevna—Sveta's teacher.

Georgi Levshik (also Gosha)—street kid and friend of Svetlana.

Elena Mikhailovna—ballet teacher, Central House of Ballet.

Polina Sergeevna—ballet teacher, Bolshoi Academy.

Vasily Vasilievich—rector of the Bolshoi Academy.

Natalia Davydovna Gerasova—friend of Vera Kravshina, former Gulag prisoner, KGB official under Khrushchev.

Maksim Naryshkin—KGB official, head of Psychological Intelligence Unit.

Viktor Fyodorovich Dukovsky (also Vitya)—Svetlana's boyfriend.

Arkady Danilov—artistic director of the Bolshoi Ballet.

HISTORICAL:

Joseph Stalin—general secretary of the Communist Party, dictator of the Soviet Union until his death in 1953.

Boris Pasternak—twentieth-century Russian writer, author of *Doctor Zhivago*, banned in the Soviet Union and awarded the Nobel Prize for Literature.

Pyotr Ilyich Tchaikovsky—nineteenth-century Russian composer of *Swan Lake* and *The Nutcracker*.

Sergei Prokofiev—twentieth-century Russian composer of *Romeo and Juliet*, his Spanish-born wife was arrested in 1948 and sentenced to the Gulag.

Galina Ulanova—*prima ballerina assoluta* of the Bolshoi Ballet until her retirement in 1960, Hero of Socialist Labor and Artist of the People.

Nikita Sergeevich Khrushchev—successor to Joseph Stalin and leader of the Soviet Union from 1953 until 1964, forced into retirement by hardliners.

Leonid Brezhnev—successor to Nikita Khrushchev and leader of the Soviet Union from 1964 until his death in 1982.

A glossary of Russian words and phrases can be found at the back of the book.

PROLOGUE
VORKUTA 2015

In a dimly lit dressing room in a dank Siberian theater in the twilight of an Arctic summer, Lana Dukovskaya marvels at the speed with which the answer to one question can reveal so many others.

For eighteen years, she peered through a veil of secrets. Then, in the short span of a spring week, this was revealed: her inscrutable mother, her anonymous father, and the thing that came between them—the woman sitting silently before her now, a grandmother who disappeared before Lana was born.

Almost overnight, Lana had gained a family. And she inherited all its secrets.

Now it is time to unpack that inheritance. Whether by fate or coincidence, Lana's traveling dance troupe has brought her to the doorstep of Svetlana Dukovskaya—a former prima ballerina of the Bolshoi Ballet, a fallen Artist of the People. Lana feels the veil strain under her fingers, as if she might rip it in half. But she is about to learn that her family's secrets did not begin with Svetlana Dukovskaya; they are older and deeper than she had imagined.

"You have a daughter named Marina," she says, taking the

old woman's hand. She feels paper-thin skin, knuckles locked stiff, and an uncertain pulse at the wrist. She searches the heavily lined face for familiar features, calculating quickly. Her grandmother would be close to seventy years old.

"Marina is my mother," she continues. "Do you remember her, your daughter? Do you remember Marina?"

The old woman turns away. Lana watches her face drain of expression and imagines the worst—that this chance encounter has come too late. That the years of imprisonment, psychiatric treatment, and abandonment have stolen too much and that her grandmother has forgotten everything—even the stage. It is the same stage upon which Lana and her mother Marina both danced. But neither of them made the stage of the Bolshoi Theatre a throne, as Svetlana Dukovskaya had.

Until she was removed from it.

Lana probes gently: "I danced with the Bolshoi once, too. Before I joined the troupe that you saw tonight, I was in the corps of the Bolshoi Ballet."

The old woman's eyes dart around the dressing room. A portrait of the president—shrewd and reptilian, not a fan of the ballet—hangs on a water-stained wall. Next to it, a closet stands open, its door sags on a busted hinge. Underneath the closet is a dusty runner with a hammer and sickle motif. The dressing room has not known a decorative thought in thirty years.

Her grandmother's gaze lands on the mirror before them. Lana asks, "Do you remember dancing with the Bolshoi?"

"Of course I do."

Her voice is louder than Lana expected.

"I remember everything."

Svetlana Dukovskaya peers into the mirror as if searching for something beyond its reflection. She taps the glass with one finger and says, "I am nothing but memories. Memories that aren't even mine . . . I am a rememberer."

She closes her eyes, but they are not still. Lana can see them dance under age-spotted lids. She can see the memories ripple across her grandmother's brow and tremble on colorless lashes. When they open once more, Svetlana Dukovskaya's eyes are bright. She turns from the mirror and raises both hands, light and pale as lunar moths, to touch her granddaughter's cheeks.

"Dochka," she murmurs—the word that can mean daughter or, simply, a girl too young to know better. Then she corrects herself: "Granddaughter."

"Shall I tell you what I remember, granddaughter?"

ACT ONE
ORPHAN
MOSCOW, 1958–1959

ONE
POX

It was a strange coincidence, the news coming on the same day: there was smallpox in Moscow, and my mother was back in town.

We'd heard about the quarantine in the morning: *Restricted civilian movement until otherwise reversed by the Protectorate of Moscow Region Health Inspectorate and Population Control as ordered by the Ministry of Health, USSR.* So by dinnertime, when Matron took me aside to tell me that my mother had been released, there was no way to know if that meant I would see her in a matter of days, or of weeks.

I wasn't sure which I preferred.

Of course it was possible I wouldn't see her at all. She didn't have to come looking for me. My mother had been gone eight years, and in all that time her name was unmentionable. Not since I was seven years old had I heard it pronounced. When Matron said it aloud, it sounded every bit as archaic and unlikely as "the pox."

"Vera Konstantinovna Kravshina has been released," is what she said. "It is her right, as a rehabilitated citizen, to reclaim you from the state's ward. Because you are not yet of legal age,

Svetlana, you have no input in the matter. If anyone is going to deny your mother's petition, it will be me."

I could smell dinner being prepared in the kitchen at the end of the corridor. The smog of stuffed cabbage was as familiar as the tang of old books and wet wool, but for years afterward the smell would cause me a moment of panic. A moment when I felt I was about to be thrown to the wolves.

"Do you understand, Svetlana? It is entirely my decision whether you rejoin your mother and her compromised history . . . or you stay here with us, in the House. The matter is in my hands."

But she was wrong, Matron was. It was not entirely in her hands and neither was I. There were others making the decisions. I just didn't know it yet. Just like I didn't know for sure who was the wolf.

LATER THAT AFTERNOON, IN the courtyard with Oksana, I repeated Matron's words about my leaving the House.

"A pox on both your houses!" Oksana retorted.

It was her favorite new curse. Our teacher, Lydia Timofeevna, had passed out the scenes from *Romeo and Juliet* the week before the smallpox outbreak. Most teachers in the tenth class assigned stories about handsome farmers, clever shepherdesses, and brave soldiers; tales full of burbling streams and birch trees. In these stories there was plenty of collective achievement securing the glory of the Motherland . . . but no teen sex. No duels. No angry curses on aristocrats.

But Lydia Timofeevna had ignored the Soviet Ministry of Education's standard fare and handed us a soap opera from Verona.

"Shakespeare, boys and girls, was an English imperialist dog," she declared. "But he was a dog with perfect pentameter, razor-sharp satire, and the barbed tongue of a true class warrior. And that, children, is something to make note of."

Oksana had made note. She had memorized whole passages, sharpening her barbed tongue. She even dug up the original and mined it for its most peculiar Shakespearean phrases, which she then taught to me. I was a poor student, but in memorizing one simple phrase: "I do bite my thumb, good sir," I effectively doubled my primitive English vocabulary.

When Matron posted the STATEMENT OF QUARANTINE AS PERTAINING TO ALL MUNICIPAL HOUSING BLOCKS in the meeting room, Oksana greeted it as Mercutio would: "A pox on both your houses!"

Which meant, of course, a pox on *our* House.

There was only one House for me and Oksana. It was a pale yellow four-story brick of a building on the end of a quiet street that curved with the river. There were other houses on the street—squat piles from the last century in various states of dilapidation—but there was only one House. The sign on the gate identified it: THE HOUSE FOR ORPHANED CHILDREN, #36. It was no secret what kind of orphans we were—solo not because of death or abandonment, but because our parents were political suicides. Orphanage #36 was exclusively for the children of Enemies of the People. It had been my home for more than half my life.

By then, eight years seemed like a long time to stay put in one house. In our Soviet Union, the authorities were always plucking citizens from their beds and rearranging them according to some mysterious political calculus. I sometimes wondered how many times my mother had changed beds, stared at new walls, made new neighbors. I knew from her letters that she had passed through at least three different prison camps, maybe in three different time zones.

Enemies of the People pay for their crimes with hard labor and countless kilometers.

But by the autumn of 1958, they were making the long trip back. Comrade Stalin was gone, and the new leader had called for an era of forgiveness. Hundreds of thousands of prisoners were released from the prison Gulag, my mother among them. We had seen them, the lost souls turning up on the train platforms of Moscow looking like ghosts from a darker time. They didn't look forgiven. Forgotten, maybe. But even that wasn't really true. We had only pretended to forget. About Stalin and the nights when our neighbors were dragged away in their pajamas. About the photographs we burned and the letters we hid. About the time when they asked us if we had ever heard our parents whispering, and we nodded, once: *yes.*

Anyway, it made no difference. Whether they had been pardoned by the State or forgiven by the People, it didn't change who *we* were: We were, and always would be, the children of Enemies of the People. We were wards of Orphanage #36. We were tainted.

A pox on our House, indeed.

OKSANA HANDED ME THE ping-pong ball and propped up the sagging net with a twig. A gust of wind blew a fresh shower of leaves into the courtyard. November nibbled at my fingers as I bounced the ball on the dilapidated table. She said, "The busses are still running. In theory your mother could show up any minute."

I made a spastic serve and she went to fetch the ball. On the other side of the brick wall, the antennae of a passing trolleybus sparked against the electric cables hanging over the street.

"Is it the number twelve?" I asked.

The #12 trolley left from Kursky Station. It was the bus that my mother would take if she were coming to the House.

"Fie, 'tis no number twelve," said Oksana, now the bard of public transport. "That fine beast is a noble stag cut loose from a primordial wood."

"And I suppose you will be comparing it to a summer day?"

We were both at the gate now. Oksana looked out. I didn't. There was no way I was going to star in some maudlin scene: anxious mother, pale-faced daughter, hands gripping iron bars, tearful reunion. All forgiven. All forgotten.

But Oksana said, "Look," so I did. A woman was climbing off the bus at our stop.

"Is it her?" whispered Oksana.

The bus pulled away. The woman's face was hidden. She had bent over to rearrange the contents of her shopping bags. I noticed her stocking, which had slid below her knee. I noticed a dried brown leaf that had fastened itself to her coat sleeve. There was nothing else to notice. She was a lady with baggage. She could have been thirty or a hundred and thirty. She could have come from the Gulag or from the other side of town. I had no idea if she was my mother.

"Is it her?" Oksana said again.

The woman lifted the bags. She was crossing the street, facing us, closing the gap. In a moment she would be at the gate, and now I noticed everything: the slight limp, the thin lips, the fatigue, and the impatience. I noticed carrot greens sprouting from one of the net bags. The woman glanced at the plaque on the gate and halted. She looked me full in the face. Then, the woman who was not my mother spat deliberately on the ground and kept walking.

"Parasites," we heard her mutter.

A single potato dropped from one of her net bags and rolled toward us. Oksana lunged through the gate and grabbed it. She hurled it at the woman's back. She missed.

"It doesn't matter," she said, slipping an arm around my waist. "In a matter of months we will be sixteen. Old enough to go wherever we want. Neither Matron nor your mother will have any claim on you. We'll pack a bag of liverwurst and gingerbread and set out for the Altai, just like the sleeping twins of the Phoenix Plains."

I didn't answer. I had never heard of the sleeping twins of the Phoenix Plains, but I loved that they wandered somewhere in Oksana's clever head. Still, I knew that was not our fate—a life of vagabond gingerbread. Our fate was to be a number in a ledger of Orphanage #36. We might soon be free of its walls, but we would never be free of its stigma. Even far away in the Altai.

Unless.

"Unless what?"

I hadn't meant to say it out loud.

"Unless what, Svet? Unless your mother makes you go live with her in some barrack halfway house for the officially pardoned outcasts of the Gulag?"

"No." I shook my head. My idea of escape was wilder than an official pardon, and Oksana knew it.

"Oh, right," she said. She stooped to pluck the ping-pong ball from the weeds. "I forgot. There's no ballet out on the Phoenix Plains. Guess I'll have to find another twin."

I had only been studying ballet for four years. But I knew I was good. Really good. Just last week I reached a new level: a triple pirouette level; a sustained 120-degree side extension level; a level of musical and physical connection that had, at its hot core, an epiphany. *This. This would save me. Ballet would be my ticket. My exit.* I blazed through that lesson like a fire. I was no nomad of the Phoenix Plains—I, myself, was the phoenix, the firebird.

Sure enough, at the end of the lesson, Elena Mikhailovna had kept me back to tell me that if I continued to progress through the winter, she would recommend me for the Bolshoi Academy in the spring. Since then, my hazy horizon was crystal clear. No mirage on some fairy-tale plain.

"I have a chance," I said. "The only chance I will ever have."

"All right then," Oksana said, her face serious. "I'll stay, too. I'll stay right here in Moscow. And when you get cast as Juliet at the Bolshoi Ballet, I'll be your Mercutio."

I laughed. *Romeo and Juliet* might be ideologically suspect as a play, but as a ballet, it was the sensation of the season. As long as the bourgeois lovers were silent and choreographed by Communists, the Soviet Ministry of Culture approved of their star-crossed plight. Even celebrated it. Especially if Galina Ulanova, the Bolshoi's leading lady, danced the role of Juliet.

"I'm not sure Ulanova will approve of your plan," I said.

"Ulanova!" cackled Oksana. "She's forty years old, Sveta! You do realize that Juliet is supposed to be fourteen? Now please tell me how Galina Ulanova, fabulous as she may be, can pretend to be a fourteen-year-old virgin?"

"Ulanova's unsurpassed technical maturity brings depth to an emotionally underdeveloped character," I said, but Oksana just rolled her eyes and gave me a look that said: *balls.*

"Besides," I said, "Juliet loses her virginity halfway through the story, remember? Why else would she be willing to die for that moony-eyed Romeo?"

Oksana twirled her paddle and wrinkled her nose.

"Well, all I know is that when *you* dance Juliet, nobody will have to praise your 'technical maturity' because *your* Juliet will actually be a teenager. A real teenager with raven hair, a face as fair as the east, and a body the boys die for. Just like Bill-chik, that imperialist hack, intended."

We played until the dark swallowed the ping-pong ball completely. Then we went inside. Another day had passed and we still hadn't caught smallpox. And I still hadn't seen my mother.

"WELL, CLEARLY, THIS OUTBREAK just shows that we have gotten too friendly with India. India's Communist Party apparatus is still unformed and it will never catch up with the Soviet Union in technological, scientific, or medical achievements."

That was Lara V., of course. Lara was a model student. She got excellent marks, wore her hair in perfect plaits, and was the best speaker in Orphanage #36's chapter of the Communist Youth Union, the Komsomol. She also had a beautiful singing voice. I liked Lara all right, but mostly when she was singing.

"That is an informed answer," said Andrei Samoilovich with nasal ambivalence. He tapped his pen on his cheek, a nervous habit that had given our geography teacher a permanent set of inky freckles. "But we cannot state, explicitly, that the outbreak of this ancient disease, which has no place in our highly developed society, necessitates a change in foreign policy. It is, after all, the duty of the Soviet Union to assist all countries trapped in a backward system to further their political and economic growth until they have achieved the same level of socialized harmony and Party unity as the Communist Party of the Soviet Union."

Lara nodded. Oksana stifled a yawn. I wrote the words "Party unity" on my slate and gave them a mustache like Comrade Stalin's. You could do that now. Now that Stalin was dead and his "excesses" exposed, you could make jokes. Like the one about his mustache wandering off his face to snack on the crumbs in his lap. That kind of joke. You could even call the new leader— jolly, bald, gap-toothed Nikita Khrushchev—by silly nicknames: *Nikitinka, Nikitushka, Nikitulka.*

"In this instance, we have to consider the recklessness of the individual who brought this scourge upon us," continued Andrei Samoilovich. "Was it not the fault of the citizen himself? This artist, whose productivity was minimal at best? Was it not his responsibility to be more vigilant while on foreign soil and prevent this terrible biological contagion?"

His beady eyes were roaming. I ducked them. I didn't want to answer the question, though its answer was obvious. The answer was: "Yes, Andrei Samoilovich. It was the comrade-artist's duty to be more vigilant while on foreign soil."

But I felt sorry for the poor bugger who had brought smallpox back from India. He was a ceramicist or something, traveling with a delegation of artists to a conference in Delhi. He died a week after they returned. So did half of his family and an old man who lived in their communal apartment. That's when the posters appeared in the subway and the announcements began on the radio. That's when people began talking disapprovingly about "cultural exchanges" and "folk art."

All I could think about—beyond the horrors of the disease that, according to Rosa D.'s medical textbook, turned your skin to scabs and bled you from the inside out—was how that ceramicist must have felt when he was told: *Your art is exceptional.*

Your talent will be rewarded. You will represent your country and your people on the world stage!

What I wouldn't give to hear those words, to be recognized and chosen.

But that's something you didn't admit if you were a good Soviet citizen. You couldn't suggest that you were better, let alone exceptional. And you couldn't be jealous of someone else's achievements, because there's no envy among comrades. A true Soviet knew not to covet good fortune—better to be smug at bad luck. Better to sneer slightly, like Andrei Samoilovich did when he pronounced the word "ceramicist."

I imagined the artist I secretly envied exploring an exotic city, meeting fellow potters from all over the world, buying his wife a silk sari maybe, or lotus tea, and thinking the whole time, *today New Delhi, tomorrow—the world!*

It didn't work out, though, for the poxy potter. Instead, it was *today New Delhi, tomorrow—the grave.*

So when Andrei Samoilovich called my name I just said, "Certainly it was his fault. He's dead, after all."

TWO
CHIP

They lifted the quarantine two weeks later. I was sitting on my bed with my mother's old letters spread before me when Oksana came in with the news.

"Just in time, too. Misha has a friend with four tickets . . ."

My head jerked up. "Tickets to what?"

I knew better than to expect tickets to the ballet, but I hoped.

"The Conservatory."

I grunted. The Conservatory was nice, but it wasn't the Bolshoi. Tickets to the Conservatory could hardly distract me from the bigger news: the quarantine was over. Vera Konstantinovna had telephoned. Matron had given her an appointment.

I saw Oksana's eyes dart across the letters arrayed on my bed, but all she said was, "Can I borrow your red cardigan?"

I grunted again.

"Misha wants to meet at the café at six, so get a move on."

I nodded and shuffled the letters like cards in a game of solitaire.

For the first two or three years they had come frequently, the letters from my mother. They said things like, *Darling Sveta, the northern lights send their kisses . . .* and *I dreamt last night that we were together at the farm. You drank a whole glass of milk and got the hiccups . . .*

But eventually the letters slowed down. I told myself that she knew I was too old for shooting stars and happy cows, and that she had lost interest in pretending to mother an already-grown girl so far away. But I knew that wasn't really what happened. I was the one who had lost interest. I had stopped writing. What was the point? *Dear Mama, I hope you are well and in good spirits. I'm being a good girl and a grateful resident of Orphanage #36.* What kind of a letter was that? What kind of a relationship was that? In our country, in our time—a completely normal relationship.

I looked at each of the envelopes. My mother's handwriting had faded in the miles they had traveled over slow-moving trains across Siberia. But the dates of the censor's stamp were still bold. I could read the timeline of our drift into silence. There had been no letter since two years ago, since the moment when everything began to change. When the weight shifted. When the dark lightened. When the ice, as people now liked to say, *began to thaw.*

Up until that day, there had been nothing to melt, nothing to move. Nothing, I sometimes thought, to wake up for. There was Oksana and Matron and the House; there were the two weeks in summer when we all took a train from Kursky Station to the countryside and stayed at a lakeside cabin with canoes and more mud than you could imagine; there was the puppet theater once a month and bird's-milk cake on Saturdays and the endless assurance that, thanks to Comrade Stalin, life was getting better and brighter.

That's actually what they said: *Better, brighter, and more cheerful.* We said it, too, all together. We even sang it—every morning before school, at the top of our lungs: "Long live Stalin, our joy, our leader! Long live hard work and our happy future!"

But I didn't believe it until that day three years ago, when

Stalin was already dead and Comrade Nikita Khrushchev said it himself: that life would be better. Things would change. Because on that day, Elena Mikhailovna invited me to join the top class at the Central House of Ballet and presented me my first pair of pointe shoes. On that day Matron looked at me with surprise and even pride, saying, "Things will change for you now, Sveta. For all of us." Stalin's promise came down off the banners and landed in my lap. Life had become better . . . brighter. And I had stopped writing to my mother.

"Did she call yet?"

I lifted my head. Oksana wasn't looking at me. She was plucking lint from my red cardigan. I felt my palms break out in sweat, just as they had when Matron told me.

"Yes," I said. "She is coming tomorrow."

Oksana sucked in her breath.

"She's coming here? Are you . . . pleased?"

It was probably the best word. "Excited" was not a word we used. "Enthusiastic," maybe, but that was a word reserved for the passion we felt toward Marxism-Leninism, Party discipline, and the Vanguard of Communism. I might have said I was "happy" if Oksana had asked me about the new skating rink being built near the depot. I would have certainly been "delighted" if offered a ticket to see Ulanova in *Romeo and Juliet*. But we were talking about my fallen, forgotten, forgiven mother coming to see me.

Was I pleased? I nodded, once: *yes.*

Then I snatched up the letters and slid them back into my trunk, where they had yellowed and thinned, out of sight and out of mind. I pulled my best skirt from the trunk and hurried downstairs to persuade Cook to iron it for me. Cook was a genius with the iron.

THE CAFÉ WAS FULL. Oksana and I stood awkwardly in the doorway looking for Misha in the crowded, steamy room. He found us first.

"*Devushki!*" came his voice from the corner. "Girls, over here."

We started toward the table where Misha sat with a slouching stranger.

"Oy. He's brought a scruffy one," observed Oksana.

Misha rose to greet us, but his companion stayed seated. He pushed the chair opposite with his foot—an invitation, I guessed. I regarded him coolly, with what I hoped was the right measure of disdain. He still didn't stand. Just lifted his glass of tea in a wordless salute. Then he tossed it back, emptying the glass in a single shot. His eyes watered and I smirked.

"Bit warm on the gullet?"

"First shot of the day, and no chaser."

It was the line of a degenerate alcoholic and only mildly funny. I rolled my eyes.

Misha was helping Oksana with her coat. "Girls, this is Georgi Levshik," he said. "Georgi, meet Oksana and Svetlana, the prettiest and most cultured girls you will find in the concert hall tonight."

Georgi seemed disinclined to agree.

I sat down across from him. His hair was long and his cuffs frayed. His voice was gravel and his lips were chapped. There was an edge to him that went beyond scruff. He kept his eyes on me as he took the last bun from the plate, ripped it through the middle and offered me half. I shook my head. I might come from Orphanage #36, but I was no gutter rat. I dropped my gaze and smoothed my skirt. But I was thinking that Georgi Levshik's eyes were a strange color. Amber, maybe.

"Georgi," piped up Oksana, "I can't tell you how glad we are for your invitation. We have been looking forward to this evening so enthusiastically!"

I flinched a little at the word, but Georgi snorted.

"Good lord," he said, "such *enthusiasm*. You sound like you've come straight from the sticks. A night on the town from the collective farm, maybe? First time to the Conservatory?"

Oksana laughed it off, but I stared daggers at him. Misha, who happened to be the son of a diplomat, was already apologizing.

"Georgi's used to more cynical company," he said, clapping him on the back.

Bad company, I would have said, but I didn't. I respected Misha, who had never, *would* never, expose the truth about Oksana and me. The fact that he associated with us was his own secret. We were not exactly appropriate companions for the son of a Foreign Ministry official. But Misha was a true believer in the grand human harmony we were creating right here in the Soviet Union. He seemed willing to ensure it single-handedly— one disreputable acquaintance at a time.

"Oksana is crazy about the theater," he said. "And Sveta here is an advanced practitioner of the arts . . ."

Georgi turned his gaze back on me, curious. Oksana was still enthusing: "It's just that it's been ages since we've enjoyed anything cultural, right Sveta?"

"Oh yes, ages," I said, deadpan. "Since before the plague."

Georgi laughed at this. When he did, I saw flecks of a less insolent humor in his unusual eyes.

Misha took my joke literally. "Isn't it remarkable! Smallpox in the USSR! Who could imagine such a thing? Just when you think you have banished all the medieval devils—feudalism, witchcraft, religion, idolatry . . ."

"French wine," added Georgi, his finger raised in mock lecture.

"My point is, it's unbelievable that such a thing could happen here, given our advanced infrastructure." Misha leaned in, all earnestness. "I'm telling you girls, thank goodness our Health Ministry and medical facilities are fully prepared for such things. Lesser societies would have buckled. Succumbed to a rampaging epidemic."

"Buckled under five cases?" Georgi shook his head. "Misha, dear boy, the only real danger the virus ever presented was exposing the fact that more than half of the state supply of vaccine procured last month came in through the black market. Believe me. I have seen the supply chain."

He sat up and stretched, as if to emphasize how casually he had just slandered the state and confirmed criminal activity that officially did not exist. But Oksana was leaning across me and whispering conspiratorially. "Do you know what I heard? I heard that it didn't even come from abroad. I heard there was an accident at—*blin*, Sveta!"

There was tea in Oksana's lap. I said I was sorry for knocking over her glass, but I wasn't. I'd had enough of this conversation. We had all heard the rumor about a mishap at a government research lab, but only a fool would believe it, let alone repeat it.

"Drop it," I hissed as I blotted Oksana's damp skirt.

I glared again at Georgi, who made no move to stop the river of tea as it spread across the table. Oksana got up and went to the ladies' room. Misha rose to pay the tab. Georgi and I were left alone. He pushed the only full glass of tea across the table toward me and said, "drink," as if he had just found me dying in the desert.

I took the glass and drank.

THE CONSERVATORY WAS DOWN the street from the café, just far enough for Georgi Levshik to worm deeper under my skin.

"So where do you live?"

"East. Near Kursky."

"And you know Misha how?"

"Through Oksana."

I ventured a glance. His hands were in his pockets. His eyes were on Misha and Oksana ahead of us.

"Oksana. What she was about to say . . . about the goof-up at the lab. You didn't want her to say it. You think she's just . . . speculating."

I considered his choice of words: *goof-up*, like a massive public health threat was nothing more than human error.

Speculating, and its double meaning. I said, "I'm pretty sure you are the only speculator among us."

He raised his eyebrows. "So. You're not afraid of bad words after all. Go ahead, say it. Say *black market*. I dare you. Call me a black marketeer. Call me a parasite. Go ahead."

I didn't. I didn't say anything.

"Well, then call me Gosha," he said finally. "Nobody calls me Georgi except my grandmother. And Misha, of course. Hell, Misha sometimes calls me by my full name—name, patronymic, gives me the whole phony comrade thing."

I spun on him. "Misha is, in fact, a very sincere comrade. And if he chooses to call you Georgi Whoever-ovich, you should appreciate it as a sign of respect. One that you probably don't deserve."

"Oh, believe me, Svetlana Whoever-ovna, I know about respect. I know plenty. I have nothing but respect for people who get it. People with whom I share a certain understanding. And those are exactly the people I don't bullshit. Those are the people who call me Gosha."

I didn't answer. I was puzzling over what made him think that we shared a certain understanding. We were standing in the middle of the sidewalk, obstacles forcing the crowd to stream around us.

"You carry yourself like a dancer," he said.

It seemed like a peace offering. I allowed a small smile. "You mean I hold my head high?"

"No. I mean you have a chip on your shoulder, Svetlana."

I didn't flinch. "I guess I have a certain understanding of the world."

Georgi took a step closer and I smelled smoke and cynicism, damp and dirt. It was all I could do not to back away. He pulled the tickets from his jacket pocket.

"First balcony, smack in the center."

It wasn't the seats reserved for Party officials that impressed me. It was the hand that held them. Georgi had bitten nails and freckles on his wrist. He was a big talker with the hands of a kid. I took the tickets. There were only three.

"Let Misha sit in the middle. A gal on each arm."

"Aren't you coming?"

"Maybe another time."

I felt relieved. Also offended.

"Tell Misha something came up. He'll understand." He pulled a battered cap out of his pocket and tugged it over his unruly hair. "It was very nice to meet you, Svetlana."

It was the first civil thing he had said. I should have left it at that, but instead I blurted: "Where are you going?"

He thrust his hands in his pockets and gave me a slow smile that I didn't quite like. "You could come with me," he said.

"Where?"

"I thought I might take in a card game. Or roll a few foreigners." He rocked back on his heels like a *muzhik*, like a regular guy just passing the time.

"Who the hell do you take me for?" My voice was ragged. My face was hot.

He shrugged. "Someone with a little curiosity."

Around us the chattering crowd crested like a wave ready to crash. I heard Oksana calling me from the entrance of the Conservatory and wondered why I was still standing there in the middle of the sidewalk, my hands full of pins and needles and my tongue frozen.

"My mistake," Georgi finally said. "Enjoy the symphony. It's Tchaikovsky. A real lullaby."

I JOINED MISHA AND Oksana at the coat check. They were watching the women clustered at the full-length mirror. Oksana had a comment for each: she approved of the tall blonde's updo, she wasn't so certain about the redhead's shade of lipstick, she felt sorry for the mousy woman who kept getting jostled to the back.

I said, "Your friend Georgi's ditched us."

Misha just screwed up his lip and shrugged. "He's not a fan."

For a minute I felt that same small insult. Like maybe Georgi wasn't a fan of girls. Like maybe he wasn't a fan of *me*. Because I lacked . . . curiosity. I looked for it in the mirror—the chip he said he saw. I saw a pressed skirt that flattered my figure. I saw my clear skin and wide-set eyes. I saw my dark hair done up in a stylish twist that made up for my worn-out shoes. I liked what I saw. Including, maybe, that chip.

Oksana gaped when I showed her the tickets. "That Georgi's connected!"

I nodded, wincing at the truth. That hoodlum was connected, while I was a ward of the state.

I gave the tickets to Misha, who handed them over to the usher, who raised his eyebrows at the prestige on the paper. For a moment I wondered if he would confiscate them and throw us out of the building. But he didn't. He handed us a program and invited us to enjoy the concert. I took my seat as if I never sat anywhere but smack in the middle of the first balcony.

The audience was high-strung after the long confinement of quarantine. We greeted the orchestra with a prolonged ovation. Finally the maestro directed us to sit. When he turned his back, the hush was alive. He rose slightly on tiptoes, hovered briefly over the silence, and launched his orchestra into Tchaikovsky's second symphony.

I wished Georgi was there so I could correct him: Tchaikovsky's second is no lullaby. For me, at least, all Tchaikovsky was ballet. Tchaikovsky was *Swan Lake* and *The Nutcracker*, and even without the dancers, I heard the drama of his music. I could hear the queen marrying off her son and the rich man buying off his daughter. I heard the music like my own cue and imagined myself onstage—promenading, entreating, seducing, despairing. I saw myself strutting through the strings, the lead-in to a little-known work called "Girl with a Chip on her Shoulder."

Georgi's taunt festered, dragging my attention from the music to unwelcome thoughts. I closed my eyes and a memory waited for me: A red glass flower vase in the middle of the table in the kitchen of my childhood. A chipped vase with deep ruby facets. And my mother's low whisper. We were sitting at the table, and my mother was instructing me to forget. To forget my father. To forget everything. As for the things I could not forget, she said: *Ni slova, Sveta.* Not a word.

It was not long after those instructions that my mother, Vera Konstantinovna Kravshina, wife of General Evgeny Kravshin, was taken away, and I was delivered to Orphanage #36. I was issued a uniform, a cot, and a file. I was fingerprinted and photographed and told of the implications of my parents' crimes on my bright, happy Soviet future. I didn't say a word. And in time I did what my mother had asked—I forgot.

I thought I had done the right thing. How would it help to remember my father as the man who stood just behind and to the right of Stalin during the parades on Red Square? What could I gain from knowing what my mother had done to be sent to the camps? Nothing. But I had a lot to lose. Despite the dreadful insinuations of the stone-faced apparatchiks and leather-clad police, my life had not ended when they entered my name in the register of Orphanage #36. My life was not hard. I was not unhappy. I was not broken like those lost causes at Orphanage #4 who had to be roped together when they went out for a walk so they wouldn't stumble, drooling and blathering, into the canal. Matron took care of us. Cook fed us. There was that fat woman named Marfa who hugged us every day . . . until she went away.

What was there to say? *Ni slova.* Not a word.

And what about my mother? After eight years would she now have something to tell me? Or would I hiss her warning right back at her: *Ni slova.* Not a word.

Maybe Georgi was right. Maybe I was a girl with no curiosity.

Or maybe I was a girl who knew how to take good advice. You can't tell something you don't remember. Just like you can't forget something that never happened.

The music stopped. The audience observed the pause between movements with the sound of a hundred hard candies being unwrapped. Misha handed me one, too. I popped it in my mouth, dropped the crinkly wrapper on the floor and pushed it and all thoughts of my mother under the chair with my foot.

By the last movement of Tchaikovsky's second symphony I could no longer hear the dancers hidden in the notes. I could hear nothing from the music but tension.

The maestro stood at the podium, taut as a human spring. The orchestra, too, was precariously wound. I felt agitated, uncertain as to who was in control—The maestro? Or the music? The tempo was uneven. The musicians were racing, like the cavalry into battle, like stallions toward a precipice. The cymbals crashed and clashed, and I saw the maestro flail. Was he driving them forward? Or was he trying to pull them back from the brink? In the hurtling hall, the podium was the only fixed point. Dizzy, I closed my eyes but I could still see:

The maestro, a general.
The orchestra, his army.

Suddenly the music turned on him. Each instrument. In unison. Confronting the conductor. My eyes snapped open and I saw the general exposed, his arms lifted in an arrested command. In the silence of a pause, he moved a fraction of an inch and was transformed: he was a prisoner, caught in surrender. The horns blared, and the prisoner collapsed against the podium.

The audience roared in approval as I sat motionless, shocked.

I had just witnessed the conductor executed by his own trumpets.

Against a wall.
In a hail of bullets.
Like my father.

About which I had never said a word.

THREE
PIROUETTE

I couldn't land the triple pirouette the next day. Elena Mikhailovna kept me after class and made me practice until I was dizzy.

"Never relinquish what you've attained, Svetlana. If you let it go, you will never get it back."

I was pacing, hands on hips, ankles wobbling with effort. The temptation was there—to cut and run. To wander the Phoenix Plains, far from the world. Then I remembered what happens to people who quit. People who drop out and dare society to judge them. *Go ahead, call me a parasite.*

I took fourth position preparation, bent, sprung, turned, turned, and landed badly.

"Again."

I groaned in frustration, but Elena Mikhailovna had no sympathy.

"No tears," she snapped. "Save your tears for real pain." She sat in the chair at the front of her room and patted her thigh. I came forward and propped one foot on her knee for inspection. She squeezed the toe of my shoe and shook her head. "I'm surprised you can do a single in these. The box is shot. They have as much support as potato skins. Did you ask for money for a new pair?"

I hadn't.

"You can't dance in these, and I don't have a spare pair. Not in your size. I will see what I can do, but it could be weeks before the next supply. The shop on Petrovka, behind the Bolshoi, has good, solid shoes for six rubles. Do I really have to give you my wages as well as my Saturday afternoons, Svetlana?"

"No, Elena Mikhailovna, I will ask Matron. I will get the shoes."

"Good girl." Elena Mikhailovna patted my rear end in dismissal. "Come back Tuesday and we will catch that runaway pirouette."

AN HOUR LATER I was sitting in Matron's office. The room was dark, despite the large window looking out onto the street. It was a quarter to four, and the sun was nearly gone. I shivered, though I wasn't exactly cold.

"She will likely tell you stories from your childhood," Matron was saying. "She will ask you if you remember this time, or that time, when you and your parents were happy and together."

Matron's eyes were hidden by the bright edge of the lampshade between us. I knew they saw right through me. I had never hidden anything from Matron. But then again, I had never had anything to hide. *Did I now?*

"I want you to remember that every unhappy family has some happy memories. Remember that even the most treacherous, pernicious saboteurs are also human beings. Your father, Svetlana, helped our troops liberate Berlin from the Fascists before he was arrested as a traitor. Did you know that?"

Did I know that? Had I forgotten? Which was worse?

I knew that my mother spent the war years with her infant daughter in a closed compound surrounded by soldiers and provisioned with daily trucks full of food. I knew that in my father's hometown, south of Moscow, there was once a statue of him in the central square. I knew that my father sometimes read fairy tales to me from a leather-bound book of *skazki*, but that one spring morning when I was six, General Evgeny Kravshin went to work in his long black car and didn't come home. Soon after, there was a picture on the front page of *Pravda* of Stalin and all of his men, and though Voroshilov and Zhukov and the fat man I knew as Uncle Vova were in it, my father was not.

Now, Matron was talking about my father *before*. No one had ever mentioned my father *after*.

"My father is gone," was all I could think to say. "He will not come claiming me."

"But your mother is outside that door."

"That doesn't mean she will claim me," I said.

Matron sighed. "They don't come if they don't intend to claim you."

She would know. She had held dozens of these reunions. Two full years had passed since Khrushchev's order to empty the camps, and they were still coming. There were so many prisoners. It was such a long trip.

I watched Matron shuffle papers on her desk and wondered what it felt like for her. Did she welcome the chance to hand us over? Or did she worry that she would soon be out of a job? Would she decide my fate based on my wishes? Or based on a thick file of directives and quotas from the Ministry? Was *successful family reunion* now a line item in some domestic five-year plan for Orphanage #36? And what did I want, if she even asked?

"Are you ready?" she asked.

"*Da*. I'm ready."

Matron stood and went to the door. "Citizen Kravshina, you may come in."

I heard a second pair of footsteps cross the floor. I felt unable to move, but when Matron told me to stand and greet my mother, I did.

I recognized her—under the faded kerchief covering faded

hair falling across a faded face was the pretty woman who used to spend an hour in front of the mirror before taking me to the park. I recognized the deep-set eyes, so full of fear as she searched the picture in *Pravda*. I remembered, with a small flutter in my stomach, the secret kiss we shared—cheeks tickled with lashes. "Butterfly kisses," we called them. I took her hands and moved toward her, but then balked. I shook both her hands together—awkwardly, like a dishrag.

I used the formal address: "*Zdravstvyte*, mother."

"*Zdravstvuy, dochka*," She kissed my cheek quickly. Furtively. "You look wonderful."

Matron gestured for us to sit. We did. She began her interview.

"Vera Konstantinovna, have you registered with the Moscow political division?"

"In which district have you been granted living quarters?"

"When do you expect to receive formal notification of rehabilitation and acquittal for your crimes?"

"What are your employment prospects?"

"Do you intend to rejoin the Communist Party?"

My mother answered each of Matron's questions. I wasn't fully aware of her responses, only that she delivered them with certainty and poise. Matron took notes with a black pen. Eventually she put the notes in the desk drawer. She cleared her throat. She looked at me, and I thought maybe she wanted me to speak. I didn't. So she did.

"Svetlana's progress here at the House has been the topic of much discussion in the past month. She is an average student and a quiet voice in our Komsomol activities and political discussions. Her last examinations were not distinguished, and she slept through Young Pioneer activities on five occasions last summer."

My nails bit into my palms. Did Matron want me out? Or was she blocking the door to keep me in?

"But we have discovered that Svetlana has undeniable talent.

She has been studying at the Central House of Ballet for four years now. Her tutor, Elena Mikhailovna, states that she is quite gifted. In fact, she may be a candidate for the Bolshoi Academy."

My hands were still fists, but I saw my mother's fly toward me. She gripped my forearm and said, "Oh, Sveta! That's wonderful, *milaya*."

Milaya, she had said. Darling.

I met her smile. But then Matron asked, "Are you, Vera Konstantinovna, in a position to forward your daughter's candidacy for the Bolshoi Academy?"

I saw her hesitate.

"I would, of course, make her study my priority," she began. "In terms of conveying Svetlana to classes, and accompanying—"

"That's not what I had in mind," interrupted Matron. "Svetlana is nearly sixteen, she does not need a chaperone. The Bolshoi Academy, as you certainly know, is reserved for dancers of the highest caliber and potential. It is the cultural extension of the State and the Party. Entry into the Academy implies not just artistic inclination, but social maturity, Party discipline, and, above all, a spotless family profile."

I felt the sun sink somewhere. The room was dark. I heard myself ask, "Are you saying that my mother's . . . record . . . will disqualify me from attending the Bolshoi Academy?"

"I'm saying it doesn't help your chances."

Matron was looking directly at my mother, but Vera Konstantinovna did not say a word. I felt a flash of anger and didn't know where to direct it.

"You are fortunate, Svetlana, that we at Orphanage number thirty-six have an excellent reputation with the State Coordinator for Adolescent Socialization. Thanks to our close relations and shared objectives, our young men and women are now able to take an active part in furthering Soviet advancements in science, industry, and culture with negligible repercussions for the time spent as wards of the state. Furthermore, it is no longer our policy . . ." here Matron coughed into her fist, struggling somewhat with the unfamiliarity of official mercy, "to discredit former prisoners and their family members as de facto 'antisocial elements.' Rehabilitation, in short, is not only possible but recommended. However, I cannot clear every obstacle for you."

She fell silent. And though she had not asked, my mother and I answered as one: "I would like to ask for more time . . ."

". . . to consider," I said.

". . . to reacquaint myself with my daughter," my mother finished.

Matron stood from her chair. "You are welcome at the House every Sunday, Vera Konstantinovna. Kindly submit your request by Friday afternoon. As for you, Svetlana," she continued as she ushered my mother to the door, "your mother and I will decide what is best for you. There is nothing for you to consider, aside from your lessons and your studies."

In the doorway, Matron spoke some final words to my mother. I didn't hear them. I was wondering why she had decided to allow my mother a role in this decision. I was watching them, the two women standing side by side. My mother's hair was the color of dirty snow. Matron's face was somber and lined. I wondered if I, too, would one day appear as aged as these two women who were not yet forty years old.

THE NEXT MORNING, I returned to Matron's office. I saw from her face that she would not discuss my mother's visit, and I was relieved. Perhaps my mother had failed a test. Perhaps I had. In any case, I didn't want to know just yet. I told myself I had more pressing concerns.

"Elena Mikhailovna says I should not come back to class until I have new shoes," I said.

"And isn't that her responsibility?" Matron asked. "Does she think I have a closet of pointe shoes in my office?"

"She said I can buy them myself in town. They cost six rubles. If I leave now I can be back for lunch and afternoon lessons."

Matron gave a small sigh and pulled a long wallet from her apron. She counted out the bills, and I thanked her. I assured her that the new shoes were absolutely necessary. Then I thanked her again.

It was only when I was at the door that she spoke. "I don't imagine that Vera Konstantinovna is in a position to afford such an expense. What do you think, Svetlana?"

I tried to remember what my mother had said about her employment prospects. "She has a job, right?"

"Yes. She's a platform attendant in the Metro."

I nodded. I had no idea what the wages for a subway worker might be. For all I knew it was six rubles a week. I had never considered how much money they took home—those bossy ladies with the yellow vests and lollipop wands who all seemed cut from the same underground cloth. In school we were taught Marxist materialism and the merits of a command economy. The economics of putting bread and pointe shoes on the table as a second-class citizen were not in our curriculum.

I felt the bills in my pocket, clutched them like a drunk fists his bottle money. I thanked Matron again and bolted for the trolleybus.

IT WAS AN UNUSUALLY mild day for mid-November. The sun ducked in and out of fast-moving clouds and the river glowed deep green like a gem. I felt the warm air through the open window. My hands moved restlessly in my lap, doing their own adagio. I imagined the new shoes on my feet, solid and supportive. Enablers in my escape. Ushers to the exit.

Trolleybus #12 had only two directions—toward Orphanage #36 and away from Orphanage #36. But at the city center, where I got off, there were as many options as points on a compass. There were plenty of routes to the store on Petrovka, behind the Bolshoi. The quickest was by Metro, but I didn't want to go underground. The last thing I wanted was to run into my mother waving her lollipop wand along the platform. I had time, so I crossed the busy avenue and plunged into the warren of narrow streets in Moscow's heart.

I arrived twenty minutes later at the shop on Petrovka only to find the door locked.

Cupping hands to my temples, I peered through the streaked window of the storefront. In the half light inside I could see a woman standing at the counter. She was unpacking a medium-size cardboard box, from which she pulled out a pair of pale pink pointe shoes. She examined them, feeling the seams and rapping the toe box on the counter. I knocked on the glass door and she looked up. She circled the counter, but when she reached the door she leaned down, picked up a fallen sign from the floor, and hung it directly in front of my face.

HOURS OF OPERATION 0900–1700, LUNCH 1200–1300.

I checked my watch. It was 9:15. I stood on my tiptoes to see above the sign and knocked again. The woman ignored me. She picked up the box and entered a back room, out of sight.

"*K chortu,*" I muttered.

I was used to being ignored, being made to wait—small slights were my daily bread. But the sight of the shoes had made me hungry. I leaned my back against the door and cursed her again. *To the devil, to hell, to rot*—that's where she could go . . . just as soon as she sold me my pointe shoes.

Five minutes passed and then ten. I knocked on the door again, in vain. The bells of the Kremlin struck the half hour and I sent them and the woman both *k chortu.*

Ten more minutes passed. I was beginning to despair when another customer joined me on the sidewalk. I eyed him—squat and bow-legged in ill-fitting pants and a leather jacket, pocked face, unshaved cheeks. I knew the type, but you didn't run into them in dance shops often. He yanked the door, and, finding it locked, cursed an uglier curse than I had. To my surprise, the woman he had just called a smelly hag emerged. She ushered in the man but blocked me at the threshold, insisting I wait until "public hours of operation."

"I've been waiting twenty-five minutes," I protested. "I just need one pair of shoes, it won't take a minute. Please. Size thirty-four."

"*Nyetu,*" she sniffed, still barring my entry. "We are all out."

"But I saw a whole box of them. You just opened it. Surely one of them is my . . ."

"That was a designated shipment," interrupted the woman. "A reserved inventory for special appointment."

I could see straight up her flared nostrils.

"But my teacher, Elena Mikhailovna of the Central House of Ballet . . ."

"Is responsible for obtaining shoes through the official channels of the Department of Physical Culture." Her tone suggested that I planned to use the precious shoes to dance a striptease. In the mud. After curfew. Drunk. "Now, I suggest that you leave before I call the Bureau of Truancy and report you for skipping school."

I was still on the sidewalk. The door was locked. The shoes, packed in their cardboard box just fifteen feet away, might as well have been secured in a Kremlin vault. *This* was Communism: prohibit people from owning anything, and they will jump at the chance to deny everyone else ownership. I pressed my face up against the glass and fumed. There was Comrade Leather Jacket, manhandling the shoes like they were spare parts for his crap car. The "special designation," I understood, was the black market. The nasty woman had probably just sold them for a weekend pass to some Crimean resort.

K chortu. To hell with you.

I gave the store a last thumb under my chin and started to walk away. Halfway up the block I stopped. I couldn't leave without the shoes. If I did, I would relinquish that triple pirouette. If I ran away, spitting and cursing, I could kiss the Bolshoi goodbye. If I gave up on the Bolshoi, life couldn't possibly get better or brighter . . . in fact, I couldn't imagine a bleaker future.

I turned around just as the leather-clad jerk with my shoes

left the store. He was headed south toward the Bolshoi Theatre with the box under his arm. Such brazenness: he had just cleared out the Bolshoi's supply closet and now was taking the shoes right into the theater, where he would probably double the price. I hurried after him, wondering what I could possibly offer for a pair of shoes out of that box.

Just before reaching the theater's back entrance, the man turned under the arch between the dairy store and the post office. I followed, but when I came out into a large cobbled courtyard, he had disappeared. I turned in a circle and spied the only place he could have gone—a metal garage in the far corner of the courtyard. Its doors were open.

I crossed the cobblestones, practicing my pitch under my breath: *From each according to his . . . to each according to . . .* What was it Lenin said about ability and need? *Comrade, consider the true value of . . .* God. How do you arrange an illegal transaction in a public courtyard? *Name your price . . .*

When I reached the garage, I could hear voices inside. Two voices. The first decidedly rougher than the second. The second certainly younger than the first:

"You sayin' you don't want in?"

"No. I'm saying that if I'm in, I want a fair split."

"Whaddaya mean by fair split? A fair split down your face?"

"I mean a third. I mean one-third of the take."

"You're outta your mind, you little shit. I put up the front. She put up the goods. You put up what? A needle and thread. That's all you got, you punk. You think you can put a thimble on your finger and call yourself a player? You get paid by the stitch. And if you get greedy, you get paid in stitches. Get it? Stitches up your face. Stitches up your skull. And you don't want that, kitten, 'cause I'm clumsy with a needle. Scar you for life, I will."

I backed away from the door. But whoever Leather Jacket was threatening seemed unconcerned. "You know you can't sell those blocks of wood for any more than seven rubles without the name. If you wanna do that, go ahead. Sell the whole bunch without the labels and buy yourself a bottle off the profit. But if you want eleven-ruble Elites, you have to cut me in for a third."

There was a nasty expletive and the crash of something thrown against the wall directly behind my head. I jumped, yelping, directly into plain sight of the garage.

"The hell?"

I stood there stupidly, blind to the shed's dark interior, until Leather Jacket emerged at the doorway. "Can we help you, kitten?"

"I'll buy a pair."

"You'll what?"

"I'll buy a pair. Without labels. Just as they are."

I held out the bills. "Six rubles."

"They ain't for sale, doll. Not at that price. Now beat it."

"You can't get more than seven rubles," I said. "You said so yourself. Take this and I promise I'll come back tomorrow with the rest."

I begged him, silently, to take the money. He rubbed his chin and grinned, showing a golden incisor. He was pretending to consider my offer.

"Nah," he said finally. "We got other plans for these shoes."

I felt his refusal like a punch in the gut. *Parasites, speculators*, I thought as he yanked the metal doors behind him. *Worms, worm-eaters. I bite my thumb at you!* My eyes smarted. To burst into tears would be mortifying, so I turned and hurried away. I was nearly at the arched exit when I heard the doors clatter open again and light feet run across the stones toward me. I whirled and recognized him—the boy with dirty hair and torn pants who got paid by the stitch. Georgi Levshik stopped before me and yanked a pair of pointe shoes from each pocket.

"They're standard jobs, not Elites," he said thrusting them into my hands. "But I can meet you later and give you fake labels. Ribbons, too."

I looked at the shoes. They were simple. They were beautiful. And they were my size. How did he know?

I said, "I only have six rubles. I can't pay for both pairs."

"Consider it a bonus." He shrugged. "For having to deal with . . . middlemen." He glanced over his shoulder at the ugly mug watching us from the garage. "Now, do you want the labels and ribbons?"

His hands were still on the shoes, holding mine by pointe-shoe proxy. I was either embarrassed or ashamed when I said, "Do I look like a girl who gives a fig about fake labels?"

"No, Svetlana. You do not look like a girl who gives a fig about what I've got to offer." His voice was angry. "Not even the ribbons that will hold those black market blocks on your pretty feet."

He hadn't moved, but it felt as though he had taken a step closer, too close. Then he dropped his hands. It felt as though a huge gap had opened between us. The shoes were mine. I grappled with words.

"I'm . . . thanks," I finally managed.

But Georgi had already turned his back. I watched him walk through a sudden block of sunshine all the way back to the garage. I saw him ignore his ugly partner with a dismissive shrug. I saw Leather Jacket spin him around with a leather-clad arm and drive a fist into his face. I saw a splatter of blood hit the ground, and I ran.

THAT AFTERNOON ON MY way to class I stopped at the fabric store near the Central House of Ballet and bought a yard of satin ribbon. It was decent ribbon, slightly discolored, but I was glad to be buying it myself. One of the two new pairs of shoes was in my bag, bumping against my thigh. The other pair was in my trunk, wrapped up in an old cardigan like a mute rebuke.

In the studio, Elena Mikhailovna examined the shoes with approval. She handed me a needle and thread. "You'll take the whole class on pointe today, Svetlana. We will finish with pirouettes."

I sewed on the ribbons, trying not to think of Georgi's boyish hands and bloodied nose. *From each according to his . . . input? Output? Goof-up? Put-out?* I still couldn't remember the phrase, though it was straight out of Lenin's primer. The point was: every profession has its price. I examined my bare feet with their black-and-blue nails and angry red blisters. Not pretty at all. Every bit as ugly as a busted nose.

I snipped the ribbons, stuffed some quilted padding into the toes of the shoes, and tied them on. I stood, rose on relevé, and jumped in place. I pranced across the studio like a wild pony, banging the boxes on the wooden floor. I rolled my neck and shoulders like a featherweight fighter. I felt the hard pointe and the supple support of the arches and did a *cabriole* in celebration.

"Thank you," I whispered. I could feel the eyes of the other girls on me. Not on my shoes, which were really nothing special, but on me.

A thin man with thinner hair and worn slippers shuffled into the room and sat at the piano.

We took our places at the barre. Mine was directly in front of the garret studio's only window—a drafty spot but I loved the view. In spring, the park below was alive with orioles and wagtails. In the summer, swifts rose from the hedges and the chimney pots for hours. But now the cold had moved in and the little birds had moved out. A raven cawed. I lifted my leg onto the polished barre. I stretched and my fingertips found the dimpled elastic of my new shoe.

Elena Mikhailovna came in clapping. The door slammed behind her. The lesson began. By the time it ended ninety minutes later, one of the ribbons had frayed and popped from its stitches. There were blisters on my blisters and my feet screamed with the effort of victory. I had nailed the triple pirouette five times in a row. I was elated. I was elite.

FOUR
WORDS

Vera Konstantinovna returned to the orphanage the following Sunday. It was another warm day. A rain shower had passed into speckled sunlight so I suggested we take a walk along the river.

She waited for me in the front hall, surrounded by the little kids who were making the grimy floor grimier with the help of a dirty mop, while I ran upstairs for my sweater and scarf. When I opened my trunk, the packet of letters was waiting for me. I hesitated. I could bring them along. The things we had once said might help us talk again. But I wasn't sure I wanted to be talking again.

The night before, in Matron's office, I nearly asked her to call it off. I had assured Matron that if she would just wait until June, I would leave the House of my own volition as a sixteen-year-old released from the ward of the state and . . .

"And what?" she had asked. "And join the other girls from the provinces without families to support them in a dormitory somewhere to wait out your probationary status? You are a capable girl, Svetlana. I know you will work and contribute to society—you will have no choice. But it will be lonely for you."

In all my years at the orphanage, I had never heard the word.

It was not just contrary to our reality; it was not in our vocabulary. We were never alone. Hence, never lonely. But there was Matron sitting on the edge of her desk and saying it: "This 'rehabilitation' that is promised—it will ease the burden of your name in time. But there are heavier burdens, Svetlana. There are so many of you—orphans of our great sacrifices. No other people in the world have sacrificed as much as the Soviet People. You should not pay more than you already have."

Regardless of whether or not my mother was owed anything, Matron thought I was owed a mother.

I picked up the packet of letters and slid it under my sweater into the waistband of my skirt.

WE WERE AT THE river when I realized that Vera Konstantinovna had forgotten how to make small talk. Not that pointless platitudes about the weather were something our society much valued. We didn't go in for bourgeois blather. Encounters were purposeful. Communication was useful. Maybe that was what her silence meant. That there was nothing useful to be said. Or maybe, on the contrary, there was something very important still to be communicated. Something that didn't get said while you stroll along the riverbank. I suggested we sit.

Vera Konstantinovna sat down on an empty bench. She folded her hands in her lap. The sun emerged from under a cloud and her words came with it, tumbling out in a rush: "You don't have to call me Mother if you don't want. I will understand if you don't. But I would like it if you did."

"What did I call you then?" I asked. "Before?"

"*Mama*, of course. All children call their mothers *mama*."

"And . . . *papa*?"

"And *papa*, yes."

She turned to face me, one eye squinted against the sun. "Tell me. Did you miss him terribly?"

I was surprised. He was gone. She was here. Did she not want to know if I had missed her? And then I remembered: I was supposed to have forgotten.

"I don't remember him," I said, but the image of his hands, holding the leather-bound book of *skazki*, floated before my eyes. I let it pass.

I said, "What I do remember is the day they came for you."

I heard the quick intake of her breath. "Your seventh birthday."

I nodded. They had been waiting for us in the stairwell when we returned from the park. I was still holding my balloon, which had lost most of its helium by the end of the day. They told my mother to pack two bags. One for her; one for me. When we left, I turned for a last look at my home. I saw the balloon hovering in the hallway, its string slack. For weeks afterward I imagined it wandering our empty apartment like a forgotten pet, hungry and alone. I couldn't remember when I began imagining my mother all alone.

"Did you come straight home?" I asked eventually. "To Moscow? Or did you live somewhere else for a time? I mean . . . were you just released recently?"

She was looking out over the river. There were geese on the far bank, nearly camouflaged against the mottled bark of the forest. She retied her kerchief—a deep red square, Soviet red—over her colorless hair.

She said, "They released us late last summer. They gave a speech, thanking us for our labor. Then they put us on a train. We rode *platzkart*—three bunks high. There was a car at the back where the commandant traveled. We lined up and went in one by one. He had our affidavits ready—typed statements that in our years of internment we had not been harmed, we had been treated respectfully, we had been remunerated for our labor, and we had benefited physically and politically and socially from our fraternity with fellow workers. We had to sign the paper or get off the train. Nobody refused to sign, but some people did get off the train. Some people were frightened. They didn't want to go so far . . . again."

She spoke calmly, evenly. Almost as if she were in a trance.

"A few days later, there was a new document to sign. It was much shorter. It said that the only person we held accountable for our criminal record and our sentencing was Joseph Stalin. That was when we knew he was dead. We all signed that one, too.

"In Ekaterinburg they told us to get off the train. They gave us some money and new papers. I bought a dress and a coat. I had a dress and a coat and two affidavits and seventy-five rubles. I asked a man with a truck to take me as far west as he was going. He took me all the way to Moscow. But they stopped us at the city limits and I spent two weeks in a quarantine facility, sleeping and signing more papers."

There was a squawk and an explosion of wings. The geese skimmed the water and Vera shifted. "Someone wrote that once," she said. "Long before me. He wrote: 'A Russian consists of a body, a soul, and some papers.' Sometimes I've wondered about the soul part, but mostly I think he got it about right."

I waited to see if her story would keep going. If it would travel on trolleybus #12, along the river to the House, to me. But she was finished. The packet pinched under my arm. I didn't take it out. The packet had no soul or sympathy. Only more papers.

I felt something like guilt. For what, I wasn't sure. Maybe for not writing. Maybe for sleeping in one bed all these years.

"I'm sorry," I said.

She answered briskly. "Don't be. What happened to me did not happen to you. It is not your memory to bear. I won't speak of it again. My past is not yours, Svetlana. It is not for you to remember."

"But I am, all the same—I'm sorry."

"Of course you are. You are a good girl, better equipped to lead our country into a proud future of economic plenty, social equality, and perfected brotherhood—Communism."

It was a barrage. I had heard all these words before. I had

recited them myself for years. But I was a Pioneer and she was a Prisoner. Coming from my mother, the words sounded neither empty nor optimistic. They didn't even sound familiar. They sounded like dissonance.

It was on the tip of my tongue to ask: *What did you do? What did my father do?* But she spoke first. "And, of course, our security, too. It is in your hands."

"Security?"

"Yes. The Motherland's security. Protection from our enemies. The Motherland is always under threat, Svetlana. And our enemies are very strong. But our defenses are even stronger. The enemy is no longer *within*, Sveta. It is the enemies *without* that we must fight."

I pictured the endless column of tanks, troops, military equipment rolled out for Victory Day. They were there to fight armies and bombers and foreign invaders. But even as my mother warned of enemies *without*, I understood that we—all of us— were still afraid of enemies *within*. Hidden enemies.

Enemies in our mind?

Enemies of our mind?

As if she could read my thoughts, she reached out and grabbed my hands.

"Did you tell, Sveta? Did you say anything about your papa?"

"No," I said. "What? What would I tell?"

She moved quickly to put a finger on my lips. As she did, the image of the maestro, his hands raised, flashed through my mind.

Were they raised in surrender? Or as a command?

Was my father executed? Or the executioner?

All I knew for sure was that my mother, after all she had been through, was still scared.

THAT NIGHT, AFTER SUPPER, there was a meeting in the big room. I knew I should speak up. Matron had warned me: my lackluster participation in political activities had been noted.

If I was going to erase the black marks in my personal file I had better start now, because it would soon be under scrutiny.

But my mind was still on the riverbank, with my mother's paranoia.

Andrei Samoilovich encouraged a few ringing endorsements of our health officials for containing a "vicious plague from beyond our borders." Then he asked Lara V. for the highlights of last month's trip to the Museum of Soviet Electrification. The final item on the agenda was a resolution denouncing the writer Boris Pasternak.

The resolution, read aloud by Lydia Timofeevna, stated that the wards of Orphanage #36 were united in their demand that Pasternak reject the Nobel Prize in Literature, which had been bestowed upon him as part of a Western plot to "wreck the common purpose of Soviet literature to raise political consciousness among the proletariat."

Lydia Timofeevna looked paler than usual when she asked, "And what would be a suitable punishment for Pasternak for allowing his antirevolutionary novel *Doctor Zhivago* to be smuggled out of the country and spread like a reactionary virus?"

It was an interesting choice of words—*virus*. I thought of the dead ceramicist and the biological virus he had allowed in. Apparently the words of a poet spread outside our own borders were even more dangerous. I remembered my mother's warning: *Now the enemies are without.*

The others all had something to say about Pasternak's treason; Lyosha spoke, Lara spoke, Fedya and Masha both spoke.

I didn't. I didn't say a word. *Ni slova.*

HOURS LATER, I CRAWLED into bed with Oksana.

"Sleeping?" I whispered.

"What's up?"

I didn't say.

She turned over to face me. "What happened with your mother today?"

I still didn't say. Oksana moved over, offering me half the pillow. She pulled the blanket up to our chins.

"What?" she whispered.

"There's something I can't remember," I began. "And I know that it's something I can't remember because I only just remembered it. Just—out of nowhere this memory that I can't quite remember. You know what I mean?"

"Um. Do you mean like déjà vu?"

"Maybe."

I thought again of the moment at the Conservatory when I confused the maestro with someone—someone who was both puppet and puppet master, soldier and general, victim and perpetrator. It wasn't déjà vu. It was a memory of something that happened. Just not to me.

"Do you know what your parents did, Oksana? To be sent to the Gulag, I mean?"

"*Blin*, Svet, I mean jeez, I don't know. Maybe they said something about Stalin. Or maybe they got drunk on the job or maybe they really were, you know—bad elements. Like deserters. Or terrorists. Or spies. Maybe they wrecked an aluminum factory. Maybe they poisoned some Party bigwig. I was four, Sveta, how would I know?"

They had returned last year, Oksana's folks. But they never came to fetch her. When she went looking for them herself, she found a gaunt woman nursing a wreck of a man. The man was half dead from drink. The woman was not fully coherent, but when she said Oksana was better off without them, Oksana didn't argue.

"The Gulag," she whispered now. "It's a place where people are sent to have their minds changed . . ."

We lay listening to the familiar sounds of the House at night.

"The thing I remembered. Or . . . can't remember," I began again. "I think my mother either wants me to remember, or else she wants to tell me. But either way, she doesn't want me to tell. That's what she wanted to know today—if I had ever told anyone about my father."

"What's there to tell?" asked Oksana.

I still couldn't say. "Maybe she just needs time to adjust."

"Or maybe you need to cut your losses."

I felt my palms sweat. *Was there more to lose? Was my mother a test—more important than a triple pirouette? Was everything at stake? Or just my peace of mind?*

"Break with her?" I asked. "Disavow her formally?"

Oksana pulled the blanket up over our heads. "Tell me what it is you remembered," she whispered.

"A firing squad."

Oksana drew a deep breath. "Yeah. That's something you want to forget."

FIVE
BIRD WITH THE DIE-CAST EYE

I didn't forget.

November passed and we slipped into winter. When Misha invited us again to the Conservatory I declined. When he proposed we join a new discussion circle he had formed on "cultural initiatives to promote Marxism-Leninism," I joined, much to Oksana's amazement. On the way home from each of these meetings I breathed a blank circle onto the frozen windows of the bus and made a mark with my finger. Three tedious discussion circles, three points for my political maturity.

But I didn't forget.

The question haunted me: *Which side of the firing squad was my father on when he became an Enemy of the People?*

And just as haunting: *Why, after eight years, was this a question? Is this curiosity? Or is this something . . . stranger?*

As for my mother, I couldn't bring myself to disavow her. Nor could I fully embrace her. So I avoided her.

In the weeks after our talk on the riverbank, I threw myself into schoolwork, into political groups, marches, and other "socially progressive activities," but mostly into my lessons with Elena Mikhailovna. On Sundays, I stayed late after the other girls left, practicing alone, without accompaniment, until night-fall.

"Those shoes must be shot at the rate you are going," noted Elena Mikhailovna one night as she passed through the studio.

I leaned over to squeeze the box of the shoe. It was not really a box any longer, but its broken-in softness molded my toes perfectly. Shedding it would be like shedding skin, but I knew she was right.

"I have another pair at home," I said, rising on relevé to show the strength of my arch. "I'll be fine until the end of the year. There will be a new distribution by then, right?"

"That's not the point, Sveta. The point is, you are eating up more than your allotment. Not just in shoes. In time, too. And in what I can give you, pedagogically. You are getting more than your share, and still you need more."

She was using the voice she used for corrections, but I heard it as a confirmation.

"From each according to his ability, to each according to his needs," I replied. Misha's discussion circles had tidied up my Leninist slogans. I felt a flush of confidence. I had given it my all, so I must get something back. My advancement was imminent. "Elena Mikhailovna, would you watch my adagio once more before we leave?"

She nodded. I took center and moved fluidly through each expression of the two-minute monologue that is a perfect adagio. I didn't leave out a single step and I breathed life into each pause; my extensions didn't waver and my *port de bras* didn't stall. My alignment was correct, my turnout sustained, and my face, each time I caught a glance in the mirror, radiated effortlessness. I rose on relevé as smoothly as if on demi-pointe and controlled a profound depth at each *plié*. Even without music, I felt musicality flowing through my muscles.

"Perfect," said Elena Mikhailovna when I was finished. "Technically perfect. But I wondered what was on your mind as you danced."

I didn't know what to say. I knew *not* to say that even as I danced I was imagining Matron declining, civilly but without an ounce of sympathy in her voice, all of my mother's requests to visit.

Unfortunately, Vera Konstantinovna, Svetlana's Sundays are now completely taken up with her ballet classes . . .

No, I am afraid that weekday visits are impossible . . .

Yes, we may be able to accommodate a Saturday visit. Just as soon as your work schedule allows it. Yes, Comrade Kravshina. I will ask Svetlana to return your call. Yes, I still have the phone number . . .

Sure enough, when I returned to the House that night, Matron called me to her office and sat me down in the bright puddle of her desk lamp.

"If you do not wish to see Comrade Kravshina again, I will tell her exactly that. There is no reason for you or me to torment the woman further. There is no reason for you to pretend that you are open to a relationship with your mother if you are not."

"Did she call again today?"

"Once in the morning. And once in the afternoon. The next time she calls I will inform her of the new regulations."

"What are the new regulations?" I asked.

Matron didn't answer. She just leaned back in her chair with her hands in her apron pockets and looked at me. I understood: there were no new regulations, but Matron had nonetheless changed her rules. She would not be making this decision after all. Matron was leaving the choice up to me.

She picked up the receiver of the phone on her desk.

"Will you, or will you not, return Comrade Kravshina's phone call?"

It would have been so easy to end it. Perfect retribution after all these years: *Ni slova.* Not a word.

But I didn't. I took the receiver from Matron's hand and called my mother.

"IT COULDN'T BE MORE perfect." Oksana was bouncing on my bed with excitement. "You'll tell Matron that we are both going to Vera Konstantinovna's for the New Year and that she has invited us to stay the night."

It was partially true. My mother had asked me to come celebrate New Year's with her in a week's time. And she had, in fact, suggested that I spend the night. She hadn't asked me to invite a friend. She hadn't asked if I had any friends.

"But then, just before midnight you tell her that Matron decided she wants you back at the House," continued Oksana. "You can even say that she's sending a car for you—why not? It's not impossible. Ivan the handyman has a car and Matron could easily conscript him as a chauffeur for her eldest, most trusted young ward. So—a kiss on the cheek, a 'Happy New Year, Mama dear,' and *hop-pa*! Sveta, my most special semi-orphan—you and I have the whole night out to celebrate!"

I shushed her. Most of the kids were already downstairs decorating the New Year's tree, but there was no such thing as being totally alone in the House.

"Sorry," she whispered. "But c'mon, Sveta. This is a golden opportunity. I mean it's landed in our lap. It's New Year's! And Misha has a friend with a car!"

"And what happens when Matron finds out that I didn't spend the night at Vera Konstantinovna's?" I asked.

"That's the beauty of it. She's already as good as told you that she won't. Isn't that what she meant when she asked you to decide? Sure—she will be watching. She will always be watching. But she trusts you. She won't call, because she wants you to understand this is your own choice. That's my bet."

Oksana was probably right. It gave me that sudden pang of panic again—like the wolves were at the door and no one could be bothered to bar it. I wished I hadn't accepted my mother's invitation, but what else could I do once I had taken the phone? Oksana's scheme would at least cut the visit short.

ON NEW YEAR'S EVE, I met my mother outside Kursky Station. Together we chose a spindly tree, the cheapest available at the stand on the boulevard, and carried it forty minutes by tram to the quiet neighborhood where she lived. Inside her building, we rested a moment on the bottom floor, our ears burning in the sudden heat of the building's over-stoked furnace. Then we shifted the tree in our sticky gloves and carried it up three flights of stairs to the communal apartment Vera Konstantinovna shared with a dozen other comrades.

My mother's bedroom in the *kommunalka* was tiny, but we managed to squeeze the tree into the corner by the window. It listed stubbornly to one side, propped in a tin bucket we found in the hallway. Aside from a narrow cot-bed and an uncomfortable wooden chair, there was only one other piece of furniture in the room—a small wardrobe, about two feet deep and five feet tall. When Vera opened it, I could see how few were her possessions. Fewer even than mine. I felt again that thing that was not guilt or shame. That thing I couldn't name.

I hadn't been certain, when I left the House a few hours ago, whether I would mention the memory. The one that I couldn't decipher, but that I knew had to do with my father and a hail of bullets. But when I got off the bus and saw her there, on the wrong side of the street, searching the festive evening crowd, I was struck: my mother was not sure that I would come. She would never be sure. That's what her life had taught her. That you never know when you are seeing someone for the last time. She would live out her life in uncertainty.

I didn't want to wonder. I wanted certainty or the closest thing to it. So now, with the tree installed, the New Year fast approaching, and the laughter of Vera's *kommunalka* neighbors drowning out my thudding heart, I asked. "How did my father die?"

She didn't answer. She walked to the bed and sat heavily next to me. In her lap was a box wrapped in brown paper.

"I hadn't thought of it in all these years but then, just before you came back I had this . . . vision. Papa. And a firing squad."

It was as if she had woken from a trance. She ripped the paper from the box and threw it to the floor. Her hands shook. "That's not possible."

"What's not possible? That Papa was shot?"

"That you could remember. You didn't witness it."

"How can you be sure?"

There was laughter in the corridor outside. Another group had arrived with bottles and bundles. There was less than an hour left in the old year.

"Because I did. I was there."

She lifted the lid of the box to reveal six glass ornaments. There were balls and bells and a star and a bird. She brushed her hand over the fragile ornaments and said, "Before they sent me to the camps I spent several months in Lubyanka Prison."

"Were you with Papa?"

"He was there. But I wasn't allowed to see him. They wanted me to denounce him. They wanted me to say that he brought conspirators home and that they were planning counterrevolutionary acts in our kitchen. Can you imagine?" Vera pulled the bird from the box. It was the color of the red vase that once stood on the kitchen table.

"Did you?" I asked.

"Never."

I took the bird from her hand and crossed over to the tree, where I hung it just in front of one of the miniature candles we had clipped on the sparse branches. I thought about what a seven-year-old girl could have told the men in Lubyanka's interrogation chambers if they had asked. Would she have told them that her father could spin two tops downhill at once? That he let his daughter wear his hat with the wide bill and red star? That he read fairy tales at bedtime? That he burned military papers in the stove and sometimes came home angry from work? That his wife had hissed: *Ni slova*. Not a word.

"One day, instead of taking me for questioning, they took me into the courtyard," my mother continued. "There were three riflemen. Your father was already in place. There was a dark spot on the wall behind him. His hands were bound and his face was covered. They made me watch. It was over in twenty seconds."

I felt dizzy. The tree was too bright. There was a black ring squeezing my peripheral vision. "It was a brick wall," I said thickly.

"Perhaps," said Vera. "Yes, probably it was. But you weren't there Svetlana. You have just . . . what's the word? Internalized—visualized—your loss. Such things happen."

There was a knock on the door. A kindly face, plain but pleasant, poked into the room. "Vera Konstantinovna. Bring your daughter and come to the kitchen. It's almost time. Come celebrate with us."

The door closed and my mother rose.

"It's not something I imagined," I said. "It's something I saw."

I turned and looked her directly in the eye. They no longer struck me as the eyes of a woman who would never know. They were the eyes of a woman who didn't want to know. I recognized them—they were much like mine. "What I saw . . ." I continued, my voice low. "He didn't have anything covering his face. His hands were not tied, they were raised. Like a command."

I crossed the room and put my hands on her shoulders. I knew as I did it that I was the one who needed to be steadied. I was the one who was going to run away, but not until I said it: "He was the maestro. He was the conductor. He was the general. It was Papa who said 'fire.'"

She didn't look away when she said, "That's impossible."

"Impossible? Or wrong?"

She didn't answer. She turned away and I didn't stop her. It was enough for now. I wrapped myself back up in the uncertainty like it was a winter coat.

Now she was standing in the open doorway. "Out with the old, Svetlana. Let's welcome the New Year."

When she left I looked again at the ruby-red bird hanging all alone. This time I saw its flaw. The calibration must have been off at the factory and the dye had missed its mark. The bird was half-blind: one eye socket was empty, and a black blotch sullied its beak.

SIX
NEW YEAR'S, 1959

It wasn't hard to make my exit. Vera seemed almost relieved when I told her that Matron expected me back at the House. I couldn't blame her—after the bomb I had dropped, she wanted only to recover. When the clock struck the New Year we drank champagne and sang with the neighbors. A quarter of an hour later, she walked me to the door.

"Come again, *milaya*," she said. "I wish you all the happiness and health and success that the New Year can bring."

There were no hard feelings in her voice. Just safe words. There was no butterfly kiss. Just a peck on the cheek.

It was twenty minutes past midnight and I was out on the street. The frigid air hurt to breathe and my teeth were chattering, but I felt flushed. Maybe it was the champagne. Maybe it was adrenaline. Maybe it was being out in the city after midnight with hours ahead until morning. Whatever it was, I celebrated it with a reckless *grand jete* right there on the icy sidewalk followed by a series of hurried, nervous *echappés*, the ones Elena Mikhailovna called "escape jumps."

I turned for a last look at my mother's building. It was a bleak structure, but its windows were full of light, leaking laughter and singing. I was glad that my mother was here on Snowfall Lane, and not in some windblown barrack with only a feeble oil lamp to light up the dark. But now I wanted to be far away.

I found her silhouette on the third floor, leaning against the windowsill. I waved and blew a kiss. Then I started up the road, repressing another leap.

There was a vehicle entering the quiet compound at the end of the road. A Pobeda with only one headlight. The car stopped about ten feet in front me. I watched three people spill out of the backseat. None of them was Oksana or Misha.

"I should charge you double," cried a not-quite-young woman as she adjusted her skirt under a patchy fur coat. "My new dress is ruined."

Her companions were two men with red faces and no hats. They swayed behind her on the sidewalk. She gave one of them a light push and he toppled over. She leaned into the driver's window. "Listen, boychik. You're going to have to collect in the New Year, love. I'll be lucky if I come out in the black tonight with these jokers."

I couldn't hear the response, but the girl with the torn dress did. She turned and eyeballed me from head to toe. She nodded. "Sure, I get it." She pulled a few rubles from her pocketbook and handed them into the car.

"Bit late in the night isn't it, schoolgirl?" she said as she sauntered toward me. When she smiled I saw lipstick on her teeth. "Just make sure he buys the good stuff," she said.

I had clearly made a mistake. I crossed the street in front of the car and walked quickly toward the main road. I heard the car shift into gear. I lowered my head and willed it to disappear. Instead, its cyclops beam lit a wide arc through the naked trees and lit the path ahead of me. Dark and breathing, the Pobeda pulled up alongside.

"Svetlana."

My eyes were glued to the pavement.

"Svetlana, it's me. Hey, sorry about that—just business."

My fingers were frozen but my palms were in a sweat. I turned and saw it was true. Georgi Levshik was driving an enormous car in my mother's housing complex on New Year's Eve.

"Misha . . ." I began.

"Is a lousy driver."

Georgi's words were a frozen cloud. He was still talking, but all I could focus on was the glittering frost between us. I heard the passenger door open on the other side of the car. "Get in."

I thought about the movies. How the boy always got out of the car to open the door.

"Svetlana, come on. The party is in full swing. Misha's at the piano and your friend Oksana is guarding the last piece of cake with her life."

On the sidewalk across the street the girl with the torn dress was struggling to get her two companions on their feet. Behind me my mother might still be watching from her windowsill. I couldn't afford for her to wonder what the hell was going on outside her window. Directly ahead of us was the white noise of the main road, leading to my friends and the New Year. I stepped back in front of the Pobeda and climbed into the passenger seat.

"*Poshli,*" I said. Let's go.

He eased the car through the dark residential maze, glancing once in the rearview mirror.

"Where on earth did you get a car?" I asked. "Do you even have a license?"

"Sure I do. I've been driving for nearly a year now. Spotless record, too."

I stifled a snort. I had a pretty good idea of his record.

At the end of the block Georgi turned right onto the Ring Road and accelerated. I gripped the handle next to me. I had never ridden in the front seat of a car before. Once or twice I had been in the backseat of Ivan's car, when Matron took me for documentation. And of course I had bumped along in a truck bed on countless Saturday Pioneer projects in the countryside.

But this was different. Like being a copilot. The road was massive and empty. It insisted on speed. I braced my feet on the floor, but a gasp of surprise escaped. Georgi grinned and stepped on the gas.

"Don't worry, I'm a great driver," he said. "Truly. My auto-vehicular skills are exceptional. Though you probably don't have much to compare them to."

I shrugged and tried a joke. "I know plenty of trolleybus drivers."

"Ha. They have leashes, for crying out loud. They couldn't go off the rails if they tried." He swerved into the inner lane of the four-lane road as if to prove his point.

"I'd like to see you climb up on the top and reconnect those electric cables," I said. It came out as a yell; the Pobeda was a loud car. "You have to be an alpinist to be a trolleybus driver."

"So I'll get my bus license next. Anything to impress you, Svetlana."

I stole a glance. I had forgotten his face after all these weeks. Obscured by the shadows and light-play of the wide highway, it hinted at bruises. The tender kind. I wanted to apologize for that day in the courtyard when he got a punch in the face for his generosity, but I couldn't find the right words.

"Where are we going?" I asked.

"The kids are at a pal of Misha's. Some Foreign Ministry apartment on Prospekt Mira. I suppose we are going there?"

He looked at me. I nodded. Then I turned to watch the city unfurl like a moving picture.

It was so different, Moscow, at night and at this speed. The landmarks I had always used for orientation were now more like ornaments. Especially the Stalinscrapers—the sand castles of marble that Joseph Stalin had built as monuments to the Victory over Fascism. Floodlit and topped with Soviet red stars, they were static streaks of lightning in a city that trapped most of its light close to the ground. As we passed the one at the Red Gates I craned my neck to see its pinnacle.

I imagined the marble foyers, the crystal chandeliers, the elite elegance inside reserved for the cream of Soviet society—the cosmonauts and commissars, the generals and the ministers. The fighter pilots. The Party bosses. The prima ballerinas. Oh yes. *To each according to their . . .*

"Have you ever been inside?" Georgi asked.

"Never. You?"

"Sure," he answered. "Piece of cake. It's *staying* inside that's the trick."

His eyes were on the rearview mirror, not on the Stalinscraper. I realized he was navigating not by the road in front of us, but by the lights behind us. I looked. There was only one other car on the road, and it was gaining on us.

"Police?" I asked.

"Nah," he answered. "Better."

He inched over to the curb. The car on our tail pulled up alongside and then parked directly in front. It was the same model that we were in but it had two headlights, a fresh coat of paint, and an official hat: TAXI. The brake lights went on and a man in a quilted coat and cap got out of the car.

Georgi opened the door. "I'll be right back."

A cold blast of air filled the car as I nervously watched him approach the taxi driver. They exchanged a few words and then leaned into the trunk. I knew what this was. The taxi driver earned much more off the black market booze he ferried around than he did on passengers. Few people who could afford a taxi actually needed one. But anyone could afford a three-ruble bottle and then stagger home on foot. Anyone except me, that is. I couldn't afford that kind of trouble.

"*Blin*," I muttered. I looked into the backseat where two empty vodka bottles lay forgotten on the floor. *Make sure he buys the good stuff.*

My stomach turned over. I grabbed the door handle, but I couldn't make out how to open it. I thought of the House, locked up. The Metro, closed. My mother, asleep. *K chortu.* How did I get myself into this? There was nowhere to go but with Georgi in his brothel on wheels.

The car door on the driver's side opened. I closed my eyes, afraid of the proof that a two-bit hustler with a "spotless record" was about to deliver me a fresh black mark for my already blackened biography.

"Hey." His voice was quiet, concerned maybe. "Svet. Svetlana, you awake?"

Something soft brushed my cheek and my eyes flew open in alarm. Roses. A whole bouquet. He dropped them in my lap.

"Happy New Year, Svetlana."

BY THE TIME WE arrived at the party on Prospekt Mira, the table was sticky, Misha had surrendered his place at the piano to the son of the Spanish ambassador, and Oksana had drunk too much champagne.

"Sveta! Hurrah! Come dance the tango with me!" she shrieked, dragging me into a dramatic promenade. Then she collapsed, giggling, into Misha's arms.

I rescued my trampled bouquet from the floor and went looking for the kitchen. It wasn't hard to find. There are only so many layouts for a generous prewar four-room apartment. I knew them from the movies. And, of course, from the first seven years of my life, not everything of which I had forgotten.

The kitchen, it appeared, was full of poets discussing the merits of Boris Pasternak's verses and the crimes of his prose. The name "Zhivago" was on everyone's lips, and I was surprised at how openly they talked. *Doctor Zhivago* and its counterrevolutionary message was a taboo subject. A good Soviet would only discuss it in formal settings, where there was a comrade secretary to record each denunciation verbatim and with attribution. But in this diplomat's apartment, occupied by a colleague of Misha's father, the kids were talking freely. Earnestly. And none of them was calling for the writer to be exiled.

"It's over for him already," said a boy in thick glasses standing next to the sink. I slipped past him to run my flowers under the tap. "He was one of the most revered writers in the Soviet Union, but he gave it all up for a silly, reactionary, romantic doctor. Now he's just a hack. He'll never be published again. He'll never come out of the basement. His scribblings will always be passed hand to hand."

"That's what a manuscript is," I heard myself say. I closed the faucet and turned to a whole room of strangers looking at me. "*Manuscript*. It's Latin. Written by hand and then . . . read by hand." I fingered one of the thorns and felt absurd.

"Good point," said the boy with thick glasses.

"Nice roses," said a girl wearing a beret.

"Sveta, I think Oksana needs you," said Misha from the doorway.

Back in the large sitting room, Georgi was hovering over the remnants of the banquet. He scraped the last of the potato salad and chopped liver onto a plate along with the dried-up end of a pork roast. I realized he was hungry, and with a shock, I recognized it as chronic hunger.

Oksana slouched next to him. Her face had a green tinge and she was licking her lips. Her eyelids fluttered.

"Not good," she whispered.

"All good!" Georgi replied cavalierly.

Without putting down his plate, he reached across the table and picked up a glass. He sniffed at its contents then poured it into the vase that I had just placed on the table. Then he grabbed a bottle of mineral water, filled the used glass, and handed it to Oksana. "Drink," he said. But Oksana just sunk farther into the sofa. "*Blin*," she said. "I'm going to . . . I'm going to be sick . . ."

Georgi put down the glass. He put down his plate. He put his hands under Oksana's armpits and lifted her from the sofa. Misha watched, wringing his hands, as Georgi marched Oksana to the toilet and shut the door. I ran to follow, but there was no room to open the door with the two of them in there.

"Let me in," I insisted nonetheless.

"Hands full here, Svetlana."

"Let me. She needs me."

"Nope. She needs this perfect porcelain bowl and then a shot of vodka."

I pushed the door open a crack and watched helplessly as Georgi straddled my best friend from behind, holding her hair from her face with one hand. I closed the door and hoped no one else had seen.

When they emerged a few minutes later, Georgi steered Oksana into Misha's arms. "She needs a bed," he said.

"Right. Yes," agreed Misha, accepting Oksana's languid body uncertainly.

"Try the last door at the end of the corridor," suggested Georgi. I wondered briefly if he knew his way around the coveted apartments of Prospekt Mira from the movies or from his nocturnal activities.

"Let me help," I said.

Georgi took my elbow. "Leave them," he said. "Time Misha learned the hard part of being a gentleman."

I shook off his hand, but I didn't follow them. I stared at the greasy plates and empty bottles on the table in front of us. I glanced at the clock. It was not yet two o'clock. The New Year was an hour old and I had already made a colossal mistake. In the foyer some of the poets were bundling into coats. They must live nearby, I thought, since the Metro was closed and the last bus had trundled down Prospekt Mira an hour ago. *What the hell was I supposed to do until morning?*

"Don't worry," said Georgi. He sat back down on the sofa and reached for a carcass of dried fish. "I'll take you home. Take her, too, after she's slept it off a bit."

"No, that's all right," I said. It wasn't, though. It wasn't all right at all. "I'll just . . ." I didn't finish. I didn't know what I would do.

He stopped his inspection of the fish to inspect me.

"Oho!" he exulted after a moment. "So you're not a perfect

Pioneer after all, are you? Not averse to breaking the rules when it suits? Let me guess—you told your mother you were staying at Oksana's house. And she told her mother she'd be at yours . . . is that it?" His face glowed—like in the movies, when pirates open an old chest and find it full of gold.

"No," I said angrily. "No. It's not like that at all."

He stifled his grin, smug. "So it was actually Oksana's idea. Yeah. That makes more sense. She's got a thing for Misha docsn't she? Well, good. Got what she was after. Too bad she's too blotto to enjoy it."

He stood up from the sofa and then was sitting again.

"You pushed me," he said, genuinely surprised.

I wanted to do it again. I wanted to shake him, punch him, blacken his other eye. I wanted to draw blood, or at least an apology.

"No, you pushed *me*. How dare you, you bastard."

He threw the stupid fish on the table. He passed a hand over his eyes. I almost expected him to make some comment about "shrews" or "broads."

"Hey kid, relax. I don't care what you girls get up to. Honest. Do what you gotta do to enjoy yourself, all right? It's better than doing what you gotta do to survive. Believe me."

The front door opened and a whole new group tumbled in to celebrate. More Spaniards. The new arrivals brought more bottles, more flowers, more tango music. Misha returned to the room and introduced Georgi to one of them who declared, in broken Russian, "I give good price for Russian rubles and Russian love!"

I inspected Georgi as he had me. I saw a boy with freckles and unwashed hair. A boy who carried a wad of rubles but ate from other peoples' tables. A boy who had bought me roses with a prostitute's wages. He met my gaze.

"What? Did you think I came just to play chauffeur for you?" His voice was soft. But defiant. "No, Svetlana. I had a New Year's agenda. Just like you."

I imagined what he must think of me. A girl with a chip on her shoulder, breaking curfew. A girl who had used him as easily as the Spaniard who was asking, "You want my money or not, Russky?" A girl who had never shown an ounce of gratitude.

"I never thanked you for the shoes," I whispered.

"Or for the ride. Or for the roses," he agreed. "Now. I am going to step out onto the balcony with this pansy-ass Don Juan and make a transaction. Then I am going to leave. If you want a ride home, get your coat."

"Where do you live?" I asked.

"Kursky Station."

"Like me."

"No. Not like you, Svetlana. I live *in* Kursky Station. In the shed. Behind the baggage depot."

I saw him now, fully. A boy who fed himself, clothed himself, and could be a midnight captain of the Ring Road because of that. A boy with hard luck but in control of his destiny. An outcast like me, who had never been offered the protection of the state. Or, if he had, had rejected it. He was the ward of no one.

I looked around the room full of strangers. Even Misha, who I had known for years and who knew my secret, suddenly seemed a stranger to me compared to this boy who did not pretend to be anything other than what he was: a hustler.

"Okay, Gosha." I said. "You can drive me home. But we have to kill six hours first. Because I live in Orphanage number thirty-six and the doors are locked till morning."

SEVEN
ACADEMY

In the end, the decision about where and with whom I would live was made not by Matron and not by my mother. It was the Bolshoi Academy that decided.

The letter came in May, a week before the end of the spring term. *Svetlana Kravshina*, it said, *is among an elite group invited to join the Academy's summer intensive ahead of the full cohort of the incoming class.*

Elena Mikhailovna didn't even try to hide her astonishment.

"Sveta, you minx! I knew that you would make the final round. I figured you had a solid chance against the others, the younger ones. But to think—the summer intensive! That's likely to be a fast-track. They're practically pushing you into the company! And at your age! What the devil did you do in that audition?"

"I may have let a triple pirouette get away from me," I said. "I think I stopped at four. The ballet master asked if I had been trained by a man."

Elena Mikhailovna let out a loud laugh and wagged her finger. "And you told him that Comrade Elena Mikhailovna of the Central House of Ballet has trained you selflessly, conscientiously, steadfastly . . ."

"Joyfully . . . forward into the future of a more graceful Communist society!" I finished in my clarion Komsomol voice.

Elena Mikhailovna threw her arms around me and squealed.

I tried to imagine Vera Konstantinovna expressing such happiness. I hoped she would. I hoped she would never know what else I had told the auditioning committee: that I had broken all communications with my mother, a former Enemy of the People.

I told myself it had nothing to do with her, anyway. I was the one who would have to live with it—never knowing if it was my pirouette or my redemption politics that got me into the Bolshoi Academy.

MATRON WAS MORE GUARDED with her congratulations. She was pleased, of course. It reflected well on the House when one of her residents flourished. She would likely be commended for her role in transforming a ward of the state into a bona fide Soviet artist. But her parting words were wary.

"You are entering another echelon, Svetlana. A different world. The Bolshoi is a great leap from Orphanage number thirty-six—even for a girl with . . ." she scanned the letter for the specific commendation: ". . . excellent airborne extension."

I stood before her desk—my suitcase by my side, my bright future outside the gate. She could have told me I was being thrown, with excellent airborne extension, to the wolves; I would have still welcomed it.

"You have been granted access to an elite realm, Svetlana. The Bolshoi Theatre might be a cultural palace for the working class, but its stage is no place for democracy. You must comport yourself with the same deference that you would if you were being inducted into the Central Committee of the Communist Party itself. You must be prepared to make adjustments . . . in recognition of your higher profile."

I kept my face serious, but my heart was headstrong. I heard the words "deference" and "Central Committee," and pictured rows of jowly Party apparatchiks and medaled generals falling over themselves to throw flowers at my feet. I was an unknown star, a bolt from the blue, a blazing comet. There would be no crashing to earth. But I nodded in deference; I recognized my higher profile. I raised my chin and promised Matron, "I will not disgrace you. I will be a tribute to the House."

I resolved never to mention Orphanage #36 again.

I WAS THE TALLEST girl in the class. The tallest and the oldest and, on the first day of the summer intensive, the one on whom the highest hopes were riding. I didn't know that, of course. I don't think anyone in the Academy knew it. Not yet.

I slept in a room with five other girls. Three were from Moscow, one from Voronezh, and one was from the back of beyond. The name of the town that Nadia came from changed every time we asked: Bogdanova or Bogdanovka or Novaya Bogdorsk. Anyway, it was far, and Nadia cried every night. The girl from Voronezh cried, too, but she hid it. Then, in the morning, she bullied poor Nadia from Novobogdannaya.

It was strange, after the House, to live so closely with girls who kept so far away. I guess we all knew that on some level we were not comrades. We were rivals. Friendship was not something any of us came to the Academy for. I didn't mind. I welcomed the space that discipline had carved out. But there were days a smile would have been nice.

Elena Mikhailovna smiled quite a lot, I thought one afternoon toward the end of the first week. The teacher, a woman named Polina Sergeevna, who at age thirty or so was the youngest coach at the Academy, was shouting. She was shouting, "That's exactly right Sonya, perfect!" But her face was a grimace.

On a whim, I turned to the mirror and flashed a thousand-watt smile at myself.

"What the hell is that, Svetlana?"

"Cramp," I answered, flushing.

Now Polina Sergeevna was beside me, running her thumb up my calf, looking for the charley horse. She didn't stop at my thigh but pressed higher, her thumb like an awl all the way up my back. It felt as though my vertebrae might flake onto the floor, like the shaved chocolate Cook left on the counter when she made the New Year's cake.

"You feel that?" she asked. I nodded. "That's your spine. It is an iron chain. When you pull it from top and from bottom it is rigid, unyielding, exacting. But when you loosen the grip . . ." Polina Sergeevna drew her thumb in a circle around my collarbone and pressed her palm flat against my sternum. "When you unlock that top link, the chain is molten iron. It is strong but it is pliant." She pressed harder, bending my shoulders out and over, beyond my sacrum, and steadily, steadily, farther—until my eyes were on the corner of the ceiling directly behind me and the crown of my head neared my ass, and still she pushed.

"Your spine is like steel, girls," she announced to the room as my thighs screamed under the pressure of my fully arched back and the blood rushed into my head. "And it should remain strong at two hundred and thirty degrees, *en arrière*."

She held me a second longer as she asked Larisa if she understood the math. "Two hundred and thirty degrees, Larisa. What do I mean?"

"Oof," breathed Larisa, who, incidentally, was standing fully upright.

"I mean that your fingers should brush the floor in a perfect back bridge. I mean that elongation and strength are partners. I mean that one hundred and eighty degrees is never enough. Thank you, Svetlana."

Polina Sergeevna helped me stand upright and patted my rear.

There was still an hour of class left for the morning. And three more in the afternoon. That night Nadia from Bogdanovka sat down on my bed and said, "Did you know you could do that?"

TWO WEEKS LATER, EXHAUSTED and sore, I called Oksana in tears and begged her to meet me. She hurried out of the Metro at Smolenskaya, took one look at me sulking in the sunshine and burst out laughing.

"You goose! Sveta! How can you possibly be unhappy? What's the matter? Do you miss Andrei Samoilovich? Is that it? Or homemade kasha by the bucketful? Can't sleep without everyone passing the front gates whispering about the poor souls inside? Maybe you long for the camaraderie of two dozen irritable girls all on their period at the same time?"

"Hardly," I said. "Most of the girls in my group haven't hit puberty, and the coaches want their bodies to stay that way. No tits, no hips."

"Ah. So no cranky communal hormones. No wonder you're lonely."

"And they don't feed us any better than Cook," I said. "Malnutrition, it turns out, produces great ballet bodies. Peas and carrots every day. One egg in the morning. Meat twice a week and it's not a nice color."

"I guess I'll have to start bringing you charity packages. Fancy some pickled beets from the Central Benevolence Committee?"

I glanced at her, chastened; my Oksana was as alone as I was. As always, she managed to have a better attitude.

"What's the news?" I asked taking her arm. "Tell me everything."

We crossed the Ring Road, chattering about Lydia Timofeevna's new gentleman friend and Lara V.'s bronze medal. "She wears it everywhere, which is funny because it's a medal for exceptional humility."

We fell silent out of habit before the Foreign Ministry, one of Stalin's gargantuans. I shielded my eyes, trying to see the top. Oksana flipped her skirt, trying to catch the eye of the soldier on guard. I giggled. I was thinking of the night when Georgi Levshik and I skidded across the foyer of the Stalinscraper at the Red Gates.

"How's Misha?" I asked.

"Absent," said Oksana. "Busy. Otherwise engaged. Studying.

Not home. That's what Misha is. I haven't heard from him in over a month. *Ni slova.*"

I squeezed her arm. "Bastard," I said.

"Who's a bastard? Not Misha. Misha's busy, Sveta. The bastard—he's the one you're really asking about, aren't you? You want to know if I've seen that bastard, Gosha."

Her tongue waggled sarcastically over the word *bastard*. I had stopped using it on New Year's Day.

"Want me to pass on your number if I ever see him? If I ever see Misha, that is."

"Good lord, no," I blurted. "I don't have time for bastards with concert tickets."

Now Oksana giggled. "He had *awfully* impressive concert tickets, didn't he, Sveta?"

We turned into the Arbat, and the busy city fell away behind a heavy curtain. This was low-lying Moscow, full of courtyards and pocket playgrounds, prams and benches. There were no cars on the roads and the pedestrians in this part of town walked to enjoy themselves, not to get somewhere. It was quiet in the heart of the capital.

On Ostozhenka Street we stopped before the heavy drapes of a fancy restaurant. Though it was not even noon yet, we could smell that evening's menu.

"Chicken cutlets and potato puree."

"Pork chops. With crispy fat."

"Caviar and blinis. Meringues in cream."

"Pitchers of punch."

We saw the dining room as clearly as in the movies. There would be waiters standing by in every corner and an elaborate fountain in the middle of the room. There would be a crooner in a sharp suit making the rounds, doling out long-stemmed roses to the ladies in their fur wraps and pearls and long gloves. Chandeliers winking.

Ochi chornye, warbled Oksana, strumming her belly like a gypsy guitar.

I smiled. I would dine at those tables, one day. In a backless dress that would show off my steely, supple spine.

Farther down Ostozhenka we came to a small shop. The awning said BOOKSHOP, but the elegant script, with its *K* like a knight in armor, promised printed materials older than the Soviet Union's modern presses. Old maps and foreign stamps, most likely.

"Let's take a look," said Oksana.

The shop appeared to be empty, but a voice close to the ceiling said, "Watch out for the cat. He's not friendly."

An elderly man was perched on a ladder that ran on a rail along the width of the wall. A large ginger cat stared at us from the corner, its tail switching irritably. I knelt and held out my hand. The cat swiped me.

"*Chort*. You devil," I murmured.

"What's the matter? No ears in your head?" The man pulled a rolled-up tube from a high shelf and blew a plume of dust from it. "Whatever you're looking for, I doubt we have it." He eyed us from over his glasses. "Or perhaps you're not looking? Just lurking?"

"Actually, I would like to see the rarest stamp you have," said Oksana smartly. "Like, almost-extinct rare."

The man seemed to warm to the challenge. "There are many kinds of rarity. There are limited editions, typography errors, discontinued presses, contested origins . . ."

"Let's see one of those, could we?" asked Oksana.

"One of what?"

"A contested origin. Is that like where the stamp comes from a letter to the duchess from her lover, but she swears that it actually belongs to her lady's maid?"

The shopkeeper reached the floor. He looked quizzically at Oksana.

"She's read too many comedies of error," I explained.

"I don't know whether to laugh or cry," he responded. He wiped his hands on his smock, pulled a stool from behind the counter and gestured for Oksana to sit. I left them to their quasi-instructional conversation.

Avoiding the cat, I crossed the room to where a big glass case, the kind you found in museums, stood in the window. It was full of yellowed maps. I recognized the obvious outlines—Europe, Kamchatka, Scandinavia. Others were indistinct, but still familiar—a city cleaved by a river, a coastline of fjords. I leaned in to examine a simple drawing, striped like a tiger's face in flames of gray. The legend was written in German. I decided that the flames were stylized arrows, defining a military advance.

There was a radio on the counter. It was the classical hour on Channel One.

Dear comrades, music lovers of Moscow, purred the voice of Sunday afternoon. *The time is 1400.*

It was a tranquil voice. Soothing as an invitation to sleep. I listened to it announce the coming concerts and segue seamlessly into a biography of *the great composer and our national genius, Pyotr Ilyich Tchaikovsky*. My eyes closed as I felt myself transported—not physically or emotionally, but mentally, temporally. I was drifting back in time, remembering another Sunday serenaded by Tchaikovsky. Another Sunday in May. Another spring day, at two o'clock in the afternoon.

On this Sunday a handful of military men, faceless but grave, shed their wool jackets and wide-brimmed hats and gathered at a table. They took turns drawing lines around the city of Berlin. Their cigarettes dropped ash on the black-and-white map. There was birdsong out the window and a piano concerto on the radio. And then one of the men spoke. He said: *And when the tyrant Hitler is defeated, we will turn our victorious tanks on the tyrant in the Kremlin.*

The voice was deep, dulcet, calm. I knew that voice. I knew it as well as the progression of chords at the end of the concerto as they shift from major to minor and back . . . It was my father's voice. It was Evgeny Kravshin calling for the overthrow of his generalissimo, Joseph Stalin.

There was a fierce yowl as I bolted from the store. The nasty cat had left its tail in the doorway. Outside on Ostozhenka, nothing had changed. I watched the pollen blow. Oksana hurried out, alarmed. I assured her it was just dust and fatigue taking its toll.

"Poor thing. They really are starving you, aren't they?"

I wondered if there wasn't relief under her concern. Or hope. Oksana would call in the cavalry to rescue me. She'd have a ladder at the window and a sack full of gingerbread. We'd escape together to the Phoenix Plains.

"I skipped breakfast," I said. "It's my own fault. I need to go home now."

A full beat passed and then I clarified: "I have to go home to the Academy."

"Okay, *milaya*. Whatever you say."

When we reached the Ring Road, Oksana threw her arms around my neck.

"No long goodbyes or I'll be the one to burst into tears," she said. "Now, I know they've got you dancing like a monkey in a circus, Svet. But if you don't summon me for your birthday, I swear I will never speak to you again."

I promised and kissed Oksana on the cheeks. As soon as she was gone through the swinging doors of the Metro I turned and walked slowly back to the corner of Ostozhenka. I peered back into the quiet green light dusted with pollen, waiting for the memory to reappear. I tried to picture, once again, the men and the table and the map. I fixed it in my mind like a single frame in a filmstrip, searching the faces for my father's. But the image was volatile. When I closed my eyes, it bubbled on my lids, like a negative that's come too close to the projector's bulb. Melting, popping, disappearing.

I TOOK THE MAIN roads back to the Academy, where there was no danger of tranquil radios and time travel. I turned my mind to business.

I needed to spend the rest of the afternoon in the studio,

working on my *port de bras*. The two-week assessment yesterday had not been a triumph; my *port de bras* was the weak link. Polina Sergeevna had crossed her legs and frowned and said, "Svetlana's arms will grow. Her spine is quite elongated and capable of extension. The arms will come."

But Vasily Vasilievich, the aging ballet master who, as rector of the Academy, pretty much ran the summer intensive like his personal fiefdom, disagreed. Vasily Vasilievich liked to pinch the skin below my elbow and hold it for the duration of an entire adagio. "Chicken wing," he called me.

Vasily Vasilievich was a bastard.

Elena Mikhailovna never complained about my arms, I thought angrily. Then I unbuttoned my coat and, like a deranged crossing guard, began moving through my full *port de bras* in the middle of the Ring Road.

I arrived at the Academy with my arms raised to fifth position.

"I was about to give up on you."

I shaded my eyes against the sun, which had turned my mother into a dark silhouette by the gate.

"I didn't know you were coming."

"It's Sunday isn't it?" she said. "When else would I be allowed to interrupt the sacred schedule of a trainee?"

I hadn't seen her since New Year's. I had planned to tell her about the Academy in person, but . . . but I didn't. I told her by phone, and when she said, "Looks like I didn't kill your chances after all, *milaya*," I didn't know if it was humor or sarcasm or just a statement of fact. The same was true now.

"Hello, *dochka*," she said cheerfully as she stepped out of the glare. "I hope it's still visiting hours? Invite me in for tea."

I took my pass from my pocket and waited while she signed the visitors' book. I tried not to think about what that signature would say to Vasily Vasilievich or the people he answered to. I started down the corridor toward the canteen, but Vera Konstantinovna wasn't in a hurry. She was moving slowly, studying each of the portraits on the wall. She stopped before Galina Ulanova's.

She cocked her head slightly and studied the picture. I wondered if she even knew who it was. Vera had been gone so long—did she even recognize the heart-shaped face framed in soft curls as the greatest ballerina in the world?

"One day it will be you," she said.

"My friend Oksana says the same thing."

I waited for Vera to acknowledge my idol, to praise her grace, or her theatricality, or the fact that she was both a Hero of Socialist Labor and Artist of the People.

Instead, she said: "She's a cool customer."

"What do you mean?"

Vera shrugged. "She knows when to speak. When not to speak. She doesn't make waves, and that's good for her career. You don't get two Stalin medals without a good head on your shoulders. Or, of course, a black hole in your heart."

I was stunned. My mother, judging Ulanova. A Gulag returnee speaking with derision about political correctness. And in the halls of the Academy, no less.

"She's a brilliant artist. An amazing dancer," I said hotly, though there was no proof in the static photograph of a woman whose beauty was revealed onstage, not by the camera. "The absolute best."

"Absolute. Yes, so they say," nodded Vera. "You've seen her?"

I felt my cheeks burn. "No, actually. But when the new season begins in September, we will all go. We have special student tickets. Perhaps I can get one for you, too."

"Thank you, dear. But that's not necessary. I have a connection."

She gave Ulanova one last look and then threaded her arm through mine. "In fact," she continued, "I should be the one offering you tickets. They are sure to be better than student seating up in the chandeliers."

We had missed lunch and the canteen was nearly empty. At

the buffet counter Vera pointed to a plate of sticky rolls with raisins. I was still trying to process what she had said about getting tickets. It had sounded like the boast of a hustler. What sort of connection could a Metro worker have at the Bolshoi?

"Someone you should befriend, Sveta," she said as if reading my thoughts. "She is what you call 'interministerial.'"

"What does that mean?"

"It means she has authority in multiple state agencies. Including the Ministry of Culture."

I knew what that meant. That meant my mother knew someone who could change my life. *But how, and since when?*

I watched Vera place two cups of tea on a tray and proceed to the cash register. She pulled out her change purse and frowned.

"Sveta, *milaya*, do you have ten kopecks?"

I handed over the change wordlessly.

"Thanks," she said. The woman who had just disparaged student tickets.

"How do you know her?" I asked when we were sitting at a table in the corner. "This interministerial friend?"

"From the camps, believe it or not. It's not just ice and snow out there, you know. When a third of the country is living in the Gulag it becomes a surprisingly cultural place."

I stirred sugar in my tea. I felt her eyes on me. I felt her judging me. Was it my fault that I developed my "natural airborne extension" at the Central House of Ballet and not in some godforsaken Siberian hovel? I felt the miles open up again between us and I didn't know what to say.

"It's decided then," said Vera. "I will introduce you. I will take you to the Bolshoi for your birthday."

She looked proud. Happy, even. But I was angry. I was angry that after planting enormous obstacles for me, she thought she could knock them down with some "friend" from the camps. Matron certainly hadn't considered that possibility. She had thought Vera Konstantinovna was a liability. So had I. In fact, I had deliberately avoided my mother to get where I was. Now

I had to consider the possibility that it was she who had put me here.

"Now tell me," she said as she plucked a raisin from the roll and popped it into her mouth. "What did you see and do today, on your day off?"

I looked her straight in the eye. I imagined her stricken face and frightened words: *Ni slova.* I was spiteful, and I wanted to see that fear again.

So I told her exactly what I had seen earlier that day: a clandestine meeting from the past. And I told her exactly what I had done: remembered that my father was a traitor.

EIGHT
CONNECTION

"Your technical review is quite good. All of your coaches give you high marks. The consensus is that you are hard-working, motivated, and, importantly, open to choreographic critique. We've seen that you are quick to incorporate corrections."

Vasily Vasilievich may have been a great dancer in his day, but I couldn't say when that was. He still had the posture of the stage, but his face had gone to flab. The hair on his head was as light as his lisp. Now he was revealing my fate.

The four-week assessment period had come and the Academy was making cuts. That morning we had watched three tearful departures—girls who hadn't made enough progress or showed enough grit. Nadia had been among the dismissed, but she didn't cry. In fact, it was the first time I had seen something like happiness on the poor girl's face. Or maybe it was relief. Relief to be back in the familiar tight embrace of Bogdanovsk's obscurity. I hugged Nadia goodbye and hurried to class, where I attacked the allegro. The combination was a gauntlet of jumps and zig-zagging directional changes. At the end of it I caught a quick glance in the mirror: my arms a lasso, my back a parabola, my legs perfectly parallel to the floor three feet below me. A split second of airborne perfection.

The last time I stood before the rector I had tried to hide my arms, my "chicken wings." Now, with the sweat of the allegro still slick on my brow, I let them dance at my side. They were strong and supple—my reinforcements, my deliverance.

Vasily Vasilievich closed the file before him. "This is an interim assessment. It is, as we say, early days."

I nodded. I could scarcely remember my life pre-Academy.

"You must be very grateful to the members of the Committee for Scouting Young Artistic Talent and the Benevolence Society for the Restitution of Compromised Progeny."

"Yes, I am," I said, though I had never heard of either.

"Such is the progressive understanding of our cultural leadership today—to recognize promise in unpromising circumstances. You do realize, Comrade Kravshina, the great favor you have been granted? That in addition to overlooking your unreliable family history and your mixed political pedigree, we have waived certain standards of involvement . . ."

I swallowed. "Involvement?"

"Yes. Involvement." He smacked his lips over the syllables. I wondered if he had always had this prim nastiness. I imagined him as a younger man, a third-rate dancer relegated to character roles: the village gossip, the informant in the doorway, the one who is always frozen in the pose of whispering behind one hand.

"I'm speaking of your political immaturity, Kravshina. Your lack of interest in Party matters and nonexistent record of communal endeavors. Most of our students here are, naturally, far too busy with their training to dedicate much time to Komsomol activities or political lectures. This is understood. But for a student in your position . . . well, you have too many black marks already to allow yourself the simple excuse of being busy at the barre."

I nodded. I sensed bad news, but not disaster.

"Luckily," he continued, his lips pursed, "there are solutions."

Solutions. That meant there were problems.

"There are ways to expunge your truancy, to demonstrate that you are neither an apolitical individualist nor an ill-intentioned element. And one such solution, Svetlana, has presented itself as custom tailored for you in particular."

I realized I was staring at the floor. "I will go to more Komsomol meetings," I promised. "I will sign up for leadership positions. I will write declarations, testimonials, exhortations . . . whatever you need of me."

"It would seem that what is needed of you is a bit more . . . involved."

That word again.

Vasily Vasilievich returned to the desk and reopened the file. "I gather you have been selected for a specialized study that will run alongside your ballet training. Both courses demand your complete, unflagging diligence. It will not be easy. But then, a Bolshoi ballerina never looks for ease—am I right, comrade? Not unless she wants to leave herself vulnerable to charges of parasitism."

Parasitism. It was an easy accusation. You heard it on the street, in police precincts, among feuding neighbors or jealous coworkers. But when it came from the mouth of the man who could open the doors of the Bolshoi Theatre or close them forever, it was a terrible charge. It was an ideological conviction. A biological diagnosis—repulsive down to its suckers.

"I am not a parasite, Vasily Vasilievich."

"Of course not," he said with a flip of his wrist. "But you do have a debt to pay. And so, Kravshina, you will fulfill your secondary training." He closed the file once more and placed it in the desk drawer. "I know nothing more about its content. I gather your mother will be facilitating your schedule."

Of course. My mother would facilitate the payment of my debt. The debt that she had paid in a penal camp while I cowered behind the gates of Orphanage #36 from the taunts outside: *Come out and fight, you parasites!*

TO CELEBRATE MY BIRTHDAY I went to the Bolshoi Ballet for the first time in my life.

My mother met me at the front entrance of the theater. She was not alone. She was, as promised, "connected."

"Svetlana, I'd like to introduce you to Comrade Natalia Davydovna Gerasova. Natalia, this is my daughter."

She looked to be older than my mother, despite her dyed hair. She had a face that was not unkind and an air of infinite patience. She was wearing a blouse with a ruffled collar under a boxy suit. The lapel of her jacket held a small medal on a red ribbon, one that I couldn't read without being indiscreet. But that badge held a clue. An answer to whether this "interministerial" friend was a high-ranking Party member or a lowly clerk in the security apparatus. A clue to this woman, who was just "Natalia" to my mother.

I extended my hand. "It's nice to meet you."

She addressed my mother without taking her eyes off me. "What a beauty she is, Vera. She should, without a doubt, be onstage."

Inside the theater I tuned them both out. I ascended the grand staircase, entered the gilded stalls, took my seat in the third row, between my mother and her mysterious friend, and forgot about them both.

I fanned my excitement with the program: *Romeo and Juliet*, starring Galina Ulanova. I was sixteen years old. I was ready to see my future before me on the stage of the Bolshoi Theatre. But I didn't. I saw Galina Ulanova's past.

IT DIDN'T HAPPEN IMMEDIATELY. The first half of the ballet was everything I had dreamt it would be: lush pageantry and playful love, a moving masquerade in brocade and *allongé*.

It was all so lovely and real that I almost missed her entrance: Juliet embodied in a forty-year-old prima ballerina. She was light as a feather, joyful in ways no longer possible in an era of electricity, hopeful in degrees unattainable in our earnest times.

Galina Ulanova, arrayed in the garb of class warfare and blood feuds, leapt into a bright future, and none of us saw the Hero of Socialist Labor she had left behind in the dressing room.

At the interval I bubbled with praise.

"Isn't she glorious? My God, I won't be able to stand it when she despairs and dies."

Natalia Davydovna Gerasova laughed. "And all because of a misunderstanding. Isn't it awful? You always hope that somehow it will turn out differently."

"We've read the play," I confided. "It doesn't. They both just make the worst possible decisions."

"Vera Konstantinovna," said Natalia Davydovna brightly. "It's Svetlana's birthday. Fetch her a glass of champagne!"

I watched my mother take a place in the line at the buffet and wondered at her quiet. I hoped she had the money for champagne.

Natalia Davydovna stepped closer to me and said, "Imagine. If only Juliet had woken just a few minutes sooner. Or if Romeo, the impetuous boy, could have somehow seen what had happened in Juliet's room the night before."

"Sure," I said, still watching my mother.

"I mean so much is lost when we are ignorant—of events, of other peoples' motivations. Their actions and memories."

It was a silly thought, really. But the way she had said it made me uneasy. I turned my attention to her fully and chose my words carefully.

"Well, yes. I suppose Juliet did wake up too late. But I don't see what Romeo could have . . ."

"Oh, I'm just being hypothetical. But don't you ever wonder? Don't you wonder how many tragedies in life are caused by misunderstandings that might never have happened if someone, somewhere, had looked backward instead of forward?"

My mother reappeared with three glasses of champagne and Natalia Davydovna raised hers in a toast. "To Svetlana's bright future. May it be . . . visionary."

We took our seats for the second act. The curtains parted on another lively gathering of the corps, all paired and laced and perfectly arranged—appealing as a wild bouquet or a well-laid table. My feet pranced under my seat. I longed to be among them, to perch for a moment on a lordly shoulder.

On my left, Vera glanced at me. I smiled and wrapped my arm through hers, my eyes on the stage.

There was dancing, dueling, mime, and a secret marriage.

And then something I had not anticipated: the moment when Juliet acts with reckless foresight.

Galina Ulanova staggered from her balcony, gripping a vial in her hand. It was time for her to take the sleeping draught and enter temporary oblivion. Instead, she stepped forward into the footlights, and the stage scenery disappeared. She turned her back and was unrecognizable—just a female figure on a stark stage.

I was no longer seeing the ballet, though I could still hear its music, the repeated four-note scale of flute: time running out. I was there but not there, and onstage was a woman who was a girl. Younger than Juliet, younger than fourteen. She was seven years old and she was alone in a crowd.

I saw them, too—the specters surrounding her. I saw the red banners and the white uniforms of revolution and civil war. I saw her run from the fighting and cower among others. More young girls, standing in formation at the barre. The flute was still counting and the girls counted with it. Each note cued a single dim light above their heads until twelve notes of the flute illuminated a clock on the wall.

Tick-tick, went the flutes.

Tock-tock, went the flutes.

I counted, too, as the clock turned into a familiar portrait. The sharp features of Vladimir Lenin, leader of the Revolution. *Tick-tick, went the flutes.* And with every beat, Lenin withdrew. *Tock-tock, went the flutes.* And with every note emerged the more dreadful face of his successor, Joseph Stalin.

I could no longer feel my mother's arm. I could no longer feel the seat of my chair. The young girls stepped out of the footlights in single file and dropped into the void of the orchestra pit. All but one. That one, all alone, reached up and placed a hand on the portrait of the man who had promised a bright future. She took it—the bright future—and the hall went dark.

Applause jolted me from the trance. Everyone in the Bolshoi Theatre had seen Juliet's act of desperation. But I had seen Galina Ulanova's act of acceptance. I had seen the moment she bowed to a dictator to acknowledge her People, claiming her place as their Artist. I had seen the compromised side of heroism, but no one had died against a brick wall.

I felt my mother clapping wildly at my side. She stopped when she saw my face. "What is it, Svetlana? What's happened?"

I scrambled over her knees and fled up the aisle out of the hall.

SHE FOUND ME QUICKLY. I was in the ladies' powder room, breathing much too fast. She sat down next to me on the round love seat with the giant plant sprouting from its center and handed me a handkerchief soaked in something aromatic.

"Breathe," she said. "Deep breaths."

I swatted the handkerchief away.

"Your mother is worried about you, Svetlana."

"Then why did she send you?" I asked.

"I may be better equipped to help than she."

I reached out and grasped the medal on Natalia Davydovna Gerasova's jacket. It was engraved with a hammer and sickle framed in a star and it read *For Valorous Labor*. I wondered how literally to take it. Did they give out medals in labor camps?

"You're wondering what I've done to earn it?"

"I am, yes."

"Perhaps nothing yet," she said, patting the ribbon back into place. "But I'm involved in work that moves quickly. I am responsible for the protection of the Soviet Union against external enemies. But I have no tanks or rockets. I don't even have a military rank. You see, people like your mother and me—we have learned, of necessity, how to make use of the only resources available. I learned how to tap resources that most people don't even know they have."

"Smelling salts?" I asked, nodding at the handkerchief in her lap.

She didn't answer immediately. She just tucked the handkerchief back into her bag. I felt rebuked.

"These episodes," she said. "How many have you had?"

Ni slova, I thought. *Ni slova.*

But Gerasova snapped her handbag shut and said, "Your mother told me, Svetlana. I know."

I remembered my mother's denials. Her disbelief and then her insistence that it was all in my head. And now, it turned out, she had believed me. She had called for more help.

"Did she tell you that I saw my father before a firing squad?"

"Is that what you saw just now?"

I closed my eyes. "I don't know what I saw."

The door opened and a stout woman in a smock holding a feather duster walked in. "That can wait until after the performance," said Natalia Davydovna. To my astonishment, instead of giving her a piece of her mind, the housekeeper backed out quietly. Did powder room attendants know Ministers of Culture when they saw them?

"Who are you?" I asked.

She moved closer to me and said in a whisper that went no farther than my ear, "Your father was in Berlin. Your father was also in a secret cellar on Ostozhenka. Your father moved in circles of heroes and dens of conspirators, and men who do that leave confusing paths. All that is important now is that you have the chance to redeem him. To make this confused history final and right. Your mother wants me to protect you, and I can. If not from your father's memories, then at least from his fate."

"How?" I asked.

"By letting you protect your country."

"Because I still have a debt to pay?"

"We all have a debt to pay. Luckily for you, you have more than enough currency to pay with."

"What are you talking about?" I asked, because I knew, but I didn't understand.

"Your gift. Your special gift. Not your talent as a dancer, Svetlana. Your mental power. We want to encourage it. Foster it. Reward it."

"Who is 'we'?" I asked.

"The *rodina*."

I heard the crescendo of the orchestra. In another world, in a gloomy crypt, Juliet was awake and despairing.

I looked again at the badge on Natalia Davydovna's lapel and then at her face, patient but grave. I remembered the vision of my idol, standing firm under a portrait of terror.

Natalia Davydovna Gerasova had not said that the Soviet Union needed me, or that the state needed me, or the Party needed me.

She had used the word *rodina*.

The Motherland needed me.

Now she pulled a small card from her purse and handed it to me. "The Academy makes its final cuts on Friday. Come and see me on Thursday at 11 A.M. I will show you who we are and tell you what we do."

The doors to the ladies' room burst open letting in a flood of chattering women, some of them still tearstained from the tragic finale of the ballet. Natalia Davydovna Gerasova slipped out in their midst.

I looked down at the card. It contained a single address.

Lubyanka 1717.

"We" were the secret police, the KGB.

My *rodina* needed me.

It didn't feel like a reward.

INTERLUDE
VORKUTA 2015

*L*ana Dukovskaya *looks up at the clock on the wall. It is nearly ten o'clock.*

The story had not come out in a straight narrative. It hadn't even come out in full sentences. It was a confused, semi-lucid recitation, and now that one of her grandmother's long pauses has stretched into a nap, Lana reaches for her bag. She pulls out a notebook and a pen and writes:

EVGENY KRAVSHIN (MY GREAT-GRANDFATHER)—GENERAL (?) UNDER STALIN. EXECUTED (?) AFTER THE WAR.

VERA KONSTANTINOVNA KRAVSHINA (GREAT-GRANDMOTHER) RELEASED FROM THE GULAG, 1958.

She takes a deep breath and writes:

SVETLANA WAS RECRUITED BY THE KGB IN JUNE 1959. BY A WOMAN NAMED NATALIA DAVYDOVNA GERASOVA.

Lana lays down the pen. She pulls a hoodie from her bag and coaxes it into a pillow under the old woman's sleeping head. She walks out into the hallway and calls, "Hello?"

There's no answer.

Lana wanders the dingy corridors of Vorkuta's Palace of Culture—a relic of a Soviet past, frozen in time. "Vor-ku-ta," she says out loud, letting its three syllables thump empty on the parquet floor. Vorkuta, the hub of Stalin's Gulag. It makes her head spin. Just an hour ago her grandmother appeared at the door of the dressing room like an apparition. Now she sleeps down the hall, and it's Lana's great-grandmother who haunts the premises: Vera Konstantinovna Kravshina, the first Dukovskaya to survive the Gulag.

Lana focuses on the craziest part of her grandmother's story: The daughter of an Enemy of the People who became an Artist of the People. Only to end up right back here. In Vorkuta.

How did it happen? Was it the visions? Was Svetlana Dukovskaya that rare Soviet who actually needed to be in a psych ward?

And how much of this story did her own mother, Marina, know?

Lana needs more time. She needs to keep traveling the shadowy path of her matriarchal line. She pushes against a double door and finds herself in the empty auditorium where she had performed earlier that evening.

"Hello!" she shouts again.

A girl—the same girl who had tried to prevent an old woman from entering the visiting dancers' dressing room after the performance—steps out onto the stage.

"Oh! You're still here?"

"I am. But I need to leave. I need a taxi.

"The babushka needs a taxi," Lana clarifies when the girl doesn't answer. "The old woman who came backstage. It's too far for her to walk. She's quite elderly."

The girl looks confused.

"The woman. She's a relative. She's my babushka, my grandmother," explains Lana.

"But, you see . . . I mean—a taxi? Well, my cousin . . ."

Lana understands the problem. Vorkuta, a half century after her great-grandmother emerged from its maw and thirty years after it swallowed her grandmother, is still a backward place. There are no taxis in Vorkuta.

"*Could you call your cousin please? I can pay.*"

The girl nods.

Lana goes back to the dressing room and touches the old woman on the shoulder.

"*Babushka, wake up. I'm going to take you home to your bed. We can talk in the morning.*"

Svetlana Dukovskaya stirs slightly. "*Getting in. A piece of cake,*" *she murmurs.* "*It's staying in. That's the trick.*"

Lana picks up the pen and opens the notebook.

She writes: GEORGI THE HUSTLER — UNCLE GOSHA.

Then she sits down to wait for the cousin with a car to carry her and her grandmother through the penumbra of midsummer Siberian dusk.

ACT TWO
AGENT
MOSCOW, 1959–1960

NINE
LUBYANKA 1717

It was strange that of the hundreds of memories I formed within the walls of Lubyanka, none were of that very first day when Natalia Davydovna Gerasova escorted me into the small suite on the ground floor of the massive building's northern wing. I knew that it had happened. I simply couldn't remember it—that introduction to the headquarters of the Committee for State Security, the KGB.

It would have been a Thursday, of course. The Thursday after my birthday, just as Comrade Gerasova had instructed. Her directives trumped all others, I'd learned, including those of the rector. He was her messenger:

"Comrade Gerasova will expect you at 1500 on Thursday."

"Comrade Gerasova has sent a car."

"You are dismissed from class. Comrade Gerasova . . ."

Poor man. He had no idea why this woman had such authority, or why it was so much greater than his own. But confessing to ignorance would only deepen the impression of stupidity, so he dismissed me week after week with wounded dignity.

You could count on one hand the number of people who knew why Gerasova sent for me. Or, at least, *I* could count them on one hand. Surely there were others who knew what was going on in suite 1717. Not rank-and-file KGB, but someone, somewhere, on a high floor with windows looking west to the Kremlin. Someone who sent messages for Gerasova: *Report at 2130.* Who sent a car around to fetch her. Who expected her to show great results. Who had been briefed on the broad outlines of this unorthodox intelligence methodology called "remote viewing" and had signed off on it.

But since I came and went through a secret passage leading directly from the Metro station underneath Lubyanka's infamous prison cells, I had contact with only five people. Five, including Natalia Davydovna Gerasova herself. I never learned who else in the Committee for State Security knew that they had an aspiring ballerina working alongside them to protect the *rodina*. I had no idea who else knew about the top secret work of the Psychological Intelligence Unit. As far as I knew, I was a member of another highly selective coterie. But I couldn't boast about this one.

I'll admit it. At first, being chosen for Enhanced Memory Transference and Recognition was as thrilling as being selected for the Academy. But as the heady summer waned with the daylight, the thrill faded. Just like the ache of strained muscles or the pain of open blisters when they grow calluses.

More importantly, my "memories" were now under control. I hadn't had a single vision outside the walls of 1717. Those that I did have were monitored, recorded, and cultivated in a scientific environment by clinical specialists. They told me I was doing important work, and I believed them. They told me my mind was being sharpened like steel.

So of course it came as a shock when on that crisp October evening, I passed through the unmarked door into the familiar, dry scent of chalk and antiseptic cleanser and realized that there was a gaping hole in my memory.

"I CAN'T REMEMBER THE first time I set foot in this room," I announced. "I can't remember my arrival here."

"There's an explanation for that," said Oleg, lifting his myopic eyes from his ledger.

Oleg was one of the four technicians to whom I was neither Svetlana nor Comrade Kravshina. In Lubyanka 1717, I was the subject called "Prima." They all had different methods, different routines, even different languages for their work—which was to fine-tune my mind like a shortwave radio.

For example, Inga was soft-spoken: a psychology student who focused on the relationship between sensory input and extrasensory perception. She used music in her sessions, exposing me to different passages and composers and measuring their psychic influence. Tchaikovsky, we had found, was most effective at generating the sort of vision that we called "memory." Prokofiev, who had composed the music for *Romeo and Juliet*, was a close second.

Pavel, a small man with the long face of a hound dog, was an engineer specializing in "neural mechanics." He studied all data points, including sleep cycles, nutrition, hormones, and physical exertion. Though he had explored my cognitive powers more thoroughly than anyone else on the team, Pavel had little interest in my unmeasured thoughts. His latest theory was that physical pain was a strong conduit for telepathy. He was always asking if I had, by any chance, injured myself that day.

Maksim was the eldest of the Enhanced Memory technicians in the Psychological Intelligence Unit. He was gruff, coarse, and had no sense of humor. I guessed that his background was not in the lab or the research library, but in the halls of Lubyanka among the flat-footed bureaucrats and spider-eyed spies. It was Maksim who coined the phrase "remote viewing," and his was the broadest interpretation of just how remote a view should be. He didn't even try to hide his disgust with me when it became apparent that I had no aptitude for mind reading. When I failed to predict what color necktie the American Senator Kennedy would be wearing in his television appearance, he actually stalked out in a rage. It struck me as absurd. There was maybe one color television in the whole country, but Maksim had somehow managed to consult it, which sent him into fits over shades of blue. I couldn't see how my remote color blindness could possibly threaten national security, but I apologized anyway.

Oleg was my favorite. He was friendly, but respectful. He was efficient, but not dismissive. He shared his ideas with me, always taking care to characterize them as theories, findings, or facts. I liked that he had a high regard for logic, since, frankly, there was so much that went on in 1717 that defied logic.

"So what is the explanation?" I asked impatiently. "Is my memory being replaced by other people's memories?"

Oleg laid his thick spectacles on the desk and shook his head. "It's not a zero-sum game, Sveta. Gaining one doesn't necessitate losing the other."

"But why have I become so weird and flighty? Why did I forget to pack my lunch three days in a row?"

"You forgot lunch?" he asked. "I hadn't noticed."

I scowled at him. "What happens when I can't remember simple combinations in ballet class? I can't afford this, Oleg. I can't sacrifice my real memory for some 'enemy memory' you want to study."

He sat me down and pulled his chair up close.

He talked about exceptionalism and compensation and counterintuitive premises. I tried to listen as he spoke, but the words sounded stilted and foreign. *A pox upon you and Lubyanka 1717*, I wanted to shout. If I could have, I would have made a break right then for Oksana's fairy-tale Phoenix Plains.

"I think it's time to introduce a new stage of your training," he was saying. "A new stage of consciousness that you are ready to enter. It's what we call the 'universal mind,' and I think you are standing on its threshold."

"Univermag?" I said stupidly, thinking of the giant department store across the square. "What will I learn there?"

"Not Univermag, no." Oleg smiled. "Universal mind. A

higher consciousness shared by all humanity. Regardless of class, language, culture . . . party affiliation."

That got my attention. I stared at him, shocked at these heretical ideas pronounced in Lubyanka, this fortress of political correctness.

"*Nu*, Oleg. What on earth?"

"I know, I know," he said, waving patient hands. "It's a highly unorthodox concept. We know, of course, that there is no higher consciousness, morally speaking, than political consciousness." He rolled his eyes ever so slightly, and then covered them with his spectacles. Oleg was a scientist, not an ideologue. I never stayed angry with him for long.

"At its most fundamental, the purest science is the act of questioning," he continued. "Look at you right now, demanding answers from me. You've always had a willingness to entertain experimental methods, even blasphemous ideas, in pursuit of hidden tracks. The universal mind, as revealed by telepathy and parapsychological probing, is one such method. We must not disregard it as a means of gaining intelligence. The very fact that our competitors in the West have been exploring these same frontiers is reason enough for us to chart such a radical course."

I glanced over at Pavel and Inga at their desks. Maksim was not present that day, but his colleagues were perfect studies in the decidedly unradical pursuit of record keeping. I wondered if Pavel was as engrossed in his papers as he appeared, or if he was just pretending to work while I considered Oleg's invitation to this "UniverMind." Inga looked up briefly and I caught her eye. But she didn't react. She just rose from her desk and disappeared into the kitchen for tea.

"A radical course to the universal mind?" I said, turning back to Oleg.

"Exactly so. You, Prima, are on the fast track of that radical course. You are progressing so rapidly toward a state of permanent heightened mental alertness that you may have abandoned some memories. Ones that are in the way. Your mind is presently more in tune to the universal than to the personal."

He scratched his beard as I took this in.

"If you think about it, it's not unlike being a good Communist," he concluded.

I laughed out loud. "A good Communist with six arms and three eyes and incense burning."

Oleg laughed, too. "It's true. The most effective training for universal mindfulness requires a good deal of meditation."

I spluttered my lips in disbelief. Childish maybe, but how else could you respond to a scientist's insistence on meditation?

"I know, I know. Most decadent, I know," he conceded. "But meditation, don't forget, has its origins in the East. The West only dabbles in the art, as in everything. The CIA uses meditation like it uses hallucinogenic drugs. Irresponsibly. A pretext for pseudoscience. Soviet meditation, I assure you, is one hundred percent scientific. And it's tremendously well funded."

Oleg stood and went to a supply closet. He returned with a metronome. There was nothing fancy about it—just a simple triangular keeper of beats. I wondered where the KGB was spending all its meditation money—certainly not on fancy metronomes. Maybe on Maksim's hidden color television.

"Believe it or not, Prima, we have our work cut out for us if we are to keep ahead of the CIA's parapsychology program. So far, we've only managed to outspend them."

Oleg placed the metronome on the desk between us and loosened its needle from the latch. "Now. Are you ready to knock on the door of the universal mind?"

IT WAS A DEEP trance. It left no traces—not of my first Thursday, not of last Thursday. When I awoke, I was numb and afraid to move. I felt fragile and exposed, though Oleg and I were alone in 1717. Pavel and Inga had disappeared. Oleg patted me on the back and told me I had made an important breakthrough.

What is it? I asked him mutely.

"Take five, Prima."

With some effort I stood and went to the small kitchen. I filled a cup from the cold teakettle and drank it to the bottom. I stood at the sink, still thirsty, too tired even to turn on the tap. The clock on the wall read 8:40. I guessed that only about twenty minutes had passed while I was in this strange altered state. I felt echoes of Oleg's voice lulling me deeper and deeper into what he called the "subconscious," the heavy tick of the metronome in my own pulse. Beyond those two rhythms, all was dark and heavy.

I went back into the main room to find Oleg scribbling furiously. Not in his regular notebook, but on a special form with carbon copies and a block-letter overleaf that read ABSOLUTELY TOP SECRET.

"Is it secret from me as well?" I asked.

He looked up and pushed his spectacles farther up his nose.

"Congratulations," he said. "As of tonight, you may well be Agent Prima."

I whispered, "I'm in the dark here, Oleg."

"I understand. And I can't tell you how enlightening that is for us. For all of us. You have performed an invaluable service."

I was exhausted. "Does that mean I'm done?"

"It means you are only beginning."

I wondered if it was an apology.

WHEN NATALIA DAVYDOVNA GERASOVA arrived she was wearing the same jacket she had worn the night I first met her, the night she'd handed me her card. But this time, the badge on her lapel was less coy. It was the Shield of the Revolution resting on seven unmistakable letters: KGB USSR. She swept right past me and disappeared into her office with Oleg.

Ten minutes later the door opened. She looked pleased. "Come, Prima," she said.

I entered. Oleg winked at me as he grabbed his coat and left.

Comrade Gerasova shut the door behind me. She pulled several papers from her case and laid them on the desk. Her face had assumed its usual inscrutable expression. She could have been a clerk at a telegraph office.

"Sign here and here please, Svetlana. Using your full name of course."

I took the pen. There was almost no text on the document. AFFIDAVIT. STATEMENT. WITNESSED. DATE. There was a blank space next to each. A heavy stamp, embossed with the same shield that decorated Gerasova's lapel.

"Just sign," she said, pointing to the space. "I will fill out the necessary information."

I signed my name, as ordered. The signature looked feeble.

"Now then," said Gerasova, sweeping the paper into her case. "You, Svetlana Evgenievna Kravshina, are hereby bound to the Extraordinary Code of Intelligence Agents within the Committee for State Security, the KGB. There are reams of protocol associated with this status, but it boils down to this: The secrecy to which you have been bound since you first entered the doors remains. But the privileges and potential penalties associated with your vow of allegiance and State Service have increased significantly."

My ears were ringing. I tried to concentrate, to move beyond the part of her speech when she said, ". . . since you first entered the doors." *The secrecy*, she had said. *So secret that I scarcely remembered entering the doors.*

"Do you understand, Prima?"

"*Da*, Comrade Gerasova. I understand."

"What you saw this evening—you understand its significance?"

I felt my face flush. "How can I? I don't remember what I saw."

She flared her nostrils but expressed no surprise.

"That's important," she said. "And not in any way a black mark against you."

"It's okay not to remember what I'm supposed to have seen?"

"Yes. For now. As long as we can access it. Because what is important is that you are, in fact, able to remember memories that are not your own. You are able to intercept memories. Which means you are in a position to provide critical intelligence. The intelligence of our enemies."

I wondered whose memories I had plundered from the universal mind; I couldn't picture an enemy. Only an ogre—like from the fairy tales. I was a *skazka* psychic. I imagined myself stealing a golden goose from Baba Yaga. *How silly*, I thought. *How childish.* And then—with a start—*how familiar.* I held my breath and let the memory manifest: the leather-bound book in my father's hands, the brightly colored picture of Baba Yaga in her chicken-legged house, the trim on the fairy-tale windows . . . as deep blue as an American necktie.

"Traditional wars are won on the battlefield," Gerasova was saying, "but wars of the future will be waged in the minds of men. Our Defense Ministry comrades may be concerned with our nuclear arsenal, but we are concerned with the weapons of psychological warfare. Your gift will help us build that arsenal."

My mind is a weapon.

My father read me stories.

Which of these things was true? Which one did I believe?

"What now?" I asked.

She smiled. "You rest. And next time, we talk about Berlin."

Berlin. That was what she had spoken of long ago, when we sat in the ladies' room of the Bolshoi Theatre. Whispered about, more accurately:

My father was in Berlin.

He was among heroes. And among traitors, too.

"But there's peace there now, in Berlin?" I said. "We have an agreement, right? With the Americans."

I realized as soon as I said it that I had answered my own question. There were enemies in Berlin. *Enemies without and enemies within.*

"Do you know, Agent Prima, how many of our East German

brothers and sisters have been lured by the Americans out of our sphere of influence, across the border into West Germany? They are draining our Communist Bloc. They give false promises and lead our comrades to a point of no return. Do you know how many have crossed over?"

I shook my head.

"Millions. And they are not just shirkers and criminals. These aren't just bad elements who have rejected our Communist ideals. It's more serious than that. Our best German comrades are being allowed to escape."

I heard the slip before she did. She hadn't called it treason or treachery. Not even the new term: "defection." She had called it *escape*.

I didn't see a connection between my twenty-minute trance and the loss of millions of ambivalent Germans. But Gerasova wanted me to make one. I remembered where I was: in the bowels of Lubyanka, where my father had met with a bullet. I still didn't know: *Was he a hero? Or a traitor?*

"Whose memories did I intercept tonight?" I asked. My mind was a blank. There was only the shadow of a man with a book, sitting at his daughter's bedside.

"It is too soon to tell." She stood. "You are dismissed, Prima. From now on you will report here nightly at 1900 hours."

"But I have rehearsal every evening," I protested. "*The Nutcracker* is at the end of the month."

She didn't even blink. "I will disregard your objections," she said impassively, "except to note that, as the team has confirmed, you are not yet prepared to dance to music written by Tchaikovsky . . . or Prokofiev for that matter. As we have seen, your sensitivity is quick, but it is tenuous. You still have work to control it. Now get your things. I will walk you out."

WE PARTED WAYS IN the Metro. Comrade Gerasova boarded a northbound train and I stood on the platform hearing voices.

Passengers, beware of the platform edge warned one of the Metro custodians from the microphone in her booth. *When leaving the train, don't forget your things . . .*

Several trains passed as I stood thinking of all the things I could possibly forget while I was busy remembering a universal past. I stood, wary, on the platform edge, wondering if I was on a train I might never get off.

When I arrived at the Academy I saw that my name had already been removed from the *Nutcracker* casting announcement.

I might be Agent Prima, but I wasn't even in the corps de ballet.

TEN
NUTCRACKER

I knew that Oksana was biting her tongue. Once we were seated high in the third circle with a bird's-eye view of the stage, she couldn't hold back.

"I just don't get it, Svet. Why are we up here in the nose-bleed seats? I thought you were fast-tracked. I thought you were the golden girl, their rising star, and I'd be watching you from the curtains. But you don't even have a part in *Nutcracker*? That's like not getting picked for dodgeball!"

"Yes. It is exactly like that," I said.

"*Blin.*" She covered her mouth with both hands. "I shouldn't have said that. I'm sorry, Sveta—it's just, I can't help it. I mean I'm outraged! You're my girl. My Juliet—they can't do that to you, Sveta!"

I took the opera glasses from her lap and surveyed the hall. It was just the Academy's year-end recital, but every seat was filled. It hurt. It did. But I had gotten very good at ignoring pain.

"Your outrage is sweet," I said calmly. "But you're right. *The Nutcracker* is dodgeball. It's child's play. Toy soldiers? Dancing snowflakes?" I shook my head and patted her hand. Like she was the one who needed assurance. "Don't you worry, Oksana.

My debut on the Bolshoi stage will not be as a house mouse scampering behind a prepubescent boy in an oversized prosthetic rat's head."

Oksana giggled. She didn't remind me that I had actually been cast as the Sugar Plum Fairy before I was unceremoniously un-cast. But we both knew it.

The conductor entered the orchestra pit. I felt a tremor of uneasiness. *The Nutcracker*, as Gerasova had rightly warned, was Tchaikovsky's score. Oleg and Inga had agreed that my mindfulness had become strong enough to control unwanted memories, but that didn't mean they wouldn't come knocking. It was hard enough keeping "Agent Prima" a secret from Oksana. I didn't need a full-on episode of "remote viewing" in the middle of the Christmas Party scene to explain as well.

As the familiar music rose from the orchestra I actively filled my mind with the present: with the simple staging, the cheerful costumes, and the fairy-tale story of a girl whose dreams come to life. I used the techniques Inga had drilled with me to render the music solid and tangible. I told myself that the only paranormal activity onstage today would be from the stagehands when they make the Christmas tree grow to twice its size.

When Act One was finally over I clapped loudly for Masha, the girl from Voronezh who had transformed into a model roommate and a fetching Marie. I was too relieved about the vision-less performance to be bitter about the celebration that was going on backstage without me.

AT THE INTERVAL I was ready to pepper Oksana with questions to keep her from asking her own. It wasn't hard. Oksana was in full chatter mode. She had joined an amateur theater group, had been invited to direct an evening of one-act plays, had kissed one of her fellow thespians on the trolleybus on the way home.

"It was super. Till he called me his 'sweet little fish' and I burst out laughing."

"You should have reciprocated. Called him a 'tasty little crumb.'"

"I should have. But I was already in hysterics."

"And Misha? How's Misha?" I asked casually. "Still hanging around with ruffians?"

"Who knows? He's consumed with his studies and his discussion groups. I'm pretty sure his father has forbidden him from seeing me. He's grooming him for a career in the foreign service after all, so he can't be associated with hooligans or you-know-whats."

"Don't say that," I hissed.

"Say what? I didn't say it. I quite deliberately did not say it, Sveta."

"You shouldn't even be thinking it," I glanced warily around the crowded buffet. "It's old thinking and you have to be the one to stop. You have to change your attitude or you'll never shake it—the stigma."

"Easy for you to say. You have a future. A bright, happy future."

I didn't know what to say. Agree? Disagree? Argue that bright futures carry a price tag?

Oksana elbowed me and grinned. "It's okay, Sveta. I've got plans and they don't include Misha or the Spanish brats he's hanging out with. Though I swear, I don't know why the offspring of fascist diplomats are more suitable company than the offspring of . . ."

"Don't say it," I warned again. "Anyway, as you of all people should know—the children of fascists are not necessarily fascists themselves."

"You're right," agreed Oksana, "just brats."

She stood and said, "I need to run to the restroom. When I get back you need to tell me all about things with your mother."

Luckily, when Oksana returned from the ladies' room the bell was already ringing for the second half. After the ballet I managed to steer the conversation into a debate over whether Olya

L. was the sourest Sugar Plum Fairy we had even seen or only the second-most sour. There was no time to discuss Vera Konstantinovna.

AND WHAT, REALLY, WAS there to discuss? I rarely saw my mother. There had been an awkward call after my birthday. Vera asked if I was "getting on well with Natalia," and I answered that she had "introduced me to her friends," with whom I had "many common interests." I was surprised at how adept my mother was at deciphering this coded language. I was surprised at how adept I was at delivering it.

But when we met about a month later, she spoke bluntly.

We were sitting on a bench outside the Red Gates Metro station. She was on her lunch break. It was a somber, rainy day and we shared a small umbrella that offered as much privacy as protection from the rain. But that didn't keep her from announcing, for all to hear, that she sometimes missed her days in the camps where "at least you knew where a person was coming from."

"Mama," I whispered furtively, "what are you saying?"

"I'm saying . . . oh, lord, I don't know what I'm saying, Sveta." She dug into her bag and pulled out a pack of cigarettes. I had never seen her smoke. They were a cheap brand, Musketeers. I guessed she had smoked in the camps. I wondered if Natalia Davydovna had smoked in the camps, too. If maybe now my mother was thinking about how Natalia Davydovna Gerasova had a KGB medal and never smoked Musketeers, while Vera Konstantinovna Kravshina was left to smoke alone outside the Metro.

I could see irritation smoldering like the tip of her cigarette. A better daughter would have tried to comfort her. But I didn't. I blew on that irritation, curious if it would turn to flame.

"How exactly did Natalia Davydovna get her position?" I asked. "I mean with her record and all?"

My mother squinted against the thick blue smoke.

"She made the most of her acquaintances out there, Natalia

did. For example, she shook that poor Prokofiev woman inside out. Then she spent the information like change."

"Prokofiev? You mean the composer's wife?"

"She served eight years. Just like me."

"For what?"

"For being married to Prokofiev, of course. Stalin's favorite composer. Stalin's pet. Gave him a three-story *dacha* and commissions and awards. Allowed him to travel and to write whatever music he wanted . . . and then the war came and Prokofiev was exposed for what he is."

"What is he?" I asked, genuinely confused.

"A pig. A *svoloch*."

"Because of the formalist tendencies in his music?"

My mother grimaced. "No, Sveta. Because he let them arrest his wife when he could have saved her." She expelled another cloud of angry smoke. I sat still, but I was squirming inside. What did my mother know, anyway? She had called Prokofiev, who wrote the best score Romeo and Juliet could have ever asked for, a *svoloch*. Worse, if what she had said was true, he was one. I also suspected she was saying something else. About my father.

"She was arrested for being his wife?" I asked carefully.

"Technically, because she was Spanish," said Vera, avoiding my eyes. "It was just after the war. Spaniards were all spies. Especially if they were married to famous composers who were notorious individualists."

I considered this explanation. I didn't know how much of it was my mother's paranoia or how much was personal. I thought it might have something to do with what she had said earlier about the camps, about knowing where a person was coming from. Perhaps everyone in the Gulag was coming from a place where they had run out of luck. They'd been thrown to the wolves. I wondered about those other prisoners, if their offenses were worse than associating with *svolochi* . . . or Spaniards.

"Where exactly were you?" I asked.

"All over. But I met Gerasova and Prokofiev outside of Vor-kuta."

There was a time when I used to track my mother's letters in the House atlas. Then the atlas was confiscated and it became harder to know where my mother was going, let alone coming from. But that wasn't quite what I had meant. I meant: Where was this place, this strange world, where the wives of disgraced men banded together to cut wood, write letters, and smoke cigarettes? Where was this exile where the secret police made the introductions? *Mrs. Prokofiev, meet Mrs. Kravshina. Ladies, meet Natalia Davydovna Gerasova, who will, in due course, use you both for the resources you don't even know you have yet . . .*

Where was this Motherland run by wronged women?

But Vera was already stamping out her cigarette. "I need to get back to my post." She rose and shook the rain from the skimpy umbrella. Her raincoat flapped open, revealing the sharp blades of her collarbone under her vest.

"Fates change rapidly, Svetlana. You must never take your present position for granted. As for Prokofiev—his musical contribution may be worth all the personal pain he caused. No. Almost certainly it is." She smiled, a wry smile, and put her chilly hand to my cheek. "I know you love his ballets. I won't take your Prokofiev from you."

"No." I said. "No you won't. Like it or not, Mother, Prokofiev is firmly in the canon. He's made musical masterpieces and they belong to the people."

She looked at me sadly. "You're repeating me, Svetlana. Yes. The music belongs to the people. And the people belong to the state. So who do you belong to?"

I opened my mouth to defend myself: I had been promoted, I was Agent Prima, I was defending the Motherland. But I closed it without a word. Because in the back of my mind was the measured ticking of a four-note progression—

Prokofiev's flutes were playing games with me.

Tick-tick, as Juliet tiptoes to her balcony.

Tock-tock, as the hero taps the map.

Tick-tick, as the maestro raises his baton.

Tock-tock, as the general raises his sword. His rifle. His hands.

Tick-tick-tock-tock . . . as the Artist and the People and the Dictator all bow down before the *rodina*, pinioned and pierced on their own proud medals.

Tick-tick-tock-tock, as a father and his daughter pledge allegiance to the Motherland.

Who did I belong to?

ELEVEN
NEW YEAR'S, 1960

It was hot on the train. I tugged the scarf from my head and edged closer to the open window. The air blowing through it was just as stuffy—tunnel stuffy. But cooler.

The car was full of high spirits and complicated itineraries—everyone on the train would be making at least three stops before midnight. New Year's Eve was that kind of holiday. If you didn't celebrate it, in person, with everyone you love, then you hadn't celebrated it at all.

But I was only planning one stop: my mother's *kommunalka* on Snowfall Lane. I barely had the energy for that. My body was tired. My mind was tired. I would have happily slept through the New Year. I still just might. I checked my watch. Not yet seven o'clock and I was exhausted. I reminded myself that the New Year came at midnight. I could make it till midnight. It wasn't like last year, when New Year's turned into an all-night adventure.

The memory gave me a small thrill. It also gave me a small comfort. In contrast to everything I seemed to forget lately, I remembered every detail of last New Year's Eve: the smell of siphoned gasoline, the astonishing spectacle of Moscow from the top floor of the Red Gates Stalinscraper, even the combination of numbers on a wrinkled ruble note that I guessed correctly in the café of a bus depot just south of the river. They had all been astonished; Georgi Levshik most of all.

I smiled. It was a happy memory. And it was mine.

At the next station a horde of passengers pressed me against the far door of the train, and when we passed into the tunnel again, my reflection jumped out like a ghost. The negative lighting erased the dark circles from under my eyes. I almost didn't recognize myself. Someone behind me did: "Hello, beautiful. It's been a while."

There was no room to turn around, but I didn't need to. I would recognize his voice anywhere. "I was just thinking of you," I said, and my reflection smiled. We pulled into the next station and the crowd pushed me onto the platform. Georgi took me by the elbow and kept walking.

"Where to?" he asked with a smile.

The little thrill was sliding into giddiness. My fatigue was gone. I laughed out loud. "I really was," I said. "I was just thinking of you."

"Of course you were," he said. "It's our anniversary. Where the hell you been, Sveta? How come I run into everyone in town but you?"

"Um. Because I don't haunt dens of iniquity?"

"Nonsense. My den is your den, Sveta. You know that."

We had reached the escalator. I pulled back. "This isn't my stop, Gosha."

I saw his eyes dart upward to the street exit. He said, "Come on now, Sveta. It won't be New Year's till we've found a drunk friend to tuck into bed and some cash-poor Spaniards to rip off. I don't have wheels tonight, but I promise a proper breakfast in compensation."

I smiled again. He had left out so much: how we lured the concierge of the Red Gates from her post with a trail of roses and skidded across the marble floor to the service elevator; how we circled the Ring Road until we ran out of gas; how I'd told him the stories of the classic ballets, how he'd taught me to signal an easy target with a single gesture. He had left out how I'd watched the sunrise wrapped in his leather jacket.

It fit him better now, I noticed. I reached out and traced a finger over the worn leather scar at the cuff, the spot where a younger Georgi had rolled up the sleeve.

He grabbed my hand. "Seriously. Let me take you somewhere. Let's celebrate together."

I raised my eyes and saw an unkempt boy with dirty hair, crooked teeth, and a bad complexion. He brimmed with confidence, but he was still a punk. He interested me, yes. But he could still take advantage of me . . . and almost certainly would if there was a reason to.

And still I wanted to say: "Yes, let's."

I felt reckless. Out of habit I moved to suppress the feeling, to regain my balance. I pulled my hand from his.

"I can't."

"Why not?"

"I promised my mother."

"Snowfall Lane?"

I nodded.

"Long way from here."

"And you've already made me miss two trains," I said as another closed its doors behind us.

"Did you bring her a gift?"

There had been no time. There was never any time. "I thought I'd pick up flowers at the station," I said.

"Then you will need to come with me."

"Why?" I could tell from his voice that we weren't flirting anymore.

"Because your wallet got lifted five minutes ago and every second we stand here it's getting farther away."

I WAS STILL CURSING when we came out on the street. Gosha just bowed his head under my onslaught and turned up his collar. The snow was falling hard, too.

"Are you done?" he asked eventually.

"I should slap you."

"Let me get your wallet back first, then you can smack me. Or you can kiss me, depending on how much money is left."

I glowered.

"Look, Svetlana. Here's the truth. Yeah, I was on the train with Pupok, and yeah, the plan was to let him finance our New Year's Eve. He's got golden hands, Pupok does. Goddamn golden. You never see him. He's invisible. Admit it; you never saw him."

Even as he said it, Gosha was searching the street for the invisible pickpocket. I wondered for a moment if Pupok even existed. I was so mad I could spit. I was also embarrassed. I was supposed to be in tune with the "universal mind," and instead I had left the train, forgetting all my things.

"But I swear on my mother," he continued, "I didn't know he had picked you till it was too late. I was distracted, Sveta. I was really glad to see you and I . . . I got distracted."

"Swear on your mother, huh?" I sneered. "That the same mother that sent you packing at age ten because you're a no-good thief?"

I saw him flinch. I regretted it. Not because it was a mean thing to say, but because I suspected Georgi Levshik was proud enough to walk away from me. And I needed my wallet.

"Would you rather I swore on *your* mother?" he asked coldly.

We were even. Back at the impasse of secrets we had exchanged a year ago.

"Come on," he said when I didn't respond. "We have to hurry. Pupok's got a fierce sweet tooth and his favorite bakery is around the corner."

When we reached the bakery Gosha barged straight to the front of the line where a chubby kid with hungry eyes was taking possession of a large box tied up in string.

"Give it back, Pupok."

I relaxed a little. Pupok was younger than Gosha. Just a baby, really. He looked from Gosha to me, and then back. His disappointment was almost comical.

"But Gosha . . ."

"Give it back, knucklehead."

"It's paid for," he whined.

Gosha tweaked the kid's ear until he squealed. Then he addressed the harassed-looking woman at the counter: "*Grazhdanka*, would you be so good as to return this cake to the case and return my young friend's money? You see, he's diabetic and he should not indulge . . ."

"Already paid for," barked the woman. "Next."

The line jostled us, but Gosha raised his voice: "Ladies and gentlemen, just a moment of your patience. Comrades, a moment, please. We are all civilized people here. I entreat you!"

They slunk back a step, cowed by a teenager.

"Now, *grazhdanka*," he said, turning and stepping squarely to the counter, "good citizen . . ."

She was red faced, thin lipped, and big haired under her paper cap, and she wasn't having it. "Young man," she snapped, "perhaps you failed to notice. It is New Year's Eve. There is a long line. I have cake to eat, too. I also like to celebrate the New Year, believe it or not. If you feel it necessary to address your friend's health, you can do it out of my store and out on the street."

"Let's take the cake and go," I whispered, but Gosha didn't budge.

"Comrade cake-baker. It is hardly *your* store, now is it? Well, I wish you a happy New Year, but I warn you that I plan to report to the Confectioners Union that you have cheated a diabetic customer and that you are running this bakery like your personal fiefdom."

"Don't you threaten me, sonny. I'll call the police on you."

"Lieutenant Fedosov is off tonight," said Gosha. "So are Lieutenants Chukin and Peremyslov. I believe you have an arrangement with them, don't you? But not, I understand, with Health Inspector Kondratov? Inspector Kondratov, who has on more than one occasion threatened to close this shop on health violations?"

She shook her head. "So that's your game, you shitty, shameless punk?" She had taken off her paper cap and was rolling up her sleeves as if for combat. She seemed to have forgotten the people in line.

"What game?" demanded Gosha. I saw his tawny eyes narrow. "You don't have the right to run an unsanitary bakeshop in defiance of the USSR Department of Health and Hygiene." He waved behind him without averting his stare. "Pupok, here, has just seen a rat."

There was a murmur down the line.

Pupok took his cue: *"Kriiiiiiiiisa!"* he shouted, his voice pitched perfectly for pandemonium. "Rat with whiskers! His tail's in the buttercream! His snout's in the flour! Whiskers whiskers! There he goes! *Kriiiiisa!!"*

He was pointing everywhere at once. The restless line scattered, embracing the sudden collective shift from resigned patience to chaos. A brigade of *babushki* took up arms, wielding brooms and platters. The men went for the unattended confections. The shop erupted into rodent hysteria, which Gosha ignored. He raised his voice to demand the cake seller's food-handling certificate and union number. But she was busy defending a fresh rack of cream cakes from the mob. Pupok, meanwhile, had slithered under the counter. He had his hand in the cash register when Gosha whispered to me, "Right. Time to split."

I ran after him.

At the door he delivered his parting shot. "Civility, comrades. Remember to be civil in the New Year. It's more effective than a good rattrap at deterring pests."

"WHAT KIND OF SELF-RESPECTING pickpocket calls himself 'belly button'?" I muttered. We were well clear of the bakery, slipping over fresh snow in a quiet park on the other side of the boulevard.

"Wasn't *me* who named me. The guys did," answered Pupok. His mouth was full of cream and he had to trot to keep up. "Oy. Gosha. I got a cramp. Let's duck into Petya's huh? Cross-eyed Petya . . . he's just through the second arch up there. Close by. Let's stop, whaddaya say?"

Gosha looked at his sticky partner in crime. "You're a disgrace, Pupok," he said, taking the cake box from the boy. He turned to me. "I assure you that this one bears no resemblance to the rest of my crew—hard-boiled miscreants, all of them. Pupok here is in training. But he's an amusing little shit, isn't he?"

"So what did you mean about her having an arrangement?" I asked. "The cashier, I mean. You weren't bluffing?"

He sniffed. "That woman sells more than cakes. She fences all sorts of stuff out the back. Imported stuff. Gets it from the foreign hotels. Cops get a cut, too, that's how she does it in the open. I don't care, personally. Plenty of women stretch their salary that way. But I don't like that one. She's a mean piece of work. I've seen her throw out day-old bagels right in front of street kids and gypsies. She makes them dive in the trash."

He stepped over a chain barrier at the edge of the park and held out his hand to help me.

"I could, you know," he added. "Shut her down. But Pupok would suffer."

"Why's that?" I asked, ignoring his casual gallantry.

Pupok answered for himself. "Her gingerbread's the best in town."

I followed them across the street and down an alley, to a flight of stairs that led below the street. There was a steel door at the end of the passage and Pupok rapped on it.

"It's us, Petya. Let us in!"

The door stayed closed. Gosha hammered on it. "Cross-Eyes! Wake up! The New Year's coming."

The door opened a crack and a pair of eyes peered out. They were, in fact, crossed. Gosha lifted the cake box into view.

"Open up Petya, we brought treats."

It was a tiny room, dark and cold, but somehow still cozy. The table in the center was covered in a bright peasant scarf and there was an enormous copper samovar hissing on top of it.

Petya opened the shutters of the only window and offered me the only chair. "Who's this then?" he asked.

"Gosha's girl," said Pupok. "Pretty isn't she?"

"I'm not Gosha's girl," I said as I pulled off my gloves. "If anything, I'm this Pupok fellow's. He's the one that picked me."

Gosha hooted and Petya chuckled. Pupok turned bright red. I sat in the middle of the male triangle and wondered why I felt at ease. I wondered why I was still there. I told myself it was to get my wallet, but I knew it was something else. I smoothed the hair at my temples and placed my long braid over my shoulder.

"Could I have a cup of tea please?"

Petya rummaged through a large trunk in the corner of the room. He pulled out three tin plates and three cracked glasses and placed them on the table. I watched the ankles passing at the street-level window above his head. He found a soup spoon and a bowl of sugar. "No forks," he apologized.

Gosha handed the slightly dented cake box to Pupok, who placed it before me and untied the string with reverence. It was a lovely cake—a layered concoction dusted with cocoa and a garland of iced yellow roses. HAPPY NEW YEAR was inscribed in florid pink icing on the top.

"You have good taste, Pupok," I said with approval.

Gosha pulled a short-bladed knife from his pocket and cut the cake while I poured our tea. Then we ate and watched the snow pile up at the windowsill.

"You don't look like one of Gosha's dolls, gotta say," said Petya.

"What he means is, you aren't nagging me to buy you things," explained Gosha.

I licked the frosting from the back of the soup spoon. "What would you buy me, Gosha? With the money you picked from my pocket?"

He scratched his nose and leaned forward to select another slice of cake.

"First of all," he said, "I'm not a pickpocket. A pickpocket, while necessarily clever, judicious, quick, and discerning, is not participating in a particularly prestigious profession. No offense, Pupok."

"None taken," chirped Pupok.

"A tailor, on the other hand, requires nerves of steel, a quality kit, and a team that works like a well-oiled machine."

"A kit?" I asked.

"Of course. A razor-sharp blade and a decent needle and thread."

"Ah. Yes, I recall now that you have some experience with needle and thread."

He glanced at me. I could tell he couldn't quite figure out where we stood. I couldn't, either.

He said: "I've been known to slit a pocket wide enough to recover the budget for a full business trip plus passport and a packet of sunflower seeds and sew it back up in as much time as it takes the number seven to get to the city center from the airport."

I said: "I'll have to give you a call the next time I need quick alterations."

He held my gaze. "Give Svetlana her wallet now, Pupok."

Pupok placed it on the table. It was a pale blue, unpromising thing. It seemed quite worthless next to the cake. But it was, after all, the only reason I was spending New Year's in a squatter's cellar, which was one step below a *kommunalka* full of Gulag returnees.

"Sure you don't want to leave it here with Gosha?" Petya suggested. "We're organizing a card game. Gosha will double that for you in a night."

"Still wouldn't be worth much," I said, reaching for the wallet.

"Svetlana's been sufficiently corrupted for one night," said

Gosha. "Anyway, she doesn't need anyone's assistance to easy street. She's got it made already. She's one of those happy comrades for whom the future really is bright and beautiful. She's a paragon of the New Woman, for whom hard work will be gloriously rewarded."

I figured it for more sarcasm. But Gosha surprised me.

"Sveta is a dancer," he announced. "She studies at the Bolshoi Academy. In a few years she will be a queen on the stage with no time for tea with us lowlifes. Feast your eyes, pals. This is the last you'll be seeing of Svetlana."

Pupok gulped. "A ballerina? For real? You hear that, Cross-Eyes? I picked a ballerina!"

I shook my head. "I'm not a ballerina yet. There's a system. You start as a member of the corps, then you get promoted to coryphée, then soloist, then principal, and so on. If you are good enough you become a prima. A prima ballerina."

Pupok nodded. "Yeah, I get it. Like me. I gotta earn my stripes, too: a plant, then a sharp, then a chewer, and so on. I've graduated from lookout and I've picked loads but I don't have the skills to be a tailor yet, like Gosha. One day, though. One day I'll be a *vor v zakone*."

"A *vor*?" I said. "That's your dream? To be a thief?"

"Not just a *vor*—a *vor v zakone*. A thief of the code."

"Well," I said, lifting my glass, "here's to training."

THE SNOW WAS DEEP when we left Petya's basement. Georgi and I made fresh footprints. I was thinking about Pupok's cherub face and grand ambitions.

"Is that your dream, too?" I asked.

"Hmmm?"

"To be a *vor*?"

"Don't be silly. Do I look like a hardened criminal? Do I look like I want to be the king of a prison cell? Do I strike you as someone who would swear loyalty to a sweaty band of crooks over everything else?"

Sometimes, I thought. *Yes.*

"Is Petya a *vor*?"

"Nah. Just a gambler. A gloriously self-destructive, unreformed chronic gambler. He's lost more fortunes in the three years I've known him than I can hope to make in a lifetime."

"He seems . . ."

Gosha waited for my verdict.

"Nice."

He snorted. "You've never seen him on a bender. Believe me, Cross-Eyes after a big loss is not a nice man."

"But not a thief."

"Well, I didn't say he wasn't a thief. But he's not a *vor*. There's a difference. A *vor v zakone* has made a nasty pact. And he's every bit as bound to it as a law-abiding man. A *vor v zakone* has given up on the good life."

"But Pupok . . ."

"Forget what Pupok said, he doesn't know what he's playing at. I don't mess with those bastards. They're blackhearts with a twisted code. Their *zakon* is certain death. Me—I'm just making a living."

We didn't do that in the Soviet Union, "make a living." We made missiles and factories and set records and quotas. We made history in the USSR; and in Lubyanka 1717 we were making a secret weapon. But here in the quiet courtyard I didn't feel a part of any of that. I tried to answer in the way Agent Prima might, but my words sounded hollow. "You're making a mockery of the state. You're sabotaging the system."

"Yup. That too."

"You don't really have any loyalties, do you?" I asked. It was an honest question.

"Loyalties, yes. A law—no."

I wrapped my hand around the wallet in my pocket, glad that there was nothing in it to reveal that I had, quite recently, signed an Extraordinary Code, making me an agent of the Committee of State Security, the KGB. It seemed quite absurd. As absurd as a cake fight on New Year's Eve. As crazy as willingly spending the evening with a hustler who openly defied the law—those of comrades and of criminals both.

"Do you see?" he said. "I'm no threat. In our country the real criminals aren't the ones who bust heads or steal wallets. They're the ones who break faith."

It reminded me of what he used to call me. *The girl with a chip on her shoulder.* Did he still see me that way? Had he decided it was the chip that made me interesting?

"Did you mean it when you said that I had it made? That in a few years I'll be a 'queen of the stage'?"

"Svetlana, I'm not an idiot. I know you've got as hard a road as any of us. Nobody's gonna hand you that crown. But . . . I think you probably have what it takes to win it."

"How do you know?" I asked. The last time we were together, the Bolshoi had been a dream, a wild hope. How had he known that I'd made the Academy? Had he been making inquiries? Or did he just assume? Was he that sure of me?

"I don't *know*," he said with a smile. "I said, 'I *think*.' I certainly *hope* so. I hope you become a prima ballerina. I don't have one of those yet."

"Oh, I see," I said, punching him playfully. "You're betting on the 'glorious reward' part. Think I might be generous with my bright future."

He stopped and turned to me, and there was nothing laughing in his eyes. "No. I'm not betting on that. And here's why: because there is no glorious reward in the Soviet Union, Sveta. Whatever cup they give you to sip from will be poisoned. And the sooner you accept that, the better."

We had emerged onto the main street. A tram trundled through the fresh snow and stopped before us. We made no move to board it.

"Where are we going?" I asked.

"Snowfall Lane."

"How far is it from here?"

"Forty minutes' walk, I'd say. Want me to find a cab?"

I checked my watch. It was almost nine o'clock. I hooked my arm through his. "Let's walk," I said. "Tell me more about this life of yours. What's a 'sharp'? What kind of cards do you play? And what sort of *zakon* does a *vor v zakone* live by?"

He smiled once more. "So, I was right. You are curious after all."

"I'M SO SORRY," I said when my mother opened the door. I thrust limp carnations and a cake—a haphazard jam job we found on the way—at her, hoping they would make up for my tardiness.

"Come in, Sveta," she said. "I saved you some food, but it's in danger at this point. Slava Stepanovich is threatening to feed it to his horrible cat. Where were you? I was beginning to get worried."

I pulled off my snow-soaked coat and my boots. "I had a bit of a kerfuffle on the Metro. Had to make a citizen's arrest." I giggled. "Then, it was just so lovely, I decided to walk . . ."

She didn't look convinced. I realized that kerfuffles in the Metro and long, snowy walks were not particularly novel diversions for my mother.

"Well. You're here now," she concluded.

It was steamy and jovial in the kitchen, and nearly 11 P.M. Vera put my flowers in a vase on a table already laden with bouquets and ringed with a half-dozen tipsy neighbors.

"How's the ballerina, then?" roared the sweaty engineer who lived across the hall.

Vera served me a bowl of soup. There was still plenty of food. And music and laughter and vodka. I danced with the engineer and sang with Slava, and everyone praised the jam cake. I watched my mother closely, hoping to see her happy. She told a joke—about a rabbi and a priest and a reindeer herder, and everyone laughed, but Vera's smile looked pained to me.

It was two in the morning when we went to bed.

"What a nice night," I sighed as I pulled off my skirt and tights and crawled into the cot Vera had made up for me. "I can't remember such a nice New Year's Eve."

She was still sitting with her feet on the floor and her earrings in her hand.

"Mama? Everything okay?"

"*Da, dochka,*" she said quietly. "Everything's fine."

She stood and switched off the lamp by her bed, leaving the string of lights on the tree burning. I heard her rustling under the blanket. When it was still she said, "The boy who walked you here tonight. Do you trust him?"

I thought of Gosha's thin shoes and thick skin. I remembered his laughing eyes and told her the truth. "Almost. He's no angel, that's for sure. But he's also not someone who can get me in trouble. Not with the authorities. Not with . . ."

"The KGB," finished Vera.

We lay quietly. From the corridor came the sound of Slava Stepanovich snoring at the kitchen table. We hadn't been able to move him. I closed my eyes again and pictured Gosha in the snow outside my mother's building. His silly imitation of a prince's declaration of love. The same one I had taught him a year ago.

"He's no *svoloch*," I said.

"That does not mean you can trust him."

I rose on one elbow and asked: "What are you worried about, Mama? I am as protected as can be. I am at the top of the Bolshoi Academy's roster and I have signed the Extraordinary Code . . ."

Vera hissed. *Shhhhh.*

But I wouldn't be hushed. "Can't you accept that things have changed? I am not living under your shadow anymore. On the contrary, someday soon *you* will be under *my* protective wing."

She made a sound like a sob that was trying to be laughter. It turned into a prolonged coughing spell. She sat upright until it passed. Then she turned to me, her eyes wet and bright.

"But you don't know that, Sveta," she said. "You cannot see the future."

To that, I had no retort. She was right, after all. I couldn't. I could only, it seemed, see the past.

"Don't trust that boy, Sveta. Don't trust anyone. Don't even trust Natalia. Just do what she says and tell her what she wants to hear. But most of all, don't tell anyone, Sveta, about where you go when you are not at the Academy."

"Of course not, Mama."

I was about to put my head back down onto the pillow when something on the tree in the corner glittered and caught my eye. It was the glass bird, stirred by an invisible draft, turning on its string. I strained to make out its features: its dark blot of an eye, misplaced and erring. Blind.

WHEN I WOKE IT was still dark out. I wanted to go back to sleep, but I couldn't. So I got up and began quietly gathering my things from the chair by the tree. I dressed quickly and then, on an impulse, I pulled the glass bird from its branch and tucked it in my coat pocket with my wallet.

I crossed the room and sat gently on my mother's bed. I was shocked at the gaunt face on the pillow. Vera looked as though she had aged a decade overnight. I bent and kissed her cool cheek and her eyes flew open. I saw her fear fade to fatigue.

"Good morning," I whispered.

"I'll get up. Make kasha. Tea."

"Please don't. I am going to leave, Mama. I have to rehearse."

"On New Year's Day?"

"Every day."

Vera smiled thinly and closed her eyes.

I was suddenly overwhelmed with emotion. I felt tears prick at my eyes and was bewildered by them. My feelings for her, my mother, had always been there: confused, persistent . . . but never overwhelming. I bent closer and wrapped her in an awkward embrace.

"Next New Year's I am taking you somewhere," I promised. "Somewhere we can celebrate without neighbors. A restaurant maybe? A winter resort?"

"I don't think we will spend next New Year's together, *milaya*," she said.

"Of course we will. Why wouldn't we?"

Her response was a whisper. "Because I am dying, Sveta."

INTERLUDE
VORKUTA 2015

*L*ana Dukovskaya wakes from a strange dream in a strange room. The walls are stacked with books. The table is painted with flowers. A broken window is patched with newspaper. But a crack of sunlight filters through, and Lana remembers: she is in her grandmother's room. A room that has been Svetlana Dukovskaya's home since there was a Soviet Union.

Sitting up on the narrow sofa, Lana pulls her feet from the thin blanket. A pair of felt slippers has been placed, just so, on the floor. She slides her toes in and steps on the heels; her grandmother's feet are smaller than her own. She steps through a faded curtain into a small kitchen. The old woman is at the stove, stirring a metal coffeemaker on the burner.

"Good morning, babushka."

"Good morning, dochka."

Lana does not correct her. She knows that to a woman as old as Svetlana Dukovskaya, all old women are grandmothers and all young women are daughters.

And that is the riddle that Lana is struggling with after a restless night. The riddle of her broken matriarchy—three generations of Dukovskaya: Where did we begin? When did *you* become we? Where is your daughter in this story? Where is Marina? You and your mis-sighted glass bird and your inscrutable dying mother, Vera Konstantinovna Kravshina . . . what do they have to do with my mother?

The question nags at her. Because though Lana and her mother, Marina, have found a new bond in the questions that this woman, the first Dukovskaya of the Bolshoi Ballet, left behind, there is still a black hole in their relationship. Lana yearns to fill it. She wants to understand the full chronology of their tragedy. She wants to bring her mother and her grandmother together and to sit in the comfort that is no unanswered questions.

But right now, on this unexpected morning in Siberia, there are still questions. They don't all stem from her grandmother's meandering stream of consciousness as it burbled through the small hours of the morning and into Lana's confused dreams. They aren't all questions born from the terrible secrets about Russia's sad Soviet history. No—this much is perfectly clear to Lana: her grandmother, like her mother and like Lana herself, is a victim of their rodina's tradition of tearing down the pedestals on which heroes are placed. A tradition of recasting roles in the middle of the performance, turning orphans into primas, turning stars into spies, turning dancers into pawns.

And there are other questions. Beginning with the one Lana thought she had already solved: Like Uncle Gosha, what sort of an uncle was he? Not long ago, just before his death, Georgi Levshik had himself told Lana that he was the best man at Svetlana's wedding and that he had dandled her daughter Marina on his knee. He was, he said, the closest of family friends. Devoted not just to Svetlana, the gorgeous prima ballerina, but to her husband, the hapless engineer Viktor Dukovsky.

Lana stands next to her grandmother as she stirs the coffee in a warm beam of sunlight. She inhales deeply. "I love it strong."

To which the old woman replies brightly, "So did your grandfather."

"Tell me about him," says Lana. "Tell me all about him."

ACT THREE
PRIMA
MOSCOW, BERLIN, AND
WASHINGTON 1961–1962

TWELVE
VIKTOR

I had been coming to the cancer ward for nearly a month when he approached me. It was the second time my mother had been admitted. The first had been over New Year's, just as she predicted. That time, she had been released after just two weeks. The doctors spoke of a "remission" and gave her three month's work reprieve during which I did my best to visit her weekly, but mostly failed. She was back at work, on duty in the box at Lubyanka Metro when she collapsed the second time. An hour later I passed through the station on my way home from 1717 and nearly collapsed myself, overwhelmed by the psychic traces of her relapse. This time, no one was talking about remission. The word was as full of false hope as the promise of rehabilitation. Some cancers are never killed.

It was August and I was sweating through my dress. I juggled bags and books and flowers; my arms were bruised from where Dmitri, the boy I was partnered with, had gripped me too hard on the balance. I recognized the doctor on duty and I waved to the nurse who had been especially kind to my mother, particularly after I brought her a box of nougat from the Baltics. But I took no notice of the lanky boy flopping in the corner like a medical mannequin.

He was new to the hospital, a student at the radiology institute—assigned to a summer rotation among the three Moscow clinics with working x-ray machines. His job was to keep them calibrated and stocked with film. He had no medical training, and only a limited understanding as to how his maintenance of the hulking devices ensured the Soviet Union's primacy in medicine. But he did know a pretty dancer when he saw one.

I didn't see his eyes go wide at the sight of my thigh, exposed high above the knee by the hitch where my skirt had caught on my dance bag. I didn't see him rush to intercept me before I passed through the double doors to the patient beds. All that I would supply later, in memory. But I heard the clatter of the trash bin he tripped over in his hurry. And I heard his painful exclamation as the doors swung back into his face.

"Chort!"

I turned. There he was, reeling in the swinging gap of the doors, his hands clasped over his nose and one foot still in the litter basket.

"Oy, I'm so sorry. I didn't see you—are you all right?"

He straightened to face me, cradling his nose. There were tears in his eyes. "You . . ." he breathed.

"I'm here for Kravshina, Vera Konstantinovna. She's in bed four."

"Yes. I know." He blinked hard. He held up his hand, a gesture for me to stop, or wait, or, just, listen. I shifted the flowers from one arm to another and looked warily down the hall to where my mother lay dying.

"Is everything all right?" I whispered.

"Oh yes," he said hurriedly. "Yes, of course. I mean, I think so. I hope so. I mean, I don't know what . . . down there." He frowned, like he didn't quite believe himself. "I just wanted to tell you . . . to invite you . . ."

And then he took a deep breath and asked me if I would join him for a cup of coffee when I was finished visiting my mother.

"Coffee?"

"Or tea. Tea." He touched his nose gingerly and then clasped his hands behind his back. "I'm partial to coffee. Strong coffee. Good for the . . ."

"Yes." I smiled. He had not broken his nose. His nose was just right. I felt a warm wave of relief. Because this young man in a white lab coat bore no resemblance to the white lab coats of 1717. Because he was stumbling to explain that he would be done in twenty minutes and he would wait for me out front. Because he had to deliver some films on the second floor and then clock out and he would wait for me out front, there was a bench at the entrance but he would wait for me there, at the entrance, but I should take my time, take as long as I needed, he would be there, waiting. It was fine. Just as long as I needed. He would be waiting.

I smiled again. "Okay."

Then he backed up with exaggerated caution and disappeared through the swinging doors.

I plucked a loose petal from my forearm and made my way down the hall to bed four. I was still smiling when I reached her bedside.

"Lilac, Mama. I hope they don't smell too strong?"

She allowed me to adjust the flat pillow behind her head. There was a bald patch where her head had rubbed against the rough linen. A hot wind pushed through the open window. I dropped the armful of lilacs on the bed.

"I brought the fruit juice you like. Some poetry, too. A new anthology. Can't remember whose verses, but it's selling like mad."

I could feel her watching me as I removed the things from bags and arranged them on the windowsill. Outside, a young mother was struggling with a child in the middle of a temper tantrum. I watched them make slow progress across the road, sympathizing with them both. I saw the bench where the boy in the white coat would be waiting for me.

"You are changed," my mother said.

I turned and raised my eyebrows. "How so?"

"The way you hold your head. The way you move, too. There's a decisiveness. And your arms. They're so strong."

"I've been working on my *port de bras*," I said.

Her eyes roved over my hair, which hung loose, and then over my dress with its tailored bodice and clinging skirt. These were clothes that no eighteen-year-old without fancy parents or a well-placed connection should be wearing, and Vera knew it. I raised my chin, challenging her to question it—my abandoned braid, my newfound "decisiveness" and sartorial suggestiveness. But there was no judgment in her eyes. Nor was there surprise, or satisfaction, or resentment. There was only pain.

I was ashamed. I was the one full of conflicted emotions; my mother was just full of disease.

I squatted on my heels and kissed her hand. "What can I do for you, Mama?"

"Tell me you are safe."

I squeezed her hand and told her I was safe.

"Safe," she repeated. "In your strange little bubble of ignorance and intelligence."

It sounded unkind, but I let it go.

"I have not heard from Natalia for months," my mother remarked.

"She sends her regards," I said.

"That's not what I meant."

"Mama. We agreed."

We had. Not in words, but with an understanding. We did not discuss Lubyanka or Natalia Davydovna Gerasova or my Extraordinary Code. But Vera, after a year's silence on the subject, was having a relapse. Or fresh doubts.

"I worry that you won't be . . ."

"Everything will be fine, Mama. I am doing well at the Academy."

"That's not what I was going to say." She closed her eyes and sighed. Her lips hardly moved when she said, "I worry that you won't be . . . happy."

I was taken aback, unsure of how to respond. Where did this tenderness come from? I blamed mortality. I dropped her hand and went to the window once more, where I made a show of arranging the lilac.

"Shall I read you poetry?" I asked eventually.

"No. Tell me the news," she replied. "Tell me about the wall."

Another surprise. My mother was keeping abreast of current events from her hospital bed. She saw my face and nodded. "I told you. Building a wall to keep out the enemy. Papers and passports are not enough anymore. They're building a wall."

I knew all about the wall. In 1717, Maksim had become a regular urban planning bully, feeding me maps of Berlin. I had become an able cartographer under hypnosis and produced a detailed topography of the Western-occupied portion of the city from memory. Whose memory? The memory of the universal mind buried *Unter Den Linden.* This was the intelligence I had recovered in all-night sessions of remote viewing: decades-old memories of tunnels, alleys, hidey-holes, and basement bunkers.

It was strange intelligence, no doubt—the intercepted fragments of blueprints that had been drafted, discarded, revised, and stamped TOP SECRET before making their way to the Western occupation force that had settled in the middle of defeated Germany like a bone stuck in the Soviet throat. That's what Comrade Khrushchev had called it: "a bone stuck in the Soviet throat."

"Yes, I know about the wall," I said. I didn't add that its path—crooked, serpentine, entrapping—had been laid based in part on my intelligence.

"I suppose . . ." wondered Vera. "I mean, how long of a wall can you build?"

"As long as the Great Wall of China," I said. "But this wall is different. It's not about length. It's about enclosure. It is meant to cut off West Berlin and the Americans. They will be completely surrounded, isolated. Like a tumor deprived of blood."

I immediately regretted the analogy. Just last week, the

doctors had found new spots on my mother's lungs. The cancer was not isolated; it was spreading. When I asked how long she had to live, they just shrugged. It was cruel—being able to see flashes of the past so vividly, but not knowing what would happen to my mother in a week's time.

I sat down on the bed. There was plenty of room; Vera was already physically retreating. I patted the blanket discreetly, looking for my mother's body underneath.

"I'll be gone soon," she said in acknowledgment.

I shook my head, but I couldn't deny her words.

"I'm just sorry I won't live to see it."

"See what?"

"Your glory. Your debut. You—onstage."

I stroked her hand. It was a secret, my good news; she couldn't have known. The Bolshoi Ballet was taking me even sooner than I had hoped. My old coach, Elena Mikhailovna had been right: I was fast-tracked. But it was my new teacher, Natalia Davydovna who had put me on that fast track. Because the Bolshoi was scheduled to travel to Berlin in October—a gesture of solidarity with our Communist brothers holding the front line against the West—and Comrade Gerasova wanted her Agent Prima in close proximity to that front line. Oleg had agreed, saying, "Remote viewing has its limitations. Namely, its remoteness."

And so I was to be included in the touring company. I would be the newest and youngest member of the Bolshoi corps de ballet.

I bent close and whispered in my mother's ear: "I join the Bolshoi in two months. You will live to see it. Hang on, Mama."

WHEN I STEPPED OUT of the hospital into the smell of mowed summer grass, he was waiting on the bench under a large poplar tree. He had recovered from his earlier encounter with the heavy doors and struck an easy pose—legs stretched out before him and his arms crossed over his chest. He seemed to be studying the sparrows making a racket in the tree above. I admired his comfort and the stillness of his face. I wondered if his skin was as smooth as it looked in the dappled shade. I thought I had never seen a boy more . . . at ease.

I felt, again, an inexplicable sense of relief. "Hello," I said.

He stood quickly.

The newspaper he had been reading fell to the ground. I caught a glimpse of the front-page photograph—the proud, sweaty face of a worker in East Berlin shouldering a bag of concrete. The headline below the photo read: BERLINERS BUILD RAMPARTS AT THE FORTRESS OF COMMUNISM.

As I stooped to retrieve it, I noticed his pants, which hung just above his ankles. I also noticed his socks, which were light blue. My gangly suitor was a hipster. I stood and examined him for other signs of *stilyagi* faddishness, but his smile was not ironic. His ash-blond hair, while sprouting a cowlick at the back, showed no signs of pomaded ducktails or other "greaser" affectations. He had gray-blue eyes.

"Hello." I said again as I handed him the newspaper. "Where did you want to have tea?"

"Gorky Park?" he suggested.

I let him carry my dance bag. He slung it over his torso so that it crisscrossed the leather strap of his own satchel, making him look like a skinny, stylish packhorse.

As we walked, he asked me a million questions: Was it true I was training to dance for the Bolshoi? Was my mother showing improvement? Did I like jazz, by any chance?

I answered politely, in noncommittal tones. I kept my eyes on his long legs and shiny shoes.

It wasn't until we were standing across from the park entrance, waiting for the traffic light to change, that I asked him his name. He smacked his head and apologized. "Viktor," he said, extending his hand. "Viktor Fyodorovich Dukovsky, radiology engineer."

"And I'm Svetlana Kravshina . . . girl who is about to have tea with a radiology engineer."

BY SEPTEMBER I WAS spending several nights a week with Viktor. The tail end of summer had left plenty of free time for us both. The Academy went on two weeks of vacation, and the wall in Berlin dividing the city into enemy zones went up practically overnight, which allowed work at Lubyanka 1717 to take a pause as well.

For the first time since I left the House, I relaxed. I slept late. I stayed out late. I considered sleeping with this boy, Viktor, who danced the boogie-woogie and thought I hung the moon.

I told Oksana about him the first night I kissed him.

"He's tall. Sweet. Silly and kind of awkward. It's weird, but he feels like home. Not like the House . . . but, well, sort of, yes, like the House," I said, trying to explain Viktor's easy attraction. "I mean, when I'm with him I almost feel like my old self. Like me before I left the House. Before my mother and the Bolshoi and . . ."

"And before a certain Georgi Levshik?" Oksana replied wryly. "I dunno, Svet. Sounds pretty reactionary. You're supposed to be going ever forward, Comrade Kravshina, not backward."

"Oh, Vitya's very progressive," I assured her. "He knows all the Western trends. He's teaching me to jitterbug and his partner Liza is taking me to an atelier where I can buy one of those bobby-sox skirts with the poodles and all."

"Oh my God. He's a hipster? You're mixing with the *stilyagi*?" she exclaimed. "Sveta, that's worse than a Spaniard, you wicked nonconformist."

"So you don't want to meet him? Too cultured for the *stilyagi*, Oksana?"

"I want to meet him immediately, you poodle-wearing, bebopping strumpet!"

I introduced them on a glorious Sunday evening, on the platform at the end of the Metro line, miles from the center.

Viktor kissed me and swung me around by the waist and then turned to my best friend and said, "Oksana, at last!"

Well done, I thought. *Well done.*

From the Metro we walked to an abandoned warehouse that had been turned into a dance hall by Moscow's crowd of too-cool *stilyagi*. I had seen Viktor dance before—in cramped living rooms with his best partner, Liza. I had watched him play his records, which he carted about in that leather satchel, for small audiences in the back room of a newspaper office where the printing presses drowned out the sound of the banned music. But this—this was a gathering on a whole new scale. All of Moscow's counterculture seemed to be in attendance—from the lapsed Party kids to the painfully posturing rockers to the intellectual nihilists who couldn't resist jazz—even the upbeat sort.

The dance hall was enormous and I wore my new skirt. We were greeted with a cheer; Viktor had brought the music. Oksana watched the girls flutter to his side. "He's kinda dreamy, Svet," she whispered.

But she hadn't seen anything yet.

Viktor's friends swept him up rickety steps to the foreman's platform where they had rigged a hi-fi system up to the speakers high in the rafters—big, horned speakers that looked like they might have blared air-raid warnings during the war. Amid shouting and jostling—and squealing on the part of some high-strung girls sporting high-strung ponytails—Viktor opened his satchel. He made a show of selecting a record. The boys pounded a drumroll on the table. Viktor flipped a switch, lowered the needle . . . and with a *one-two-three-four* the warehouse was filled with "hound dogs."

Immediately, the whole place was jumping and gyrating as if the cement floor was electrified. And my Vitya was right in the middle of it all, his knees and elbows buckling and his hips doing the most amazing things.

I turned to Oksana's stunned face and laughed out loud.

"American music?" she asked, her eyes wide.

"Of course!"

Oksana's dropped jaw turned into a smile. "That boy can dance."

It was true. Even in the close confines of Liza's living room, where they had to negotiate her mother's cabinet of porcelain pigs, I had seen that Viktor Dukovsky was a good dancer. His joints were like rubber, snappy and loose, which made for more interesting choreography than a spine of steel. But the soft shoes he had demonstrated for me so far had been just a taste, a hint, of his uninhibited self. Here on the outskirts of the city, there were no neighbors to report the loud music and there was enough room for dozens of couples to let loose—whirling and jumping and flashing their garters. Here in the middle of nowhere, under the massive banners proclaiming the FIVE YEAR ACHIEVEMENT OF THE PETROLEUM QUOTA IN FOUR YEARS!, I saw that Vitya wasn't just a good dancer—he was an idol. A free spirit. A happy guy. A carefree *stilyaga*.

He was as strange to me as a merman.

From the middle of the dance floor he beckoned to me, his mouth open, begging to play. I smiled and shook my head. I pointed across the floor to where Liza had just come in. Like a puppy distracted by a squirrel, Viktor bounded to her side.

"Watch this," I said to Oksana.

It was worth watching. I could practice for days and never dance like Liza. My training wasn't having it—the bouncy abandon of her body, the raw excitement in her face. Sure, I could jump higher and turn faster than she could, and I could lift my leg onto my partner's shoulders without a running start. But for me dancing was practice and perfection. It was about performance. For Liza it was just fun. She was adorable—a cute caricature with a fire-engine red mouth hanging open and a high ponytail. But she was a "chic." I was a ballerina.

The song ended and a new one began. For a moment, I didn't even notice. I was too distracted by the long, low whistle coming nearer and nearer . . . until just as I thought a freight train might barrel right through the walls of the warehouse, the entire dance floor whooped as one: "Choo choo!" and I realized the train whistle was coming from the speakers. The approaching locomotive resolved itself in a languid question of saxophones, and the crowd formed a long conga line, asking someone named Roy how to get to Chattanooga.

Oksana was bouncing on her toes and tugging at my hand. I caught Viktor's eye and he came quickly to lead her onto the dance floor. I leaned back against the wall and prepared to be amazed by the revelation that my Oksana, eloquent scourge of artistic nonsense and capitalist dreck, was a natural acolyte of the American jukebox.

She wasn't, as it turned out.

Oksana didn't have the bop gene, and after gamely attempting the twist, she fell back on something closer to a Cossack folk dance. Viktor met her halfway, and soon they were the center of a Volga-style hoedown. The rest of the dancers formed a ring around them. *"Hoppa!"* shouted a tall boy with an even taller pompadour. He leapt into a boisterous Slavic soft shoe, which he followed by lifting a pretty redhead into a vertical salute to the ceiling. We all saw her striped knickers. That's what they were there for—to be seen. When the redhead came back to earth, the circle dissolved and regrouped into two camps: On one side of the floor the "swing" scaled fresh acrobatic heights. On the other, the exaggerated foot stomping and thigh slapping native to this abandoned warehouse grew louder in response. There was taunting and cheering as the jive surged forward, only to be knocked aside by the lockstep line of Kamarinsky hoofers.

It was a battle royal of enemy dances: an American twist, a Spanish flamenco, a proletarian polka, a Kavkazki split. A bobby-soxer slid through the spread-eagle of a *muzhik*'s flex-kneed squat like a spy in the night. It was a Cold War on the dance floor, and before I knew it I had entered the fray.

It must have been the music. There was no other way to explain the collapse of my perfect posture. My practiced turn-out turned itself inside out. I threw up my hands in surrender and found myself the partner of a young man in a suit sharp enough to cut. We danced a two-step that didn't last the third step because suddenly I was dancing with a girl wearing light green pedal pushers and deep green eye shadow.

One song rolled into the next, and I flipped partners and petticoats until I found Oksana's outstretched hands. Laughing, we spun in wild circles shouting "goodness!" singing "gracious!" If we let go, the centripetal force of this music—banned and crude—would send us out the door, out of the abandoned industrial park, out of Moscow, the fortress of the Soviet Union, and out into the cosmos . . . like great balls of fire.

And then . . .

The scratch of the needle across vinyl, as loud as a train crash. A moment of freighted silence.

"Raaaaaaaaaid!"

It took me a moment to understand: everyone had to leave. Quickly.

I watched the chaos as if in slow motion: pointed zoot boots, high-heeled shoes, ripped nylons, and broken beer bottles. We were surrounded, encircled and squeezed by a gray army of interlopers at the perimeter. I thought of the rats creeping from the wings into Marie's *Nutcracker* dreams, and then I thought of Pupok's rat: *"Kriiiiiiisa!"*

But these rats were real. And they were human.

I recognized them collectively, though I had never seen any of them before. Ordinary kids. The kind I once lived with, studied with, rode the bus with, and dozed with during obligatory political meetings. They were just Komsomol kids, but stupid and fanatical. They were Komsomol kids who saw the threat of Soviet annihilation in the gyrations of Elvis, so it was their duty to stage a raid on rock-and-roll with metal bars and wooden bats. I stood there in disbelief. Didn't they know that the enemy was *without*? That we had built a wall?

Now Viktor was grabbing me by the hand. We swept Oksana out with us as we slid under the platform and down a short flight of stairs. We burst through a metal door, leapt over a drainage ditch and crashed into the bushes. We hunkered low, listening to a sonic map of insults.

"Traitors! Bourgeois parasites! Degenerate imbeciles!"

"Slobs! Conformists! Zombie youth!"

"We know where you hide, perverts!"

"Who's hiding, morons? You're the invisible ones, you mindless peasants!"

Viktor parted the branches to reveal an empty pathway, marked by a sequined pocketbook that had been abandoned in flight. We could still hear the last song, stuck in its groove on the turntable, yelling for more.

"Damn," said Viktor. "I left my records."

I scowled. "Honestly, Vitya. I hardly think Elvis is worth getting arrested over."

"Arrested?" Oksana repeated breathlessly. But she was smiling.

"First of all, nobody's arresting anybody. Second of all, it's not just Elvis. It's the Everly Brothers . . . and Bill Haley and Kid Ory and . . ."

"Viktor Dukovsky, you are not going back in there."

But he went.

We watched him sneak back toward the warehouse, his bent frame a caricature of stealth. Oksana thought it was funny. I didn't. The whole night had turned into a juvenile escapade, and I was beginning to itch, hiding in the tall bushes. I looked away from the warehouse to the rail depot in the distance, studded with boxcars. Beyond that, a highway. Headlights moved slowly across the horizon, dimmer than the stars in the sky.

"This is absurd," I declared.

I stepped out onto the path and yelled. "Vitya!"

Seconds later he came shooting toward us from the building like a rocket. Oksana dove back behind the bushes. A lone Komsomol scout clung to Viktor's satchel—a puny little kid—looking desperate, an unwanted caboose.

"Run!" Viktor yelled, but I didn't budge. Not until they were practically on top of me. Only then did I throw my leg into a *grand battement*. Viktor's pursuer slammed to the ground with a grunt.

Viktor halted and stared at what I had done.

I knelt to see what I had done.

"My nose," the kid whimpered.

"Your ass," I retorted.

Oksana emerged from the bushes. "Sveeeeeeta," she breathed. Then she giggled. She began clapping, slowly. Viktor joined her.

"Let's get out of here," I said.

IT WAS A LONG walk. Oksana led the way, catcalling potential Komsomol outliers the whole time. Viktor hung back and apologized.

"I was going to give you the whole speech about how you were never in any danger and I'd never let you get hurt and blah blah blah . . . but clearly you know how to look out for yourself."

He leaned in to kiss me, and I pushed him away.

"If I had been looking out for myself I would have never gotten into that idiotic position in the first place."

Viktor shifted his bag to the other shoulder. "You know they can't do anything, Sveta. They have no authority. They can't arrest you or—or even report you. I mean they don't know our names or anything about us."

We were in the middle of nowhere and the raiders had vanished. But I wanted him to lower his voice. I had thought it a joke—those cartoons in *Pravda* where the long-legged *stilyagi* in their wide-bottomed pants fled the righteous, upstanding models of Communism in their red kerchiefs beneath the caption: TODAY YOU ARE LISTENING TO JAZZ. TOMORROW YOU ARE BETRAYING THE MOTHERLAND.

But it wasn't a joke. It was a warning. One that I hadn't heeded.

"The only time I've ever seen real police show up, we paid

them off," Viktor was saying. "And with records, of all things. I mean, there they were ready to break them into smithereens and then one of them is like, 'hey fellas, you know what you can get for these at Gorbushka market?' And the next thing you know they've forgotten all about 'destruction of anti-Soviet neo-fascist materials' and they're going on about 'confiscation of contraband propaganda.' And sure enough, the next day I went down to Gorbushka and bought them all back. You can be sure those cops dined on caviar that Saturday. They're jokers."

I folded my arms across my chest. I had heard this lecture before. It was Georgi Levshik's worldview, only the naïve version. The police were not jokers. They could label any pretext at all—vinyl, jazz, unauthorized gatherings—the same way: *Enemy of the People.* Playing hide-and-seek with Komsomol kiddie storm troopers might be a lark for Viktor and his well-heeled hipster friends. But for me, for someone who had everything to lose from one more black mark, it was dangerous. It was poor judgment. It was stupid.

"I should never have gone," I said.

"And so we will never go again," he answered. He stepped in front of me and took both my hands. "You have my word."

I leaned my head against his chest and felt the sense of relief that came only from him. I reached up and wrapped my arms around his neck. He lifted me from the ground and I wrapped my legs around his hips. We didn't need to dance, Viktor and me. We didn't need to argue: if I said no, he heard no. No need, either, to explain.

I still hadn't told him. Viktor didn't know that I'd once lived in Orphanage #36 and that my mother was once an Enemy of the People. He didn't know that I had a blackened biography and that I was scrubbing it daily with powerful cleansers. I could have told him, of course. I could have told him right there on the outskirts of Moscow under a starry September sky. He wouldn't have blinked an eye. Or he would have praised me for beating the system. But I didn't. Not because I was afraid to, but because

I didn't have to. Vitya had never asked. He never baited me, like Gosha did. He never investigated me, though all it would have taken was a simple file query about the patient in bed number four of the cancer ward.

So I forgave him for the harmless, subversive dance party.

I smoothed the tufted craziness of his hair and kissed him.

He laughed. "What is it with you? Breaking hearts and noses with equal flair. You really floored that punk. I would love to be a fly on the wall when he makes his report. Can you imagine? Can you picture him squirming before his thought-police minders in Lubyanka?"

Viktor put on his fake straight-arrow voice and saluted. "*That's right, Commandant. The enemy was a merciless ballerina, trained in deadly force!*"

He cracked up. "So much for your KGB career, pal!" he yelled back into the darkness.

And that's when I knew I would always have secrets from Viktor.

TH!RTEEN
BONE MUSIC

The morning before our departure for Berlin, I was a bundle of cool, steely nerves. Anxious enough to jump out of my skin, my only defense was an unflappable calm. I moved slowly, underwater. My distress felt oxygen deprived. I yawned massively.

I sat alone in the canteen, forcing myself to eat a hard-boiled egg. I made slow progress, in tiny bites, until I reached the yolk. It was gray. I dropped it on my plate and studied my empty hand. It was shaking. I stared at it until it stopped.

I was about to attend my first class at the Bolshoi. And though there was nothing so predictable as a ballet class—*pliés, tendues, frappés,* and *battements* followed by an adagio and a grand allegro—I was still nervous. Because I was taking this class at the Bolshoi, which was to say *with* the Bolshoi, which was to say with all the dancers of the company traveling to Berlin. Which was to say: I was about to take a class in the company of the *prima ballerina assoluta*, Galina Ulanova.

The yolk was watching me. I took a gulp of tea and popped the vulgar thing in my mouth. I swallowed it down, hurried upstairs, and threw up. Then I brushed my teeth and got my things together for class.

Outside it was a perfect autumn morning. The hills behind the dormitory had burst into color overnight, a dazzling backdrop for the golden cupolas of an ancient monastery that had been left alone by the bulldozers of the Revolution.

I stepped onto the street, breathed the scent of wet leaves and fungus and fresh bread and gasoline. I whispered, *pull yourself together, Sveta*, and marched off for the Metro.

On the escalator I stood on the right-hand side, letting the tardy students pummel past me into the depths of the station. When I reached the bottom, I felt: waves of pain, memories of a physical trauma. Alarmed, I turned to the guard box. Of course my mother wasn't there. She was in a hospital on the other side of the river. But the panic was heavy. And it was coming from the Metro worker. She was, an Asian woman—a Kazakh or a Buryat or some other Sovietized tribe from the east. She was leaning into the booth's small microphone, shouting at someone midway up the escalator. Her voice was doing battle with the piped-in music, and I saw her urgency escalate with the volume of the symphony. Was it Tchaikovsky? I didn't know, but I knew that I was in the middle of the Kazakh Metro-watcher's childhood memory: *the cows bottlenecking the gate of the corral, the stampede, her father injured as she looked on, helpless.*

I turned away and the vision passed.

Stay away, I begged. *Just for the next three hours, no visions or memories or evidence of that talent of mine that has nothing to do with ballet.*

I needed to focus on my own body. My own mind.

TEATRALNAYA WAS ONLY FOUR stops down the line. I came out onto the square and stood before the Bolshoi Theatre. The awe that I usually felt at the sight of its imposing classical façade felt different; the building appeared both smaller and larger at the same time. Like when a speck of dust in your eye feels like a handful of sand. I gripped the pass in my pocket and crossed the square.

I found the artists' entrance on the east side of the building, just down the street from the courtyard where I had once been given some much-needed pointe shoes. Inside, the theater smelled of oak and velvet and something else. At the desk was an elderly man engrossed in a crossword puzzle. He had an intelligent face, a face that had been handsome once. It still invited the close angle of a camera. I wondered if I should know him. Was he a famous actor? Past his prime and now checking the passes of the new generation? I showed him mine and he squinted at it over his glasses.

"Welcome, Miss Kravshina," he said. "Reporting for class, are you?"

I nodded. I had never been called "Miss" before. It was not Soviet. It was not proletarian. It was certainly not what you called a girl raised in Orphanage #36. He *must* be an actor with an illustrious past.

"Do you know your way?"

"No, actually. It's my first time."

He raised the half gate of the desk and stepped into the hallway next to me. He pointed down the corridor.

"All the way to the second stairway. Up to the third floor. You'll have to ask that lot up there for further directions. That's already not my territory."

At the second stairway I quickly climbed two flights and then paused on the landing. I could hear the chatter of dancers and the clatter of pianos. I took a deep breath and climbed the last flight. I followed a handful of dancers into a small dressing room. Only one of them paid me any mind. She had a husky voice and the body of a gymnast. I imagined she had a killer *grand jeté*.

"It's Markova's class," the girl told me. "She's a demon for ankles. Just watch that you don't go weak on the relevé and she won't be too hard on you. Not on your first day."

She pulled her hair back so tight I wondered if she could blink. She stabbed pins into the tight bun, cracked her knuckles, and extended a hand. "I'm Sasha."

"Svetlana," I said. Her grip was as strong as her thighs. "Is it all right if I follow you to the barre?"

"Yeah, sure. But if Ulanova shows up I might abandon you. I hate standing next to Ulanova."

My heart leapt. "I'd give my eye teeth . . ."

Sasha laughed. "Watch what you wish for. I know a girl who got kicked in the kisser by Ulanova and nearly did lose a tooth. An accident of course. Ulanova wouldn't hurt a fly. Not unless the fly said something sideways about her beloved Bolshoi, that is. Ready?"

I tucked in my ribbons and nodded. "Ready."

Inside the studio the chatter ended.

I felt a keen focus—the practiced concentration that rules the studio. I could almost smell the self-absorption. The door flew open and a small woman dressed in black silk strode into the room, already instructing. Her hands were demonstrating the combination; her feet were tapping the rhythm.

"New girl to the front," she commanded, "directly behind Ulanova."

I stood frozen for a half second before I understood: I was the new girl; the plain-looking woman with the frizzy hair and the faded leotard at the head of the barre was my idol, Galina Ulanova, whom I had last seen onstage in silent deference to her most dreadful fan, Joseph Stalin.

The other dancers eyed me with mild curiosity as I took my place behind the prima ballerina. Ulanova didn't move an inch, though her eyes met mine in the mirror. I felt my heart in my chest and wondered if the whole room could hear it: *tick-tick-tock-tock*.

I WAS STILL DANCING when I arrived at Lubyanka two hours later. All four technicians were on duty, but I made a beeline for Inga, who was spooling some audiotape near the sound booth. She listened to me babble. I even demonstrated part of the allegro, which I had nailed.

"Inga. After class, you know what she did? Ulanova came right up to me and told me I had 'profound musicality.'"

"And indeed you do. I hope the pianist didn't play Tchaikovsky during the allegro?" she teased.

"I was good, Inga," I said. "Really good."

I noticed her shoot a glance across the room at Maksim, who was scowling more than usual. But he couldn't ruin my mood. Not today.

"Actually, Markova—that's the ballet coach—she was a little sticky. She was suspicious of my ankles and she said it was nonsense that I had only been sent over for one class before we leave for Berlin."

"Nonsense, huh?" Inga snapped an elastic band around the audiotape and dropped it in the pocket of her white coat.

"She said it was to be expected from the amateurs at the Academy. That they were too busy measuring little rumps and thighs to give any thought to the question of professionalism. She said it was a good thing that I don't have to do anything but stand stage right and look pretty in Berlin, because my *port de bras* still needs work."

Maksim was suddenly next to me, his voice like cold water: "There's much that still needs work, Prima. Here. Today."

Inga returned to her desk. Oleg retreated to the kitchen.

"Our business is not about 'standing around and looking pretty,'" Maksim added snidely. "So let's have no more of your giddiness. You can dispel, right now, any expectations you have of wild applause and bouquets in the dressing room. True service to the *rodina* goes unacknowledged."

I kept silent, but another voice stood up for me. From the door, Natalia Davydovna Gerasova said, "Let's not underestimate the importance of appearance, comrades. Especially not with a versatile operative like Prima here, for whom it comes so naturally. As far as I know, no artist has ever endangered the Motherland by looking pretty."

She removed her coat and smiled sweetly at the room.

"I will be joining you today," she said.

WE MOVED INTO THE soundproof booth where Inga usually tested music for "impressionistic remote viewing." Maksim began outfitting me with a headset—a snug helmet with earphones and a strap of sensors that ran around my hairline. The door slid open and Pavel joined us. He removed the cover from a machine I had not noticed before and powered it on. He rubbed his hands before it as if it were a small campfire.

Maksim tightened the straps on the headset and adjusted the sensors at the nape of my neck. He consulted with Pavel as he worked, but his voice did not penetrate the thick helmet. Gerasova pulled up her chair so that she was facing me directly. She held a microphone. Static crackled in my ear.

"Can you hear me, Prima?" she said into the microphone.

I nodded.

"Let's recall, first of all, why we are here. Tell me—what is the work that you are involved with?"

"Psychological intelligence."

"That's right. And how is this intelligence gained?"

"Enhanced Memory Recognition. Remote viewing. Transference of information along asymmetric and personal channels of recalled observation." The answers came out easily, but I couldn't hear them clearly from within the helmet. I felt like a deaf person stumbling over misshapen words.

I glanced at Pavel's monitor in the corner: a constellation of blinking lights, the world under the helmet, the space in my skull.

In the fourteen months I had been coming to the Psychological Intelligence Unit, I had been photographed, fingerprinted, measured, and weighed. But my colleagues had never taken a look inside my mind. No x-rays, no scans, no tangible evidence that could link my brain to my work. All this time, what went on in my brain had been strictly theoretical. Often implausibly so. But now . . . *Were they watching me? Watching me viewing, remembering, transferring information along asymmetric channels of observation?*

"Yes," said Gerasova, as if she were, indeed, reading my thoughts. "What you are looking at is your mind at work. Pavel is using advanced imaging technology to see . . . well, to see . . . How did you explain it to me, comrade?"

"A positron emission tomographic mapping of episodic memory cross-referenced with semantic memory," Pavel said. His words were a murmur.

I heard Maksim more clearly. "The psychosphere," he said.

The monitor went dark. The only sound in the booth was of Pavel typing. In the corner, a printing machine began spitting out a paper version of my tomographic semantic memory. Its clacking echoed through the sensors at the back of my head.

"New terminologies for both of us to learn," said Gerasova, still holding the microphone. "But let's return to those that you've already been taught. Let's return to transference. And let's combine it with Maksim's useful concept—the psychosphere."

I shifted in my chair. The sensations, tiny sparks at the back of my head, were becoming more pronounced. I concentrated on the puddle of the printout on the floor. A map, I guessed, of my psychosphere.

Gerasova leaned close. "What does transference mean, Prima?"

"It means that information is moved from the target's memory to my own."

"For what purpose?"

"For the purpose of . . ." I stopped, waiting to hear my own words better, but they were still untethered from my voice.

"For what purpose?"

"For the purpose of intelligence. Knowing information. Information crucial to the defense of the Motherland and the victory of the Communist . . ."

"Yes, yes, yes," Maksim interrupted. "But that is passive transference. That is just recognition put into words and recorded on paper. It's time for you to master real transference. Active transference."

Gerasova held up a hand to silence him. Then she put the microphone in her lap and took my hand. She placed it palm to palm against her own. I read her lips, echoed by the whisper of her words through the microphone in her lap. "There is intelligence, and there is counterintelligence."

She closed our fingers into a joint fist.

"There is information," she continued, opening our fingers once more and shifting them until they nested together in a way that made mine dominant, with her thumb pinned under mine. "And there is disinformation."

Pavel turned from his monitor and nodded. He was ready. *But for what?* I wondered. *Was I ready?*

Gerasova was looking intently at me. She dropped our unnatural fist and picked up the microphone. "Today we are going to implant a memory into your brain. It will be encoded into the dendrites of the hippocampus through electric stimulation and will be, physiologically and neurologically, yours. If we are successful, we will have promoted you from a defensive asset to an operational tool, capable of offensive deception in the psychosphere."

I was suddenly aware of my breathing. It seemed impossibly loud, too loud for anything else to be heard. I looked at my fingers in my lap and saw that they were trembling. I thought of the gray egg yolk from this morning, so long ago.

I steeled myself from the inside out and watched Gerasova's lips say: "If we are successful, Agent Prima, you will become a psychosoldier of the information war."

IT WAS TWILIGHT WHEN I got home. I had missed the sunset over the western hills by an hour or more, but as I stood at the window I remembered, vividly, the glint of late sun on the golden onion domes at their base. I remembered the raucous calls of late afternoon ravens.

Normal memories, I told myself. *My memories.*

But something else told me they weren't.

They warned me of that.

Maksim had called it "asymmetric certainty."

Pavel called it "sabotage on the infrastructure of reason."

Inga had spoken of "psycho-acoustics," the phenomenon that made it possible to hear encrypted messages outside the range of audible sound. "Like a recording. A recording in which the bass line is removed, forcing your brain to replace it to make sense of a melody," she had explained. "An important piece of audible information is gone, rendering it incomplete to some listeners. But we have made sure your mind can hear it."

"A phantom sound?" I had asked.

"Yes. Or a phantom vision. Or a phantom memory."

And I had sat among them, rubbing my temples, insisting that I felt nothing new. Nothing different. Nothing missing. But now I wasn't so sure. Because now I was watching the sunset. And an early October sunset over the western hills meant it was quarter to six, but the clock on the wall said it was closer to eight. Two hours had been removed and my brain was replacing them. Psychically. I was seeing a phantom sunset. I was hearing phantom ravens.

I closed my eyes and rested my forehead against the window. I heard something else. I heard the bass line of my consciousness—the voice of a man.

He said: *Go to sleep,* dochka. *I will be home in the morning.*

He said: *Go to the west, soldier. And serve the* rodina *faithfully.*

He said: *Go to hell, commander. I will never betray my general.*

I remembered my father's face. I remembered my mother's long exile. I remembered a forlorn balloon in my childhood home. I wondered: *How can these things be more real than ravens?* And then these memories swirled into a new one: Seven-year-old Sveta standing alone in a town square waiting for the wrecking ball. A bronze man on the pedestal waiting to be toppled. He had his back to me, and no matter how many times I circled the statue, searching for a name, a face, it kept its back turned.

The man's voice spoke again: *Evgeny.*

Pieces of information had been erased. From the newspapers, from the atlases, from the history books. But I could make sense of it all: *My father had served the* rodina. *Evgeny had gone west. But who had asked whom to betray his general?*

That I didn't know for certain.

When I opened my eyes, the sunset was long gone and there was a cloud on the windowpane from my breath. I cleared a line down its middle and watched it bleed warmth into the circle of condensation. It struck me as an obvious symbol. But of what? Had I marked my presence on the glass? Or had I erased a layer of reality with one finger?

I smudged the whole riddle with the heel of my hand.

K chortu, I concluded. Outside it was dark, neither sunset nor twilight. Only October 5, 1961, and I had a flight to catch in the morning.

There was a knock at the door. A small girl peeked in. "Telephone for you, Svetlana."

I pulled the curtains against the dark and made my way downstairs. "Hello?"

"It's me. Gosha."

I slid down the wall, taking the phone with me. It had been months since we last talked.

"What's new?"

I hoped he had a long answer. Because my news was hard to explain. My news had a lot to do with why it had been months since we last talked.

"Well, let's see," drawled Georgi. "I have new digs, for a start. A cozy little place in the center, left to me by an exceptional fellow currently engaged in the export side of a profitable venture. And I have a new set of wheels, mine in the free and clear. And I have an extra ticket to the circus next weekend. Come with me?"

"I can't."

"I know."

I waited a beat, wondering if he also knew why.

"How's your mother?"

"In hospital since the beginning of the summer."

"I'm sorry to hear that."

"They can care for her there."

I stretched my legs out in front of me and bent my nose to my knee. I turned my face and considered the sideways hallway. I was fairly sure that Gosha already knew about my mother. I waited to see if he would now wish me luck in Berlin. *Just how closely was he keeping tabs on me?* But he was quiet.

"How are you?" I asked eventually.

"I find myself in a funny position," he answered.

I spread my legs into a split and rolled smoothly over my pelvis until my belly was flat on the ground. I lifted both legs from the knee and rested my toes on my ears. "Me too," I said.

"I'm down at Petrovka 38."

I sat up straight.

There was background noise on the line: quarreling and barking. Someone giving orders and someone protesting. Petrovka 38 was police headquarters. "Gosha, what happened? Are you in trouble?"

"No. I'm not in any trouble."

Again the sound of decisions being made. Disagreements being registered. *"Sign here,"* I heard, clear as day.

"It's your boyfriend who's in trouble."

So he knew that, too. "Viktor?"

"Yup. That's him. He got picked up for those x-rays."

I didn't understand. I said so.

"The x-rays. You know—to make bone records."

"Bone records?"

"*Blin.* Yes, Svetlana. Bone music. You know, rock-and-roll."

"What's rock-and-roll got to do with x-rays?"

"That's what they are made on, those bootleg records. Your boy has a little rock-and-roll factory set up in his basement. Pretty nifty setup, I have to say. He can print something like a dozen records a night, what with his steady supply of films from the hospital. He's spreading banned music like the pox."

I was speechless. What did it mean? That Viktor was not just a connoisseur, but also a bootlegger? That I didn't know this? But that bastard Gosha did.

I thought of Viktor's leather satchel, the bag that he always left the hospital with. The same bag he insisted on going back for on the night of the dance party raid. I had seen him hand over stacks of records wrapped in newspaper. I had seen him tuck x-ray films under his arm when he left the radiology wing. I had never put the two together.

Bone records. Viktor trafficked in the underground of banned music.

First you are listening to jazz. Next you are betraying the rodina.

Nonsense, of course. But nonsense that a sensible person avoids.

"What will happen to him?" I asked. "What will they do?"

"They already did it," said Gosha. "He's pretty beat up. Nothing broken, I don't think, maybe a tooth or two. I know the captain on duty. He owed me a favor. I cashed in. They're letting Viktor go with some bruises and threats. Took what was in his wallet, too. Called it 'restitution' for all the skeletons he made off with."

I felt sick. My mother's films. The scans of her diseased lungs. Viktor had used them? Had covered them in jazz? Had danced with that idiot Liza on my mother's frail bones? He may not have betrayed the Motherland, but I had betrayed my mother. I thought of the term that Inga had used: "psycho-acoustics."

It had a nasty new meaning. It was the sound of music where music had no business being. It was the sound of my brain, enraged.

"Sveta. You there?"

"Why did you call me?"

I meant: *How do you know these things?* I meant: *What should I do?*

"Why did you call me?" I asked again, my voice cracking.

"I just thought you should know. I wanted you to know that . . . I took care of it. It could have been bad, you know? But luckily, I happened to be there. And I speak their language, these bored cops."

I leaned back against the wall and remembered what to say. "Thank you, Georgi. I am grateful. But I don't know what more I can do . . ."

"I thought that you cared about him, Svetlana. I thought you might want to be with him, take care of him. Make him feel better. He's a good guy, Viktor is."

I was listening for sarcasm or jealousy or just the friendly baiting that was Gosha's mother tongue. But there was only the sound of Petrovka 38. I put the phone in my lap and listened hard to the low registers that hid encrypted messages. I heard my mother's labored breathing. I heard the syncopation of jazz skipping over bones.

I picked up the telephone.

"Gosha," I whispered. "Could you come and get me? Now?"

VIKTOR LIVED BEYOND THE hills in a neighborhood ringed with cranes, where ugly new apartment blocks grew with the unsightly steadiness of a cancer. By the time we arrived at his building, I had fully expressed my opinion of his irresponsible, careless, immoral use of private property.

"Private property!" hooted Gosha. He caught my eye in the rearview mirror. Then he turned to Viktor, who was slumped against the door on the passenger's side, a bloody handkerchief stanching the blood from the dental work provided by the louts at Petrovka 38. "You see what you've done, Viktor?" Gosha wagged a mocking finger. "You've gone and exposed this pure, honest, steadfast comrade to degenerate music and now she's spouting capitalist filth. 'Private property' indeed. Foo. Shame on you, Sveta. And shame on you, Viktor—you nasty corruptor."

"Enough, Gosha." I climbed out of the car and opened the door for Viktor. I glanced up at the darkened windows of his flat. "Your parents?"

"Out," Viktor said. "But there's no need for you to stay. Let Georgi take you home. You should get some rest before tomorrow."

But Gosha was already out of the car and standing next to us.

"I think what we all need is fifty grams," he said pulling a bottle from his coat pocket.

In the kitchen I prepared a poultice for Viktor's swollen eye while Gosha poured out vodka and rummaged in the icebox for something to chase it.

"None of them were hers," said Viktor. "None of them were your mother's x-rays. They were all made from films that were at least two years old. They were going to be incinerated."

Gosha snorted and put a bowl of pickles on the table.

"Yeah, right. Sveta—if Viktor hadn't taken the films, his boss would have. Or his boss's boss. It's valuable material, the stuff those prints are made on. Hell, I would have taken them if I had known." He ruffled Viktor's hair. "It's good to see you again, Vitya. How long's it been? Since Stalin's funeral, right? And you haven't changed a bit, except for the long legs and high pants."

Georgi handed us both a shot glass, filled to the brim, and explained to me how it was he had known my boyfriend longer than I'd known him.

"He spent the day at the canal with us. Just a snot-nosed kid and he already knew that standing at attention in Red Square with the rest of the kiddies while Uncle Joe was laid to rest was

not his idea of a good time. So he slummed it with us barracks
rats on the canal. I suppose that was the beginning of your slide
into degeneracy, eh Vitya? A ten-year-old wrecker, you were."

He gave me a smug wink and lifted his glass. "Here's to
bone music. The most ingenious medical waste disposal ever
developed. A method so cunning, so creative, so musically
cynical, it could only come from the great minds of Soviets."

He drank. Vitya drank. I took a small sip that filled my throat
and then my chest and my belly. I felt the warmth settle in my
knees. I raised the glass to my lips and finished it off.

"I want to see them," I said. "The records."

We had to go back outside and around the building to get to
the cellar door. Down a short flight of steps was the small room
where Viktor recorded banned music. He snapped on a light
and I saw a workbench. A stack of x-ray films waited under a
tea towel like bread left to rise. Viktor took a long-bladed pair
of scissors from a hook above the bench. I examined the rest of
his apparatus: a spindle, a lathe, a small net of wires like a miniature jungle gym, one of which Viktor gripped delicately and
pulled tense to attach to a turntable.

"Pretty bare-bones operation," noted Gosha.

Viktor frowned at the pun. "What should we make?" he
asked. "Buddy Holly? The Beatles?"

I shrugged. "Do you have that song about the moon?"

"Excellent choice," said Viktor with a smile. "Georgi, what
should we make it on?"

Gosha rifled through the stack of films. He selected one and
handed it over. Viktor held the transparent sheath up to the light
and I watched as he traced a shadowed human skull with his
scissors until the film was a perfectly round disc. He placed it on
the workbench and used a razor to file its edges. Then he held it
up once more and inspected his work.

"A steady hand," murmured Gosha approvingly. He pulled
a pack of cigarettes from his pocket and lit one. He dragged on
it twice and handed it to Viktor, who touched the glowing red

ember to the center of the skull, producing a small hole, which he then fit over the spindle. He opened a small box and removed a steel stylus, which he fastened to a wire resting in a carriage suspended over the film. Finally, he used a key from his belt to open a trunk under the workbench in which about two dozen records were hidden. He found the one he was looking for and placed it on the record player. He flipped the switches on both turntables and positioned the needles.

"The sound waves travel over the wires as easily as they travel through air," he explained. "And the needle responds. Just like your eardrum. It moves in sympathetic vibrations, making new grooves for your ears alone."

"Well, or for that poor sucker's ears," noted Gosha.

I watched the ghostly cranium circling under the hiss of sympathetic vibrations. *Psycho-acoustics.*

"It's just a piece of plastic," said Viktor. He reached for Gosha's cigarette. "It's a medium. There's no reason why it can't hold two different sets of information. Personal information and public information. Physical information and musical information. Visual information and aural information."

Information and disinformation, I thought, watching the x-ray rotate under a fresh set of messages.

Viktor exhaled smoke, blowing the curling worms of the steel blade's residue from the new record. Gosha ran a finger down the stack of waiting films, making the sound of a plastic arpeggio. I stood between them and listened to Elvis croon a blue moon onto a spinning stranger's skull.

FOURTEEN
CHIC

We were a large entourage on the exclusive flight to Berlin. But of the hundred-plus passengers filing up the rolling stairs from the tarmac, only thirty of us were dancers. The seats at the front of the plane were reserved for management: theater directors and deputy directors, ministers and functionaries, Party apparatchiks and cultural liaisons. They, not us, were the VIPs. Their reports, full of superlatives about the "ecstatic reception" of our "unparalleled artistry," were the real objective of the tour.

Flying in the rear of the plane was another group without whom there could be no tour. They didn't introduce themselves, but we all knew who they were. Their identical shoes and ill-fitting suits, their zip-up travel satchels and bland faces—their disguises of normalcy gave them away: they were KGB-*shniki*. They were our minders. Or, rather, our *re-minders*—reminders that no one, not even the elite artists of the Bolshoi Ballet, could be completely trusted.

We dancers were dumped between the two groups in the middle of the plane, mixed among the stage handlers and ballet masters and costumers. The guys flirted with the stewardess. The girls sprawled across seats. Katya had brought a beautiful, brand-new camera with her—a Zenit—and was busy arranging a group onboard photograph. Sasha and the rest of the corps de ballet were blocking the aisle, negotiating who would sit by the windows. Tatiana Bibikova, a star principal, was bossing the scene haulers around, making them rearrange all the bags in the bins above.

Only Galina Ulanova settled into her seat quietly with a sleeping mask and earplugs. She had made five tours already. She had been to New York and London. East Berlin, she seemed to be saying with a yawn, was not much farther than the last stop on the Metro line. I smiled at her nonchalance. It was the wall that had brought our comrades closer. It was my work that allowed us to cross borders effortlessly. And I had no intention of sleeping through it.

"Can you believe it?" breathed Sasha when the plane finally taxied for takeoff. "Flying! Whole plane to ourselves. And you, Svetlana, you just made it by the skin of your teeth. Want me to pinch you?"

IT WASN'T UNTIL WE landed in Berlin that I spotted her. We were standing around in a holding area while uniforms shuffled papers. I had nearly forgotten why I was here, in a place so reminiscent of the over-uniformed terminal on the other end of our short flight, until I looked up and saw Natalia Davydovna Gerasova.

She stood alone, halfway between the KGB-*shniki* and the Party bigwigs, which begged the question: Which delegation did the "interministerial" boss of Lubyanka belong to? I squinted to make out the pin on her lapel—was it the emblem of the Bolshoi Theatre? Or the Communist Party? Would Comrade Gerasova wear the sword and shield of the KGB outside of the protected compound of Lubyanka? I didn't think so. But something told me she had flown in the back of the plane with the other minders, where she could keep her eyes on her agent.

She looked my way, but I made no sign of recognition, just

joined the conversation of Sasha and the other girls. When, a half hour later, we boarded the bus into the city, Comrade Gerasova was not on it. Neither, I noticed, was our prima ballerina.

"Where's Ulanova?" I asked as we pulled onto the highway. Tatiana Bibikova shrugged. "Probably in a limo on the way to the only decent restaurant in town. Wish that's where we were headed."

It was well after noon when we reached the hotel, a newly built but shoddy building hidden behind a high fence on a treeless avenue. A clerk met us at the entrance, looking slightly terrified. He had "lamentable news": due to an "administrative mishap," the rooms for "the distinguished guests from Moscow" were "unprepared."

I knew from a lifetime of watching deputies reporting to someone higher that this was bad news for everyone involved. We stood in a group in the lobby and watched the stakes escalate. What was initially poor planning quickly became a diplomatic snub and then a debacle. Soon we'd have an international incident. The Bolshoi chain of command flexed its muscles; the hapless German clerk called for backup.

While the managers made threats and excuses, we retired to the restaurant. It was empty—not just of diners, but also of food. Lunch was as unprepared as our rooms. There was a collective groan. Then the sound of a suitcase being popped open. Another followed, and another, and another, and soon the tables were covered in the provisions that the Bolshoi Ballet had smuggled to East Berlin in case the rumors about food shortages were true. Salamis wrapped in newsprint, pies tied up in string, glass jars of caviar nestled protectively in thick tights. Ilya, a middle-aged character dancer and forever the jester, dispatched a junior dancer for glasses and leapt on top of a table with a bottle of vodka in hand.

"To the end of the Berlin blockade!" he announced to cheers.

We had finished off the bottle and most of the salami when a little man in a terrible toupee came hurrying in. "*Bitte,*" he said, his hand raised for attention. "Please . . . to finish the appetizing and move on to courses one and two." He smiled a smile that looked like it might have been used before to lure innocents into a dark alley. No one moved.

"You can keep your courses one and two, my pigeon," answered Bibikova, wiping her greasy fingers on her trousers. "We are provisioned by the Motherland."

But the German was not to be dissuaded. "*Nein*, comrades. I am restaurant manager. We have lunch feast prepared. Please to dine at our table. This to . . . mitigate . . ." His halting Russian halted altogether.

"Hunger?" suggested Ilya.

"*Nepriyatnosti,*" supplied Bibikova, taking pity on the man.

"*Da.* Yes. Unpleasantness," he said happy to be understood. "We do not want unpleasantness."

Flapping his hands in encouragement, he ushered us through the kitchen, out a back door, and into a neighboring building. We emerged into what appeared to be a cafeteria. Judging by the frail faces regarding us from the wheelchairs on its perimeter, I assumed it was a hospital canteen. On closer inspection, I decided that the patients weren't sick. Just old. Old enough, apparently, to have no fear of an officious busybody in a toupee telling them to clear out. They argued silently, making no move until they heard the magic words, "Bolshoi Ballet." At that, the grumpy old men and sour old women were transformed. A stooped geezer tottered forward and ushered Tatiana Bibikova directly to the hot buffet in the corner.

It was a sad feast. The best that could be said about the dishes was that none of them required much chewing. We shuffled stupidly, mumbling about our lack of appetite, until the KGB crew entered the room. They greeted the buffet with dutiful delight and the rest of us ungrateful bastards with threatening scowls. We understood: fraternal harmony with our East Berlin comrades was paramount. We were expected to exercise culinary diplomacy. Tatiana filled her plate with pureed parsnips and Rode Grütt, and we all followed her lead.

Another hour passed before another clerk—one of ours—entered to tell us our rooms were ready.

"I will read the room assignments," he wheezed. "Please do not make pests of yourselves, comrades. The arrangements were laborious, and personal requests will not be considered."

"What a surprise," murmured Bibikova, stubbing out a cigarette in her puddle of groats.

The clerk began with the top billed and worked his way down through the corps, squeezed three to a room: "Kuryakina, Sverdlova, and Prelestnaya, room 202. Tikhonova, Kuznetsova, and Larina, room 205."

Sasha was rooming with two girls named Irina.

"See you at dinner," she said as she left. "If there is dinner, I mean."

We were a dwindling group.

"Gambrovsky, Kurchagin, Semyonov, and Rodin, 401. The lifts in front reach the third floor. If you are on the fourth floor, I recommend the service entrance, but you must ask management for assistance."

I watched them leave. I watched them all leave. Even the minders in their worn-out suits.

When I was the only one left I said, "I'm sorry, I didn't hear my name called. I'm Kravshina, Svetlana Evgenievna."

The man studied his sheet. "Kravshina, Kravshina . . ." Then he raised bleary eyes and said shortly, "Room 314, third floor."

"Thank you."

I was nearly at the door when I thought to ask, "And who do I live with for the week?"

He answered without consulting the paper. "With Comrade Natalia Davydovna Gerasova."

His tone suggested that I should have already known.

I WAS ASLEEP WHEN my roommate finally showed up. She snapped on the overhead light, which buzzed with the telltale sign of a microphone bug. I wondered who was listening—the East German "Stasi" secret police? The KGB? Both? I thought of the bickering in the lobby and wondered how allies cooperate when it comes to spying on hotel rooms that, "due to administrative mishaps," take extra time to prepare.

Gerasova handed me a blue frock with white polka dots across the skirt. "Get dressed," she mouthed.

I rolled from the bed and pulled off my nightgown. The dress was tight in the bodice and got stuck going over my head. Natalia Davydovna helped pull it down over my hips and zipped up the back. She lifted the skirt and gave a quick jerk. The label was gone. Now there was no evidence that I was wearing a dress from the other side of the wall.

She rummaged in my suitcase and pulled out my cosmetics bag and brush. I began braiding my hair but she shook her head, so I brushed it loose and clipped it with a barrette low on my neck. I put on pale pink lipstick and added a sliver of silver to my eyes. Gerasova nodded in approval.

"Let's go."

We took the stairs in silence. On the landing above the lobby, we stopped. Voices from below. Russian.

"The understudies," whispered Gerasova dismissively.

I pictured them, the faceless minders lounging in a commandeered hotel office watching Soviet television and snacking on caviar confiscated from that clown, Ilya. KGB yes, but of the pedestrian order. To my fellow dancers, they were a vaguely menacing nuisance; to Gerasova and me, they were just "understudies," destined to live their life in obscurity.

"We can't afford your being seen," said Gerasova. "Go back up one level and toward the back. I will send the service elevator for you."

I did as I was told. Gerasova, I understood, was working undercover like me. I wondered what would happen if someone in the Bolshoi, or even one of the minders, found me skulking around the elevator. All I could imagine was the embarrassment

I would feel if my peers knew that, in another world, the new girl was referred to as "Prima."

A battered sedan was waiting for us behind the hotel. Gerasova opened the door and steered me into the backseat. Then she climbed in next to me and instructed the driver, in German, to head for the *kontrollpunkt*.

We passed out of the alley onto the empty avenue. It was quiet. And dark. Quieter and darker than Moscow. I couldn't shake the feeling that I was already in enemy territory, though we hadn't yet reached the wall. I peered out the dirty window at deserted streets.

"Where is everyone?" I asked.

"It's nearly midnight," said Gerasova. "This part of town is not known for its nightlife."

She spoke again to the driver, who turned into a large open space. It was a city square, but there was nothing left, only rubble and large rolls of wire fencing. I wasn't sure if I was looking at ruins of the bombing that ended the war fifteen years ago or at a construction site that I had helped launch.

The driver pulled into the shadows at the far end of the square and cut the engine. Gerasova opened the door and ushered me out. She ducked her head back into the car and spoke to the driver. Then she took my arm and led me to another abandoned street. I saw light at its end—not the hazy glow of distant civilization, but the blinding glare of a klieg light. The wall, with its armed checkpoints and shoot-to-kill guards, lay ahead.

"That's checkpoint Bravo," said Gerasova in a low voice. "We're not going there." Instead, she pulled a small flashlight from her bag and shone it along a grimy row of abandoned buildings, revealing one unpromising door after another.

"This is it," she said when the beam fell on an entryway with a small metal porthole above a brass knocker. She snapped off the light and knocked—three short raps.

The door opened and a man with a pocked face let us in.

I followed Gerasova into the dark hallway and through

another doorway into a spartan room, where another man—
this one older than the first—was waiting. He greeted Gerasova.
He eyed me. In the dim light of a single shaded lamp, I could
see that the gray in his temples was premature. He had an intelligent face, handsome despite a slight harelip. I had never met
this man, never lain eyes on him, but I understood instantly that
I knew him. I had seen him—mentally, if not actually. Not in
Berlin, but in Moscow. Perched, perhaps, at the side of a bed.
*Yes. I had seen him in Lubyanka 1717. He was part of my psy-
chosphere.*

But I, apparently, was not part of his. He rubbed his unshaven
chin. "This is her?"

"Yes," answered Gerasova. "This is Prima, your dance partner for the night."

The man put out his hand. *"Zdravstvuyte,"* he said in
accented Russian.

"Hello," I answered.

"You have two hours," said Gerasova to the man. "Return
her to the car." Then she turned to me and placed her hands
on my shoulders. "This is Eugene. He is a trusted comrade, a
good Communist, a smart operative, and a fighter for our global
cause. You are going to West Berlin with him." She saw the
questions on my face and said, "It will be easy. Easier than anything you've done at 1717."

"Do I use remote viewing? Do I gather information? Do I
transfer . . ."

"No. You have all the information you need," she answered.
"This is just a test. All you have to do is be a good date for
Eugene. You are just going dancing."

I nodded, but I must have looked concerned, because Natalia
Davydovna brushed a strand of hair from my face and let her
fingers linger on my cheek.

"Don't open your mouth except to laugh. Have a good time.
Be a fun-loving girl . . . a what do you call it?" She turned the
question to Eugene.

"A 'chic.'"

"Yes. Tonight, Prima, you are a 'chic.'"

IT WAS SO CLOSE. Down a flight of stairs, through a short tunnel, up another flight of stairs, and we were in the West.

"Checkpoint Bravo and a half," said Eugene as he closed the door behind us. We had stepped out of an abandoned building almost identical to the one we had just left. The street was as dark as the one in East Berlin where a car waited for my return. But I felt the searching lights of the wall behind us.

I turned and saw it: the seven-foot-tall shadow, topped with a roll of barbed wire. It was less than fifty yards up the street and it stretched as far as the eye could see—a cinder-block scar stitched with squat guard towers. I felt stunned; the wall I had helped build was hideous.

"We can't linger here. No-man's-land," Eugene said.

He took my hand and pulled me away, toward the lights of West Berlin, which were bright but not welcoming. I went, imagining the thousands of anticommunists who had followed this very route toward a false promise. This path had been a floodgate for traitors—"defectors" as the Western propagandists called them. We had blocked it, and yet here I was, following their tracks. I looked back over my shoulder. The sight of the wall gave me no sense of safety. I felt my ears close as if adjusting to pressure, and for a moment all I could hear was a muffled but steady tick of a metronome. I knew that if I were to sit down and close my eyes, I would tap into the universal mind right here in no-man's-land.

But that was not my mission; those were not my instructions.

Eugene spoke: "Nice dress," he said. "You'll blend in well. Just remember: you don't talk. These American soldiers speak lousy German, so there's not much chance you'll get into trouble. But giggling is the safer bet. Okay?"

I nodded.

"*Schön,*" he said, switching to German.

We came to a street full of people. Restaurants and taverns lined both sides. Cars double-parked, couples spilled out of the backseats, music blared from the radios. We threaded our way through the pockets of people and stopped in front of a frosted glass door. A torn awning above the door read UPPER CLUB.

"Here's the spot," Eugene announced.

It was crowded inside, full of soldiers in uniform, girls in pin curls, shady types, flamboyant types, and plenty of faceless wall-flowers. There was a stage with an orchestra and a dance floor ringed with tables, many with tipped-over chairs. There was a heady sense of abandon, stronger even than in the *stilyagi's* warehouse. Eugene ferried me toward the bar, greeting people as we went. Slaps on the back, kisses on the cheek. I smiled. I laughed. I nodded. *How ya doin'?*, I heard over and over. I thought I was doing fine. And then the music began—a long, low whistle of horns followed by the jaunty piano and smooth saxophone of a Chattanooga choo choo.

"Oy!" I yelled. I clapped my hand over my mouth, but Eugene just winked.

"Jitterbug!" he yelled, pulling me to the floor.

He was good. Almost as good as Viktor. If I had time to think, I might have thought, *too bad Vitya's not here.* Or I might have thought, *good thing Vitya taught me the jitterbug.* But I didn't have time to think. When the dance was over there was a crowd of men waiting for us, and all of them wanted to dance with Eugene's chic.

I hesitated, but he nudged me forward. So I danced the next number with a Yank soldier with two left feet. When it was over, Eugene was back at my side with two glasses of schnapps. He led me to a table in the corner where I caught my breath. "Drink up," he said in a low voice. "You need to dance the next one with the fellow in the corner over there."

I followed his eyes. There was more than one fellow in the corner.

"The serious one. His hair is in his eyes. Looks to be wearing his father's suspenders. He's the one you have to dance with next."

I sized him up. He was older than me, but not as old as he wanted to be taken for. He had a wide, flat face—perceptive but hinting at . . . what? Awkwardness? Defiance? Or maybe madness. He flipped his stringy hair back with a jerk and his face suddenly contorted in a spasm.

"Who is he?"

"Just a guy."

Onstage, a voluptuous woman in long black gloves stepped up to the microphone and let out a moan that was nearly obscene. I took a sip from the glass Eugene had handed me and watched him as he watched my target.

Eugene. I thought. *In Russian—Evgeny.* My father's name. Was it a coincidence? An alias? I felt his thoughts slide against mine and wondered if Gerasova really intended for me to turn off everything I had been trained to do.

"Music's starting," he said.

I didn't move. I ran my finger around the rim of the glass and thought:

There is information . . . and disinformation.

Intelligence . . . and counterintelligence.

And there are traitors and there are defectors and there are spies.

There is serving your Motherland; and there is protecting your father.

"Hey chic," Eugene said in English, "didja hear me?"

I heard him. I heard the music and I heard Maksim and I heard Inga and Oleg and Comrade Gerasova. I heard them all in my head, assuring me that I was well trained, that I was prepared, and that my first mission in the field was both important and easy. They were right. I *was* prepared. But not by them. I had been trained for this strange improvisational assignment to *be a chic* by one Viktor Dukovsky. And if I ever caught a stupid lummox cop or an ass-wipe with Komsomol credits warning

Today you're listening to jazz, but tomorrow you'll betray the Motherland, I would break his face with one well-swung kick of a Lindy hop.

I let out a peal of laughter, pitched to the key of flirt. I stood up from the table, turned, and locked eyes with the boy in the corner. In a second he was next to me and his arm was around my waist. He grabbed my hand and pulled me tight. We were on the edge of the dance floor but he was pulling me away from it, not toward it. I felt a flash of panic and covered it with another burst of laughter. The music shifted. The train had passed, and like a couple left alone on the platform, we were dancing a slow dance, a close dance. The strange boy smelled of cheap cologne and sweat, and the buckles of his suspenders bit into my breast.

I focused on the song sung by the woman in long gloves. The words meant nothing to me, but the music—reedy with the brush against the drums—was triggering something like a memory. The woman's low warble became a deep rumble—like storms converging on a river, like tanks endless and unstoppable, like Cook's cart across tiled floor.

Like the roar of a wrecking ball in the small town square where my father's statue once stood.

I closed my eyes and saw:

Berlin in ruins.

My father in smithereens.

The music stopped.

I was in a supper club in enemy-occupied West Berlin in 1961, dancing with a boy whose mind was a blank to me.

He grabbed the back of my head and pulled me toward him as if to kiss me, but instead he whispered something harsh in my ear. I jerked away, pulling on his suspenders. He gasped. It sounded like excitement. He spoke again, but there was applause all around us and I mimed deafness. Again and again, he repeated himself, his voice urgent, but I could only shrug and smile.

Finally Eugene stepped between us, a fresh glass of beer in

his hand. He handed it to my partner and slung an arm con-spiratorially over his shoulders. He spoke to the strange boy in suspenders gently and steadily, like a man trying to calm a wild horse. But his eyes, like the boy's, were on me.

I stood there as they spoke. In German. About me. It was not small talk. They were ogling me, yes. But not as a chic. They were negotiating something; I was a bargaining chip. When it was over, there was no handshake. They simply turned their backs on each other. The boy in suspenders drifted into the crowd without a word of goodbye.

Eugene and I danced one more dance. "Laugh, chic. Smile, Prima."

I did as he instructed. And then we left.

BACK ON THE OTHER side of the wall, Eugene told Gera-sova that the next meeting would take place in three days.

"Fine," she said. "Tuesday at ten P.M. We can't make it any earlier. Prima has another obligation to the Motherland. She has to stand stage right and look pretty. Isn't that right, Prima?"

I searched her face for sarcasm, but Gerasova just smiled.

"Don't worry," she said. "I won't tell Maksim."

FIFTEEN
MASQUERADE

The next morning I joined Sasha and the two Irinas for breakfast in the hotel restaurant. Natalia Davydovna sat at the table with the KGB "understudies."

These, of course, were our natural places. If you drew a Venn diagram of the Bolshoi in Berlin, room 314 was an unexpected gray zone: the place where the new girl and the middle-aged lady with ill-defined affiliations and special clearance somehow overlapped. But no one at my table asked about my living arrangements. And the minders and managers, too, seemed to pretend not to notice. Our room was like the no-man's-land that ran parallel to the wall, I told Gerasova at the end of the second day—a place of coexistence along an unnatural divide that cautious observers pretend not to see.

"You give cautious observers too much credit," she replied. "Make yourself visible as a nobody and no one will suspect that you are somebody."

I did as she recommended. I walked to the People's Theatre with the rest of the corps and stood in the back row for ovations. I grumbled about the food, just like the rest of the troupe. I avoided, along with half the company, the suggested field trips to the Monument of Soviet Liberation and Museum of Fascist Aggression by hiding out in the old folks' home, playing checkers. Ilya had taken a liking to me but Bibikova still pretended I didn't exist. I worked hard at being nobody.

But on the fourth morning in Berlin, Galina Ulanova waltzed into our geriatric hideout and proved Gerasova wrong.

"You remind me of someone," she said, taking a seat across a checkers-strewn table from me.

"I stood behind you in class last week," I answered. "The day before we left Moscow. It was my first class with the company."

"Yes, I remember. But you remind me of someone I knew before last Friday."

The rest of the dancers in the room were watching us. I thought small talk might be the best deflection.

"Are you enjoying Berlin?"

"Of course," she said. "It's a beautiful city."

It lacked . . . sincerity, this answer. I was struck again by the star's ordinary features and plain dress. She was a phenomenon onstage, startling in the emotion and plaintiveness of her dancing, but in the cafeteria of an East Berlin nursing home she had no charisma at all.

"Where do you like best to perform?" I asked as she continued to look at me blankly. "I mean aside from home at the Bolshoi?"

"I quite like America," she said.

I nodded, hiding my surprise. Ulanova's patriotism was as legendary as her dancing. She didn't express it subtly, either. When she declared her love of the Party or her belief in total Communism and a perfect society, she did it without the nuance she displayed as Juliet. She just stated it as fact. Ulanova's political enthusiasm had been rewarded, of course. She had more medals than any other prima ballerina. Most of them had been given to her by Comrade Stalin himself. And yet here she was, "quite liking" the land of the enemy.

"They are lied to, you see," she explained. "The Americans

are told all sorts of terrible things about how we live and what we lack. They don't understand what motivates us to work harder and do better." Ulanova folded her hands in front of her. "It is every Soviet artist's duty to translate our people's love of peace, art, and beauty to the Americans, who have been robbed."

"Robbed?" I repeated.

"Robbed, yes. Of high culture. Of free will. And of faith in their leaders. The American people have none of those things." Her face was a study in earnestness. "But they do have very nice hot dogs, for which I would be very grateful right now." Ulanova rose from her seat and checked her watch. "I have a luncheon to attend. The Congress of Cultural Exchange and Coexistence awaits."

I rose as well. "It was nice talking to you."

She didn't leave. She just stood there, looking at me.

"Ah," she said, snapping her fingers. "Kravshin. I remember. He was one of Stalin's generals."

The room was silent, rendered speechless by the casual, verbal recognition of a ghost.

He was . . .

"Kravshin sometimes accompanied Stalin to the theater," she continued. "And sometimes he would come backstage. He was very courteous. I remember once Stalin didn't like the production and he told us so. Just marched into the dressing rooms and began berating us. It was Kravshin who reminded him, very diplomatically, that the production was the responsibility of the artistic director, not the soloists. He was very brave to contradict him like that. We were, frankly, amazed. And grateful."

I couldn't answer.

"He had your elegance and your dark eyes. I remember him, though history has forgotten him."

I watched, stunned, as the Artist of the People walked down the corridor to the limousine waiting outside. With her went the first fond remembrance of my father that I had ever heard. Indeed, the first remembrance at all.

It was hers, not mine.

TUESDAY NIGHT WAS THE final performance of our engagement, and the theater was full. I sat alone in the dressing room at the end of Act One, in a black mood. My ten-second waltz during the masquerade ball was over. There was nothing left but to march along with the rest of the Capulets and Montagues during the funeral procession and then, as usual, stand in the back for the bows.

It wasn't that I was impatient. I wasn't ungrateful or jealous. I certainly wasn't bored. I had no complaints against the Bolshoi, which had quickly become my new family. I planned to give my heart and soul to the corps de ballet. I respected the ranks. I would pay my dues. I would work hard to claim my place as Juliet.

Ballet wasn't the problem. Ballet had never been the problem. Ballet was meant to be the solution.

But what if it wasn't?

I fingered the mask that lay on the dressing table before me. Soft crushed velvet with black feather brows and a figure eight for eyes. Onstage, it turned me into a charming masquerader. Backstage, it seemed to mock me.

It seemed to say: *You are only masquerading as a dancer. You are only given this privilege in order to hide your real identity.*

It seemed to sneer at me: *Prima.*

I picked it up and pulled it over my face.

Onstage I was a reveler. Backstage I was a spy.

Right on cue, the door to the dressing room opened and in walked Natalia Davydovna Gerasova.

"We need to leave."

"But the final act . . ."

"We can't wait. You will have to feign illness. Quickly. I'll be waiting at the stage door."

She had just left when the door opened again. It was one of the Irinas. She saw me sitting in front of the mirror and hesitated. I took off the mask.

"Oh, hello." She laughed. "For a second I didn't recognize you."

I looked at my naked face in the mirror. *Did I recognize myself?*

I looked at Irina, who had settled on the floor with a book to wait out the last act.

I didn't want to be Irina.

I didn't want to be always waiting for the last act.

I wanted to be Prima. I wanted the mask.

I grabbed my stomach and moaned.

"Hey. You okay, Svetlana?"

"I'm going to be sick," I breathed. I grabbed my bag and bolted from the dressing room.

GERASOVA WAS SILENT UNTIL we reached the house with the blackened door. We were let in by the same guy with the rough complexion, but once inside, Eugene was nowhere to be seen.

"He went missing four hours ago," said Gerasova. She pulled a mirror from her bag and ran it under the desk, the chairs, and the table—a quick search for any listening devices—before she continued.

"There are two possible explanations. One—his cover was blown."

"What exactly was his cover?" I asked.

"Eugene has been crossing the border for years," she answered. "Everyone knows he's a double agent. They just don't know *whose* double agent. His connections on both sides have been his safety net. But a safety net is no help if you're a trapeze artist with a concrete wall in your trajectory. Then you're not worried about a fall. You're worried about a collision. Perhaps he had one."

I considered the analogy: Eugene as a trapeze artist. Eugene as a wrecking ball.

"And the second explanation?"

"The second explanation is that Eugene betrayed us." Something flickered over her face. "It's not so different from the first explanation, except that we're the ones who didn't know."

I didn't like what I was hearing. *A traitor. An enemy within.* Too close to home. I had hoped never to meet another Enemy of the People. Let alone dance with one. I desperately wanted for Eugene *not* to be a traitor. Something weaker perhaps. A defector, maybe. Though I knew that to the KGB, they were one and the same.

I wanted to ask: *Which general did he betray? A good general? Or a bad general?* This, too, I was supposed to know. Wasn't I the rememberer? Wasn't I the one who should have intercepted his memories?

"Does he have it?" I asked. "Enhanced Recognition? Is Eugene trained like me?"

Gerasova gave me a disapproving look. "Eugene is far better trained than you. He has been an agent for over fifteen years. He was protecting the *rodina* when you were just a baby. That said, his activities have never intersected with our work in the Psychological Intelligence Unit. Until now, that is.

"In any case," she continued, "he must be returned. We cannot leave him on the other side."

She took off her coat and flung it over a naked chair. She addressed the silent man in German and he left the room.

"Eugene was to meet with a man named Turner. Eugene and *you* were to meet him, that is. Now you will keep the meeting, Prima."

"Turner," I said. "Is he the one . . . ?"

"Yes, your target from the last time. He is a soft target. He has access to telex cables we want. Eugene was one step away from convincing him that by letting us have them, he could save lives. Starting with yours. He told him that you were in desperate straits and that only he could help you. Like I said, this Turner is a soft target with a soft heart. An easy ear to a desperate plea."

I thought back to the night of the supper club and the alarming urgency of the boy in suspenders. Was it that simple? A classic bait and switch, a honey trap? I remembered the way they had watched me, Eugene and Turner. It had not seemed like a conversation about a helpless girl. And Turner, with his unsavory eyes and greasy hair, had not seemed soft. On the contrary, I had felt nothing but sharpness, hardness from his weakest spots. And the bite of his suspenders on my dress—a chic's dress, the costume of a damsel in distress.

"What if you are right about the second option? What if Eugene . . ." The word—"defected"—stuck in my throat. "What if Eugene told Turner the truth? The truth about me?"

"Then it's all the more crucial that we retrieve him. Before he spills more information. That is why you have to be the most convincing defector you can possibly be. You must persuade Turner to take you to Eugene. You must convince him that you are, in fact, seeking asylum together with Eugene and that everything else was a cover story."

I put my hands in my pockets. I felt the velvet mask from Act One. I balled it in my fist.

"And how will I get back?"

The silent man returned to the room and handed me a wristwatch. I studied it. It was Soviet made, a bit large for a woman, but otherwise unremarkable.

"It has a radio tracker," said Gerasova. "We will have no trouble finding you. But not until you have reached Eugene. Do you understand your objective?"

I strapped the watch onto my wrist. It gave me no confidence. It told me it was 9:12. Nothing more.

"What if Turner doesn't know where Eugene is? What if it's option one, and Eugene has been caught and this Turner guy had nothing to do with it?"

"Then at least we have our best asset in place to find our man down."

I raised my eyebrows in a question.

"Our psychosoldier, Agent Prima," finished Gerasova.

IT WAS DARK IN the tunnel. I wasn't eager to see the light, but still, it came. More quickly than I had remembered, I was climbing the stairs from the passage beneath the wall into the abandoned building on the other side. I let myself out onto the street—a casual Berliner out for a walk in no-man's-land.

There was a cold wind, and I was glad I had not had time to change my costume tights for nylons. I wrapped my coat more snugly around my gown, embroidered in the crest of the Capulets, and gripped the mask in its pocket. When I reached the supper club I hesitated. It was empty. *It's Tuesday*, I told myself, *not a night for jazz.* And only 9:30. Romeo and Juliet were dead and mourned in East Berlin, but here in the West, the party had not even started.

The front door was open and I went inside. There were a few lights on. The chairs were stacked on tables. The stage was empty.

"Hello?" I called in English.

There was a shuffling near the stage.

"Hello? Are you here?"

The shuffling resolved itself into a human figure. "Yes. I'm here."

His suspenders were hidden under a jacket. An athletic warm-up jacket of some German football club. I had no idea which side of the wall it played on.

"I'm looking for Eugene." I said in my best English.

"He's not arrived yet."

He stepped farther from the shadows, and I still didn't know. Was he there to trap me? Or to release me? Did he stoop like that deliberately? Or was there some trauma in his past that had truly beaten him down? His face was ugly, angry even, frozen in a half snarl, but also frightened. I tried, but I was blind to his past. I could not penetrate his memories.

"How did you get here?" he asked.

"Foot," I said "By foot. On foot. Footed . . ."

"Speak Russian," he said.

He was a Russian speaker. I filtered all of Gerasova's scenarios through my racing brain and rejected them all. Gerasova was wrong. The wary young man in suspenders was no soft target. He was a Russian speaker. An agent. Like Eugene. But for which side?

I felt panic. I had not been trained for this. My team at Lubyanka 1717 might have programmed my brain, but they had not taught me mind games.

You must be convincing, Gerasova had said.

You have all the information you need, she had said.

But Gerasova was surely wrong.

I had to pick a role to play on the empty stage of this supper club. In the time it took for Turner to cross the room, I chose. I rejected the desperate defector and chose a trickier character: I would be a rebel; a wrecker; an agent of the opposition. If Turner was in the Western camp, I would be, too. I stepped forward to meet him and spoke in the language of spies: short sentences, oblique references, low voice.

"You have brought high-worth assets. Cables. You think they are worth what you are getting in exchange. You think you are getting an operative skilled in remote viewing. That is misinformation. That is disinformation. I am not worth anything to you, if that is what you are here to trade. I am not here to stay. I am here to gather assets to take back to Moscow, where I am working with people to further our cause."

Now it was his turn to recalibrate. I watched him work it out, following the switchbacks that had led us both here. I saw him consider the very real possibility that I was no damsel in distress, but an agent of Soviet resistance making contact with the West.

"Which assets are you here to gather?"

"First of all, I want the KGB operative who presented me as a potential defector—the double agent, Eugene, who fed you lies. Secondly, a pact of continued assistance in toppling the Soviet regime." I paused and then threw in one last lie. One I thought would make my new role more convincing: "And I need . . . effective propaganda messages to spread among my people."

I saw his hard face soften, almost imperceptibly. Like a hairline crack in a block of ice—the beginning of a thaw. Or maybe it was just another weird tic.

"Take me to Eugene," I said.

THIS CROSSING WAS SHORTER: he led me upstairs into a large room above the club. It was full of mechanical equipment, carpenter's tools, Formica-covered card tables and marquees, advertising the charms of Marlene Dietrich, Doris Day, and Brigitte Bardot.

He closed the door behind us and said something in German I didn't understand. In response, a door in another corner of the room opened. Two large men led in a third—Eugene. They sat him in an empty chair. He looked at me with a mixture of surprise and despair, and the recognition was complete: Eugene was a Soviet operative in Germany, far from his *rodina* and his wife and daughter. I understood. I had tapped easily into his memories because they were nearly identical to those of my father's fifteen years earlier. Evgeny Kravshin, like Eugene, was once a prisoner in a conspirator's den. He, too, had said: *Go to hell. I will never betray my Motherland.*

I stood at the nexus between the universal mind and my own and decided to trust him. I would deliver him home. I would save him.

I walked up to him and spat in his face.

"What did they promise you, *svoloch*," I demanded. "What did they offer you, pig, to make you sell out?" I slapped him across the face. "Coward."

Eugene was completely still, his face to the floor. His guards turned to Turner for translation, and I felt the sweat on my shoulder blades as he spoke. *Were they buying it? Was he telling them that I was no meek asylum seeker, but a freedom fighter working inside the Soviet Union to overthrow the Communists? Did they believe this role I was playing? Or could they see behind the mask?*

I waited for him to finish and then addressed all three Germans:

"We owe you an enormous debt of gratitude for identifying this man for what he is. A turncoat."

Turner translated.

I turned back to Eugene and hissed, "What did they promise you? A luxurious apartment in the center of Moscow? A *dacha* on the Black Sea? An external passport? A seat on the Central Committee? What did they give you to betray our cause?"

Eugene lifted his head slowly. His eyes were pleading. I caught my breath, uncertain. Did he know that I knew that he would never betray the *rodina*? Or did he think I was digging his grave? *Was I? Was I digging his grave?*

"My wife," he said hoarsely. "They promised to release my wife. She has been arrested."

I faltered. *Your wife, of course. And your daughter? What of your daughter? An abandoned ward of the state, waiting for her bedtime fairy tale?* I didn't know. I didn't know if Eugene was telling the truth . . . or if, despite Gerasova's denials, he had intercepted my own. *Transference of information along asymmetric and personal channels of recalled observation moved from the target's memory . . .*

I didn't have time to puzzle it out.

"Your wife," I said. I slumped into an empty chair and addressed Turner. "You see how they work? You see their brutality? They are holding his family hostage."

"That was not his story," said Turner flatly. "Not before you came."

"You're right," I said, adjusting course once more. "I should not let my hatred for the regime affect my objectivity. My people will want him back. We need to interrogate him to see if others in the opposition have been compromised. I leave that decision to you. You caught him and we are grateful. But if I leave without anything, some . . . asset to represent our mutual collaboration . . ."

The other men were talking now. They were having trouble following our conversation. They were unconvinced. I felt the sweat trickle down my spine. If they didn't believe me, it wouldn't just be Eugene who would be trapped behind the wall; it would be me.

"My friends want proof," said Turner. "Proof that you are on our side. How do we know you are in the underground opposition?"

I looked again around the room. In one corner was a stack of film reels resting beside a projector that dated back before the war. Above a long table against the wall was a shelf full of ledgers and radios in various stages of assembly. On the table itself were a number of record players, from old-fashioned Victrolas to high-fidelity stereos. Under the table were crates of records, bins of electrical cables and cords, and several telescoped microphone stands. We were in a room that was a screening booth and an audio archive. A new possibility began formulating itself in my risky gamble.

Oh, Vitya. I could kiss you, I thought.

I crossed to the crate of records against the wall and selected one. Then I whipped the stiff plastic tablecloth from one of the tables. I located scissors, a dull needle, and enough wire to reach from one turntable to another. They watched wordlessly as the girl they had been told was a defector, a spy, a psychic—and God knows what else—showed herself to be a resourceful bootlegger.

Turner took a key from his belt and opened a heavy locker. Inside was another stack of records made of thick black vinyl. He handed me one. "It's . . . how do you say? Clean."

"Blank."

He nodded. Then he pulled a thick manuscript from the locker and handed it to me as well. I glanced at it—a typewritten copy of *Doctor Zhivago* in the original Russian.

"How much time do you have?" he asked, handing it to me. "It's a long novel."

I leafed through pages, skimming long passages describing the beauty of the Russian countryside, the love of a doctor, the upheaval of war.

For a moment I forgot the men in the room, as I wondered why these words were so threatening to our leaders. What was in this *Doctor Zhivago* that could possibly overthrow the regime? Where was the threat in this poet's prose?

"We will record only the most anti-Soviet passages, then," I said. "Please select them while I set up a microphone."

TWO HOURS LATER, EUGENE and I crossed back under the wall. We were met by a stone-faced Gerasova.

I handed over the tracker watch, which I had not needed. I handed over the banned recording of *Doctor Zhivago* that had convinced Turner's group I was an ally. I handed over the pistol that Turner had given me to escort my prisoner back across the wall.

I had held the gun to Eugene's back all the way to the wall. It was meant as a prop, to complete the performance. But when we were well out of sight of Turner and the West and "my prisoner" remained silent, I didn't lower the gun. I couldn't read his thoughts; my own were too loud. I was thinking about the pistol—if it was just a prop, who was my audience? Was this an act for Turner's crew? Or for Gerasova's? I wondered how many bullets were in the chamber, about how I didn't know how to find out. As my uncertainty climbed, I imagined myself cocking the gun, pulling the trigger.

Tick-tick: How many bullets did it take to kill a man dead?

Tock-tock: How many memories did it take to save a dead man?

Click-click: the gun was cocked.

"Excellent work, Prima," said Gerasova, pocketing the untried pistol.

I never learned what was done with the assets I secured that night. I never asked what became of Eugene, who may or may not have betrayed his Motherland, who may or may not have lied to protect his wife.

But among the lines that Turner selected for me to record that night was one that I never forgot:

What has for centuries raised man above the beast is not the cudgel but an inward music: the irresistible power of unarmed truth.

For as I read those words aloud in a rigged-up-recording booth in a supper club in West Berlin I understood that my inward music would always be that of the maestro as he lifted his baton and sealed a man's fate. In Berlin, I became that maestro. But my truth was armed. Did that make it untrue? Had I rescued a comrade or executed a traitor? Had a righted a wrong or erased a mistake?

That night in Berlin, I understood why Pasternak's Zhivago made the authorities so uneasy.

SIXTEEN
HOMECOMING

I didn't return to the Academy when we arrived back in Moscow. My things, few as they were, had already been moved from the dormitory. They were waiting at my new home—a small room with a high ceiling and a complaining radiator, located at Number 8, Cobbler's Lane.

It was the first time since I was seven years old that I had a room of my own. And it looked out on the stage door of the Bolshoi Theatre.

"There are about twenty of us in all," I told Viktor on the phone. "Maybe more. There's always someone coming out of the cracks. An up-and-coming choreographer, an oboist between homes, a visiting artist . . . Lavrovsky has three rooms in the back with a piano in each one, but the rest of us—just one. Even Nadezhda Sukhareva. She's been elevated to principal and still can't get a second room. Didn't stop her from moving a maid in with her."

Vitya wanted to know about the trip, but I deflected his questions. I had too many questions of my own about Berlin. So I prattled on about my elite *kommunalka*:

"There's also a soprano. I don't know who she is, frankly,

but she's quite good. Every morning she gargles salt water for her vocal chords. But there's just one bathroom in the whole flat so she's gone and set up a spittoon in the corridor and this morning Kostya—he's Iliana's son—was riding his tricycle up and down . . . well, I've already decided I will just run across to the theater to bathe. More privacy there, quite honestly."

"Ah yes, privacy," said Viktor. "Because the last thing a ballerina wants is an audience."

"Tease if you must. How would you like to have to put your name on a list just to use the toilet?"

"Sounds perfectly correct to me." Viktor adopted the voice of a Party bore: "*Long live the public queue! Provider of order, parameters, fairness, and discipline.* Clearly, dear Sveta, you have been deprived for too long of the great joys and important lessons of communal life. May you exchange many meaningful dialogues and share many Party praises in line for the *kommunalka* toilet!"

I bit my lip. I still had not told him about my childhood as a member of a far less prestigious collective called Orphanage #36. I was afraid that once I started confiding, the confessions would never end.

"So," I said. "A housewarming party is in order, don't you think?"

"Tomorrow night?"

"Perfect. I will call Oksana, and maybe . . ." I hesitated. We still had not discussed that other thing—Georgi Levshik, our mutual acquaintance, the petty crook who had rescued Vitya from a long night at Petrovka 38. "Maybe bring some music," I finished.

"I would. But Gosha took off with my collection. Said he could get at least twenty rubles a record."

"Vitya!" I scolded. To get involved with the black market was risky. To speak of it over the phone was riskier. "How could you be so stupid?"

"Yeah, I know, Svet. But don't worry, I'll hunt him down. Won't be a party without . . ."

"Champagne," I finished for him.

THE NEXT NIGHT GOSHA and Vitya arrived at Cobbler's Lane together. Oksana was already seated on my bed when Esther Adamovna, an ancient ballerina who had danced for the Tsar as a child, ushered them into my room.

"Guests for you, Svetlana Evgenievna," she announced imperiously. She turned to Vitya. "The flowers, young man." It was a command. "I will put them in a vase for you."

"That's fine," I told her, "I have one here somewhere."

But Esther Adamovna had already staked a claim on the bouquet and wrested them from Viktor's hands.

"She's a thief," I muttered when the door closed behind the old woman.

"How scandalous," said Gosha drily.

"How artistic," added Viktor with a wink.

"Perhaps we should invite her to join us?"

"Indeed, I think she's just your type, Gosha."

I settled on the windowsill and watched warily as the two of them parried and jabbed. Viktor knew that Gosha's game was a fix. He went out of his way to make it unnecessary for him to cheat: "Hey Georgi, here's three rubles. Go get us a two ruble bottle, will ya?"

Gosha was catlike. He fired his claws only to lick them daintily: "That's some high-quality honey you've brought to Svetlana's table," he purred, spooning Viktor's mother's home-made gift into his tea.

Oksana suggested charades, sleights of hand, and finally a drunken game of "name the neighbor." It ended in Kristina Sergeevna's slightly erotic boudoir, where Viktor and Gosha both enthusiastically modeled the actress's elaborate silk kimonos. With each passing hour, the strange song and dance that was Vitya and Gosha pretending to court me, while in fact they were courting each other, became more straightforward. Better executed. With practice, they became comfortable partners.

At midnight I was back on my windowsill, watching the trolley send sparks along the electric cable. I was enchanted with my view and weary of my guests.

"Okay boys," I said decisively. "Curfew on Cobbler's Lane. Girl's gotta get her beauty sleep. Out you go."

I expected protests, stalling, jokes, and maybe some wheedling. I certainly expected Vitya, at least, to claim his right as the last to leave. Instead, he jumped to his feet and grabbed his jacket.

"Hand over the keys then, Gosha. You're too blotto to drive."

Before I knew it they were stumbling down the stairs and then serenading one last goodbye from the street.

"Like long-lost brothers." Oksana laughed as she closed the window against the cold. "Finishing each other's sentences, hamming it up like they've been onstage together for years. And the nasty things they call each other?"

"I don't know whether to laugh or cry," I agreed.

"Oh, cry, for sure," she said. "Because we've been laughing for two hours straight and my belly hurts."

"Did it go well?" I asked. "I think it did. Better than it might have. It would be just like Gosha to start a fight for the sake of starting a fight. And Vitya can be quite jealous." I handed Oksana a nightdress. "But now I think maybe I'm the one who should be jealous. Did you see him jump up, Oksana? Did you see him grab his jacket the moment Gosha said he could give him a lift home?"

Oksana scrutinized me. "Sveta. You really are jealous, aren't you?"

"Of course not."

"Jealous!" She threw a pillow at me. She was delighted. "Well, good for Viktor then! You shouldn't take that boy for granted."

"What do you mean?"

"I mean he's a catch, Sveta."

She undressed and scrambled into my nightgown.

"Does he know?" she asked as she made up the bed.

I didn't answer. I was thinking about the things I might be taking for granted. Viktor's sunniness, his smile, his music . . . his loyalty. I was thinking of all the things Oksana might have meant when she asked, "Does he know?"

There was only one answer. "No."

Oksana sat on the bed. "None of that matters anymore. Your past is behind you now. Your life is the Bolshoi now."

I nodded. I wanted to believe her, but I knew it was only half true. The other half—the half lodged in Lubyanka 1717—was my life, too. But only my mother knew about that half, and she would soon carry that secret with her to the grave.

"They really did hit it off, didn't they?" I said to change the subject. "I mean—they really do like each other, Gosha and Vitya."

"They have to." Oksana settled into bed and yawned. "They are both in love with you. They can't afford not to like what you love."

It wasn't what she had said about the two young men that struck me. It was what she had said about me.

MY MOTHER WAS STILL alive. This posed a dilemma for the hospital. Vera Kravshina's live body looked good for their records, but it was taking up space in an overcrowded ward. They called me in and waved charts in my face.

"Comrade Kravshina has exceeded her medical quota as of December 20. You will need to take her home for one week. We can readmit her on the first Friday of January."

My friends rallied to help: Gosha arrived in a car to collect Vera and deliver her to Cobbler's Lane, where my neighbors had already scavenged an extra mattress and linens. Viktor managed to secure a week's supply of pain medicine from the clinic. Oksana agreed to skip classes to stay with my mother while I was in rehearsals. These were rehearsals that I couldn't miss.

It was *Nutcracker* season, and I had been cast as the Sugar Plum Fairy. The team at 1717 had not objected. My sensitivity to music was now classed as an asset rather than a liability.

"But what is there to gain?" Maksim had asked, the killjoy. "Why elevate her visibility? Why distract her from her priorities?" Comrade Gerasova had shot him down.

"Let's let Prima have a shot at strengthening her cover," she had said. "In time she may be called Prima outside of 1717, and that wouldn't be so bad."

I had thrilled at the suggestion, initially. Then I nearly collapsed with nerves. *What if I couldn't be both? What if I couldn't be a prima without the damn mask?* It was as terrifying a notion as being unmasked for what I was: an agent of the KGB. And now there was the sudden presence of my mother to add to my concerns.

"I am going," said Vera from her new bed with its view of the theater. "If I'm strong enough to leave a hospital bed, I am strong enough to cross the street to see my daughter dance on the Bolshoi stage."

I didn't argue. I called Natalia Davydovna, who delivered a box seat and a promise to accompany my mother to opening night.

"And in January, when Vera Konstantinovna returns to the hospital, you will return to us," she said.

So far, my two months' leave from Lubyanka were serving me well. I was taking two classes a day followed by long coaching sessions with Markova. She had polished my *port de bras*, turning my spine into molten steel and my arms into wings. I had been noticed at the theater; the other teachers were circling, ready to poach me as their own star student. My name had risen up the corps rankings, spiking to the top in the last week of November. I had been mentioned in the press: *Ogonyok, Art World,* and *Soviet Artist* had all run notices. I was promoted to soloist. My *Nutcracker* premiere was much anticipated. A respected senior dancer, Alexander Karpov, would be my prince. He actually looked like one, too. Unlike the other men in my life, Alexander had perfect posture and no personality.

The best thing about all this attention had been its ability to deflect Lubyanka. The stern headquarters of the KGB, just blocks away, was a distant reality. But I still couldn't shake the doubts from Berlin: Why had Gerasova told me that I had "all the information" needed to succeed in my mission? Why had she assured me afterward that it had all been "just a test?"

A test for me? Or a test for my partner? Had Eugene passed?

They were still there, fragments of those two strange nights when I had crossed and recrossed enemy lines. And they wanted to haunt me, those fleeting images:

A trapeze artist colliding with a cement wall.

A wrecking ball slamming into an anonymous statue in a town square.

They were connected. Of this I was sure. I had read Eugene's memories because he was a shadow of my father: a handsome man playing a dangerous double game who still cherished the rare night at his daughter's bedside. I remembered what Ulanova had said about my father—how he had been forgotten by history but remembered by her.

Would history forget Eugene? Would I always remember?

For two months I had slept on that confusion, pushing it under my pillow, burying it in my dance bag under athletic tape and cotton wool and darned tights.

But now Gerasova had said it was time to return.

THE DAY BEFORE OPENING night of *The Nutcracker*, Galina Ulanova found me in a basement studio. I was rehearsing with Alexander. She motioned for us to continue the *pas de deux*, and at its end she said, "Could I have a word with Svetlana in private?"

Alexander nodded. "Till tomorrow," he said to me.

When he was gone she said, "You have a bright future, Svetlana Evgenievna."

"That's kind of you," I said, bowing my head deferentially. "I hope I will distinguish myself."

"As Sugar Plum?" Ulanova's face showed no humor. "A walk in the park. You are a natural Sugar Plum and Alexander makes a handsome partner. Though you must be sure, in the *pas de deux*, to hold your poses to the end of the phrase. And your breathing—don't let it be seen. The audience doesn't want your efforts. They want effortless."

"Thank you," I said. I was pleased to hear genuine feedback instead of banal promises about bright futures. "Do you have any other suggestions?"

"I do."

"Please . . ."

"As you know, my time is up, Svetlana Evgenievna. I have given my resignation. I am retiring from the stage. Now, there are many others just behind me, ready to become the Bolshoi Ballet's leading lady. You are still young and developing your technique. Bibikova, Petrenko, Tsiskovaya—they are the principals. They will have the leads. But there is one thing that they cannot replace when I retire."

I waited. What thing? *Juliet?* Was Ulanova giving me Juliet?

"The Bolshoi will not have an international ambassador," she said.

"Ambassador? You mean like a spokesperson?"

"I mean that and more."

"Cultural diplomacy and all that?" I asked, searching her plain features for a hint. "All due respect, but surely those ladies are commendable representatives of Soviet achievements in the arts."

"Yes. All of them can look elegant at press conferences and spout platitudes about 'art speaking one language,' yes. But none of them are in a position to truly serve the Motherland. None of them can defend the *rodina* abroad."

I felt a tightness encircle my ribs. Heat under my skin. My face was flushed. I knew Ulanova could see my breathing. She could see my effort to appear effortless. I couldn't see hers.

"You are the Bolshoi's secret weapon, Svetlana. Do you think I don't know this? You are the only one of our artists who can defend the theater even as you serve it. The Bolshoi is like our *rodina*. When you promote the one, you protect the other. That is why I will advise the administration to introduce you to stages beyond Berlin. You will see the world, Svetlana. You will see how cold it is on the wrong side of the Cold War. And if you are a faithful servant, you will be a prima. Truly."

I was surprised that I felt it so strongly—not honor, not commendation, but anger.

"You think I owe it to our *rodina*, don't you?"

Ulanova didn't answer.

"You think because my father . . ."

"I think that your father served his country. I think your father faced enemies he could not defeat. I hope that you never shall."

And with that, Galina Ulanova curtsied low before me and left.

ON THE OPENING NIGHT of *The Nutcracker* I stood backstage, hands on hips. My entrance—my debut solo on the Bolshoi stage—was minutes away.

The four teapot-topped whirlwinds of the Oriental dance spun and flexed their way through the stage lights. I imagined myself in their place: my jet-black braid, after all, was natural. If I wore the ballooning silk trousers of the Chinese party guests, my pockets would conceal secrets. But tonight my braid was tucked under the headdress of the Sugar Plum Fairy. Tonight I was fully exposed. There was nothing but the stiff halo of my tutu covering the naked lines of my body.

I clasped my hands behind my back and pulled them over my head, bending my nose to my knees.

Behind me, Alexander adjusted his tights and all that they covered. Ilya, late on his cue, leapt past us into the middle of the Chinese mandala. His legs mimicked the shape of his fake Manchu mustache. He circled the stage twice and swept into a mocking bow. The Oriental dance was over. My prince slid a hand around my waist. We entered the stage to applause.

Throughout the adagio, I did as Ulanova had advised: I held the poses two beats longer than usual. I breathed in small sips. My lines were flawless, my mind focused on technique. I had emptied it of everything else, so that I would not fall down a rabbit hole, sucked into the phantom memories of Tchaikovsky's music.

But when Alexander promenaded me to the corner to launch a diagonal parade of pirouettes, I heard the swelling strings in the orchestra pit and understood that if I didn't ride them, they would swamp me. I saw the endless stage and my glorious nose-dive, and I felt reckless. I attacked the turns, covering the stage like a Sugar Plum Fury, and flung myself into the steady arms of my prince.

"Easy, Sveta," he whispered.

He placed me upright, and with a single turn of my wrist I fended off the music and withdrew to the wings. From the safety of backstage, I watched the Prince's solo without seeing it. Instead, I saw my thoughts flicker like fairies across the stage: a bicycle racing along the river, a corridor filled with sleep, a long black braid climbing a dilapidated fence.

Brief applause cued my entrance. As Alexander left the stage I ran out to take his place. I sprang into a *pas de chat*, and I felt them surround me, these memories of a not-so-distant past. Gingerly, I tiptoed through them, a girl sneaking into her own childhood. But as I danced, my caution turned to confidence.

This is my solo. These are my memories. This is my stage.

With a rush of adrenaline, I recognized that I was happy. That happiness carried me through the solo, which was lighter and brighter than I had ever danced it. I marveled at my body, because it was my own. I skipped across the music, because it delivered memories of *me*. I was the phoenix, I was my bright future, I was the protector of my *rodina*.

In the moment, I danced the solo perfectly.

There were murmurs from the audience. When I stepped forward to acknowledge their approval, I stole a glance at the box where my mother watched, her face gaunt and pale, but smiling. On one side of her sat Gerasova. On the other side, Ulanova. Smiling, too.

My mother, flanked by my Motherland.

The ovations at the end lasted several minutes. There were too many bouquets for me to hold. Alexander led me to the front of the stage four times, the clapping still thunderous, before the curtains finally closed.

I knew I should go look for my mother. I knew Viktor would be waiting at the Hotel Metropol across the street, holding a table for our celebration. I knew that the visions I had just danced with—the House, the river, the end of my childhood and my innocence—were gone. I knew my bright future awaited.

But I wanted to go back in time.

I didn't look for my mother. I left Viktor waiting at the Metropol. I snuck out the stage door and found the car waiting.

"Where to, Sugar Plum?" asked Gosha.

"The embankment east of Kursky Station," I said. "How long till sunrise?"

I couldn't remember feeling happier.

SEVENTEEN
SOULS

My mother died in the spring. I wasn't with her. The day she died I was fighting a bad cold. And I was fighting with Gosha. The day she died, our argument—the longest and bitterest yet—was coming to an end. I had just finished class. He was waiting for me at the theater door. He begged me to forgive him.

"I had to, Sveta. I had to tell him. He was beginning to act delusional. He had all sorts of crazy ideas. You have to understand—when you keep a secret too long, whatever it is you are hiding begins to get warped. That's what they do to us in this country. They clamp down the truth and in its absence, lies become reality. Sveta, if I hadn't told him that the only thing you've been hiding is that you grew up in Orphanage number thirty-six, he was ready to believe . . . something worse."

"Worse? What's worse?"

My nose was chapped. My eyes were slits. I knew I looked as miserable as I felt. "You had no right to tell him," I said.

He threw up his hands. He began to explain again—it was the same argument he had been making for days. Viktor had asked him point-blank what was between us. He'd assured Vitya that the only time he had tried to romance me, he had been soundly rebuffed. That he and I—Gosha and Sveta—would never be anything but friends.

"A sister, more like. We have a common childhood bond," he'd said.

That was his mistake. Forced to elaborate, he'd told Viktor that I, like him, came from the bottom of Soviet society. That I was the daughter of Enemies of the People.

I was furious. I was still furious.

Gosha lashed back at first, instinctively: It was my own fault for not telling Viktor myself. If I weren't such a coward, I would have already told the whole world.

"Look at you," he'd sneered. "You've embraced the tyrannies of our so-called classless society." He'd called me a "duplicitous diva" and a hypocrite.

But now he was pleading.

"I was wrong. I'm sorry. I was worried. I was afraid that—out of stupid stubbornness about admitting that you have overcome such odds to get where you are—you would lose him." He didn't look at me when he added, "And now I'm afraid that I have lost you."

My anger turned to despair. "You haven't lost me, Gosha. But there are things I can't tell Viktor."

He raised his eyes. I thought he might actually be frightened. "Are there things you can't tell me?" he whispered.

I threw myself against him and sobbed. He wrapped his arms around me. I started talking, telling. I don't how long we stood there, huddled in weak spring sunshine. Long enough for me to tell him everything.

"Nobody else knows but my mother," I finished.

But by then my mother was dead, and Gosha was the only one who knew my secret. I clung to him. And by the end of that day of truth, there was something else that I could never tell Viktor.

MOURNING BECAME ME. I had recovered from my cold and I was, I knew, stunning in black against the early blooms of the cemetery's lilac trees. I stood at my mother's grave. Viktor held my hand. But Gosha stood closer.

I stepped away from them both and took up the shovel. I plunged it into the fresh mound by the grave and threw dirt over my mother's coffin. I replaced the shovel in the mound. It stood upright like a sentinel of symbolic gestures. I grabbed it again and set to work in earnest. I was burying my mother feverishly.

Viktor came to my side and gently took the shovel from me.

"She's gone," I said. Then I used all the expressions—blunt, clinical, euphemistic, temporal—to say it again. "She's gone, dead, finished, over."

I looked up and saw Natalia Davydovna Gerasova coming down the path to the grave site.

I said, "Meet me back at the front gate."

Viktor began to protest, but Gosha stepped up and pulled him away, leaving me alone with my mother's old friend.

She had brought lilies, which she placed at the headstone.

"Did you have a chance to say goodbye?"

I laughed. "I've had many chances to say goodbye. Beginning on June 14, 1950."

"You're fortunate that you had this time with her. The past two years—they were something that Vera Konstantinovna dreamt of during the toughest times. I remember her telling me that she didn't need a long life. Only long enough to see you again."

I looked not at her but at my hand, numb from the rough handle of the shovel. I said, "Please don't bullshit me. My mother and I were never in any real need of each other. The truth is, I have been a better ward of the state than a daughter. I accepted the Bolshoi as my family more easily than my own. And I've been more faithful to your wishes than to my mother's."

"My wishes, Svetlana, do not contradict your mother's," she said. "It was her initiative that brought you to me. She offered your services to the Motherland. She wanted for you what you have now."

The grave digger returned to take up the shovel. His son was next to him—a kid with a face younger than his body. He was familiar, somehow. I watched the boy for a moment, wondering who he reminded me of.

"Initiative," I murmured. "How fortunate that I had such an industrious parent." I heard my bitterness and felt ashamed. I met Gerasova's gaze.

"Forgive me, Natalia Davydovna. I'm not myself. I haven't been sleeping well."

She nodded. "I can arrange for you to take a short holiday. Four days in the Baltics, perhaps? There is a lovely lake resort not far from Tallinn—exclusively for Ministry . . ."

"No. Thank you for the offer. But I cannot afford to be absent from the theater. You see, there are rumors. A whisper campaign that all my success of the last three months—the role in *Bayadère*, the All-Soviet prize, skipping ranks from the corps to first soloist—that it comes from on high. That only a patron somewhere could have arranged it so well for me. Naturally, I want to dispel this talk. A vacation in Tallinn won't help."

Gerasova smiled faintly. "Your caution is commendable." She snapped open her pocketbook and removed an envelope. "Don't worry," she said. "Not train tickets." She handed it to me. "This is a document of rehabilitation. Your mother's criminal record has been fully expunged. She earned it . . . and more. I offer you my condolences."

Natalia Davydovna put a hand on my shoulder. Then she turned and left the way she came.

I broke the envelope's seal and fingered the document inside. I remembered a rainy day on a bench, when the sky was gray and my mother, black: *"A Russian consists of a body, a soul, and some papers. Sometimes I wonder about the soul part."*

The grave was nearly filled. The grave digger's son patted the earth into place and wiped sweat from the back of his neck. He looked up and saw me watching him. He removed his cap and bowed, slightly but respectfully. There was something in it that was more than good manners. There was something tender. Something shared. As if he meant to assure me that he had buried a soul as well as a body.

Gosha. He reminded me of Gosha.

"AH YES. THE PERPLEXING, exasperating, impenetrable soul. Hunted and haunting. Awarded the Nobel Prize in Literature in absentia and in protest."

Viktor flopped from his elbow and lifted his whole face to the sky, which was pale and hot and ready for evening. I was packing up the remains of a picnic. Gosha sat with his shoulders braced against my spine. He held a picked-over bunch of Caucasus grapes in one hand. The other hand was exploring the basket I was trying to pack. I slapped it.

"Hey, philosopher-poet," he said, "I'm not drunk enough for a discourse on the Russian soul."

"And I am not sober enough to give you one, my friend." Viktor's eyes were closed. "On this summer's eve, I offer poetry only. Pure, grade-A, off-the-cuff, one-size-fits-all *poezia*."

I held out my hand. Gosha dropped three grapes into my palm.

"Let's have one then," I said.

"One what."

"A poem, silly."

Viktor rolled over and looked at me. His eyes were warm. They reminded me of summer. Soon it would be summer. Soon it would be two years that we were together. But I could see that he wasn't thinking about the future. He was thinking about last night. Last night he had apologized for his jealousy and, more importantly, acknowledged my own jealous privacy.

"I get it, Sveta," he had said. "It wasn't something you should have been expected to share—your past is your own. I only want your present."

My relief was overwhelming. And physical. So I had given it to him—my full presence. I finally took him to bed. Afterward, we had lain awake, watching the sparks of the trolleybus reflected on the ceiling.

Now he reached out and caressed my naked foot. "A poem about what?" he asked.

"Fireflies."

He smiled and flipped onto his back again. He tucked his hands into a pillow under his head and ad-libbed:

This spark of young June
This ember of twilight
This lick of . . .
Sveta, my light.

He turned his head and saw me flush. I dug a toe into his ribcage.

"Is that all?" I asked.

Stars shooting through our cosmos
Insects flaming bloodless
Beacons of an ineffable bond . . .

A grape whizzed past my ear and hit the poet in the eye.

"God help us, that is absolute crap."

Gosha got up and I fell backward.

"Vitya. You should swear us both to secrecy immediately if you don't want us to ruin your reputation as a cool cat with unassailable taste. 'Stars of the cosmos, ineffable bonds . . .' Foo, what shit. Sveta, I certainly hope this is not your doing." He stomped the blankets in a flamboyant show of disgust. "Look, kids. Enough of your romantic squeals in the dark. I leave you to your squishy sentiments and go in search of steadfast Soviet company—solid *muzhiki* and honest whores. Palms of silver and hearts of gold. Anything but pedantic poetry, I beg of you."

But Viktor, encouraged, waxed more lyrical. His firefly muse had become one with the dusk: *singular, tumescent, profound, and seismic . . .*

"Stop this instant or I will have to physically restrain your blather!"

Forever sucking my light . . .

My Sveta . . . my soul . . .
Into torrents of quantum . . .

"I mean it!" Gosha bellowed. "I can't be held responsible for my actions, you degenerate! I will either report you to the pornographers or rape you myself!"

I was giggling, pelting them both with grapes. Defending my Vitya against Gosha's heartless critique and threats. They started wrestling. Puppy dogs with sharp teeth.

"Oof, Gosha. Your tumescence!" Vitya grunted, laughing.

Gosha had him pinned. "Give us the knife, Sveta. We'll give him sideburns like Pushkin's."

He knocked over the lemonade. I protested and fired more grapes.

Viktor spat a retort, expelled by the weight of Gosha on his chest: "Give the knife to me. A knife to geld this whoremonger."

"You sonofabitch."

"You fucking thief."

"You pathetic, blind excuse of a man."

I was on my feet. "Stop it. Now."

It was over as quickly as it began. Gosha removed his hand from Viktor's throat. Viktor scrambled up. There were grass stains on his shirt. He wiped the spit from his lips. Gosha stood, checked his watch. None of us was smiling anymore. We were all embarrassed.

"I gotta go," Gosha said.

He was halfway down the hill when I called out. "Gosha! Tomorrow night."

He turned and looked at us. Me in my crown of fireflies. Viktor at my feet, his hand on my calf. His face, I imagined, recognizing what we all three knew: That Gosha would see me tomorrow night. And that he would recite poetry if I asked him to.

EIGHTEEN
SOLOIST

I began my second season with the Bolshoi Ballet confident that I had earned my position as the youngest soloist in the company's history. The months after my mother's death had provided ample opportunity to prove my dedication, virtuosity, discretion, and—perhaps most importantly for Markova and the rest of the ballet's management—my star power.

Night after night, the stage door opened on a flock of acolytes.

Week after week, *Soviet Artist* reserved space in its centerfold for supposedly candid shots of "the Bolshoi's photogenic young soloist"—at the Gorky Park skating rink, trying on hats in the Central Department Store, poring over the latest poetry anthologies at the House of Books.

"Agent Prima" was Lubyanka's covert secret, but Svetlana Kravshina was a very public darling of the People.

I was steadily closing in on the role that Ulanova had said was mine: the international face of the Bolshoi Ballet. My Sugar Plum debut was a childish memory. Even Juliet, the role that was once the object of all my desires, seemed unimportant. It would be mine when I demanded it, I figured. For now, I was stepping into shoes far larger than those of a star-crossed girl on pointe. I was not yet a prima, but I could already see myself as the Bolshoi's queen.

It began when the president of India made a weeklong visit to Moscow. His country was in good favor with the Kremlin again, forgiven for its troublesome contagious diseases. Mostly because India was quarrelling with China, just like Nikita Khrushchev. I didn't bother trying to understand the politics of the state visit. My main concern was to not collapse of exhaustion during an encore performance of *Spartacus*, which the Indian president requested two nights in a row, with me dancing the lead both nights. Of course, Maksim was not impressed. He stormed around 1717 for a half hour, demanding to know what on earth I had been doing all night if not gathering information. "Making a ballet fan out of Secretary Khrushchev," I replied, which sent him on another tirade but made Inga smile.

A month later, it was a delegation from Egypt. They requested me by name. Not just for their evening's entertainment, but as a guest at a banquet reception in the Palace of the Soviets. I wore a low-cut dress that made Viktor whine. I sat next to an Egyptian general who was pleasant enough, though I didn't care for his mustache. The next day I described for Maksim the Egyptian's dreams: of camels, sand, a ship beached and leaking.

Then, in early spring, it was Yugoslavia. There was a dashing backstage gesture from the strongman Josip Tito, meant to "demonstrate the respect of our Balkan brotherhood for Secretary Khrushchev as the leader of the International Communist Party and model of Marxist-Leninist correctness." At least that's what the paper said. I rather thought that the thin gold chain Marshal Tito had given me, along with a kiss on my hand, was a gesture of his respect for my Giselle, but I was glad that Khrushchev felt flattered, too.

At the end of the season, just before summer vacation, word came that the American ambassador was leaving Moscow. For his farewell dinner, he had requested the attendance of the

Bolshoi's artistic director, executive director, assistant director, musical director . . . and first soloist, Svetlana Kravshina.

The invitation had the 1717 team buzzing with excitement.

"He's been walking a tightrope for over a decade, but now his guard will be down," explained Comrade Gerasova. "He's got one foot out the door and he has no need to be cautious with a young ballerina. Five minutes of innocent conversation about music, art, whatever—it's in these small windows that information can be mined."

"You must be very focused, Prima," growled Maksim. "No necklaces, no compliments, and no silly camel dreams. I don't care what Galina Ulanova sees in you. Tonight you are Lubyanka's leading lady, not the damn Bolshoi's. Do you understand?"

I understood. This was not a matter of protocol or politics. This was not about representing the Bolshoi or even the Soviet Union. The only ambassador at the banquet that mattered would be the American one, and the Americans were enemies of the Motherland. The Cold War had come to my doorstep, and I was a frontline soldier. I girded myself for battle in a new silk dress. But it was Oleg who gave me my best weapon.

On the night of the banquet, he picked me up at Cobbler's Lane. Instead of driving straight to the ambassador's residence in the Arbat, he took a circuitous route over the river. In the middle of the Big Stone Bridge he flipped on the turn signal of his battered Moskvich.

"Are you planning to drive us into the river, Oleg?" I teased nervously.

"Funny you should ask," he replied. "No. I am not. I *could* drive off this bridge, but it would be a reckless move. Because if I did, I would plunge to my death along with you. It is what we call *mutual assured destruction*. And that's where we are, Prima. Our countries—the Soviet Union and the United States—are capable of obliterating each other with a single press of a button. We must be certain that this ability works to prevent, rather than assure, our mutual destruction. Do you understand?"

He turned to me briefly, and his face was grave. "I want you to listen closely to the sound of brinkmanship."

I listened. To the *tick-tick-tick* of the car's indicator signal as it threatened to make a right turn over the barrier and into the river. The sound—like the rhythm of a metronome, like the countdown of a nuclear clock—had a message:

Tick-tick: mutual.

Tick-tick: assured.

Tick-tick: destruction.

Only when we had crossed the bridge again and pulled into an alley across from the ambassador's residence did Oleg shut off the turn signal. It was quiet in the car. But I could still hear the pulse: the countdown of mutual assured destruction, the steady beat of madness.

I PASSED THROUGH THE security and joined the other Russian guests waiting to be presented to the American ambassador. The paneled walls and glittering chandeliers of the reception room were full of memories—of peace treaties signed when our two countries were allies; of the listening device planted in a plaque presented by a goodwill Komsomol delegation; of a legendary party that ended in the wee hours of the morning with a circus bear drunk on champagne; of the last farewell party for a departing ambassador, at which Galina Ulanova had been a guest of honor.

I tucked them all away, my mind as focused and even as the beat of a metronome. I waited for my five-minute window.

It came just before dinner. The ambassador, a man with thin lips and dark circles under his eyes, stepped forward to kiss my hand. "Svetlana Kravshina, it is a great pleasure."

His Russian was good. It was flat and wide, and I had a vision of open sky above the American plains.

"The pleasure is mine," I said. "Do you know I have never been inside this beautiful house? It is spectacular."

"It is, isn't it? I will miss it almost as much as I will miss the grand performances of the Bolshoi Ballet."

I saw his eyes pass over my shoulder. There were others waiting, and dinner had been laid in the hall next door. I heard the *tick-tick* of my time running out.

"Tell me, are you a dancer, Mr. Ambassador?" I asked, touching his elbow lightly.

"I'm afraid not much of one. Unless you count square dancing. My father was a rancher, you know."

"And mine was a general."

He hesitated. We both seemed surprised at this revelation.

"General Kravshin," he said. "Yes."

I squeezed his elbow, ever so lightly.

"I met your father," he continued. "Just after the war." He hesitated once more before suggesting, "Perhaps, after dinner, you might honor me with a dance?"

I breathed. I had not failed yet. I had managed to establish something mutual, something assured. Which meant I could still make a stab against destruction.

The dinner was lavish and long, in part because we could not leave the table until Secretary Khrushchev made a late appearance and a rambling toast, ending with: "And so we drink to a man whose best quality can only be said that he's the son of a farmer. Maybe we can make a good Communist of him yet!"

There was polite laughter. Then Khrushchev departed and the musicians in the next room struck up a waltz. As the guests rose from the table I made a beeline for the ambassador.

"You must be used to Nikita Sergeevich's humor by now," I said, referring to Khrushchev's parting shot.

"Yes." The American laughed. "Nikita Sergeevich and I have a long history together. It's not the first time he has made a joke at my expense. But this is the fate of a diplomat, you see. You must be prepared to be the butt in order to save face."

He had used the wrong word. He had used the word for a butt of a gun. The butt of a rancher's pistol. The butt of a rifle. The visions rained down: of a cowboy at high noon, of a soldier raising his weapon, of the order to fire, of the end of the symphony.

Of my father obliged to save face.

"Now then, Miss Kravshina, let's have that dance."

We spoke little on the ballroom floor. The diplomatic son of the rancher plodded in heavy circles, humming the strains of Tchaikovsky. I followed his lead wordlessly, the beat of brinkmanship as my true guide, probing his thoughts for assurance. In the five minutes we shared with a waltz, I learned that the outgoing ambassador had many fond memories of Moscow, including of the brave Soviet generals who fought in the war. But the war was ancient history. He was being recalled to Washington, D.C., in order to advise the president that without further military buildup, Soviet expansion was inevitable, and the United States would be the butt of Comrade Khrushchev's worst joke.

"I have greatly enjoyed this dance," he said when the music halted.

I assured him it was mutual. He bowed and reentered the fray.

I left shortly thereafter, knowing that the ulcers the ambassador suffered came from the madness of assurances that lead only to mutual destruction. And that in the summer of 1962, he heard the clock ticking toward high noon.

BY SEPTEMBER, MY NAME was on every cast for the upcoming season. I was also on the list of dancers who would be sent on a two-week tour of America. I lay on my bed studying the schedule, wondering if Comrade Gerasova's hand had guided the itinerary.

"New York, Washington . . ." I frowned, struggling with the phonetics of an unfamiliar city. Viktor leaned over my shoulder for a look.

"Poughkeepsie," he said.

"Pow-what?"

"Keepsie. Pow-keepsie. I think it is near Hyena's Port."

"What the hell?"

"Hyena's Port. It's the Kennedy's Kremlin. A lavish beach palace crawling with movie stars. And those crustacean thingies. Langoustines."

"Lobsters and Jackie O.?" I asked. "Sounds like good company."

"Yeah," said Victor. "But you're not going there. You're going to Pow-keepsie."

I wondered. If the president of the USA was lounging in Hyena's Port, shouldn't I be going there?

I was still slightly heady with the praise I had received from Maksim and Gerasova after the ambassador's dinner. They said that my account of his diplomatic impasse was crucial and was already being acted upon. I was thinking about how open his mind had been, the unguarded ambassador, despite the weight of his thoughts. I couldn't help thinking that I had helped . . . not just read it, but *open* it. It made me wonder about the president of the United States. Everyone knew that Jack Kennedy was a notorious playboy. Could I crack him open with a single dance?

"Are you sure the Kennedys don't live in Camelot?" I asked.

Viktor's head was on the floor as he searched for his shoes under the bed.

"No. That's King Arthur."

"But he was British."

"Right. Never set foot in Pow-keepsie. Or Washington, D.C., for that matter. Which is where the Kennedys will probably be when you are in town. Don't worry, Sveta, I'm sure you will have the chance to make the so-called 'leader of the free world' a slave of your heart."

Or a slave of mutual assured destruction, I thought.

SURE ENOUGH, WHEN NATALIA Davydovna Gerasova visited Lubyanka 1717 the next day, she brought news.

"We've arranged for you to meet the president's wife and daughter at the White House residence while you are in the American capital."

"Wife and daughter? Why not the president himself?"

"Don't be arrogant, Prima," said Gerasova. "It's unbecoming and counterproductive."

"I just meant that if I were able to intercept . . ." I stammered, flustered.

"We would like nothing more than for you to make a mental connection with the president of the United States," said Gerasova. "As well as his joint chiefs of staff, his defense secretary, his secretary of state, his father confessor, and his psychotherapist. But we thought we might start with his wife and daughter. They are women. They like ballet. They have busy schedules, but ones in which a half hour with a ballerina makes sense. Do you understand?"

"Yes." I felt foolish. "Yes, of course."

"So. That's Washington, last week of October. Before that, New York. You will need to be extremely attentive there. If only to be sure that you are prepared for the White House. You should employ the relaxation and meditation exercises that Oleg devised. Twice daily. Prepare to open yourself again to the universal mind."

I nodded. The universal mind. I had forgotten that part of my psychological intelligence training. The part where *I* was the one to be opened. I imagined universal fingers prying apart my skull, only to find a ticking bomb inside.

"I've got logs for you," Gerasova continued. "You will record all thoughts, scenes, visions, scraps of information that present themselves while you are in America. I have new coding sheets as well. You will follow them scrupulously, as you will be surrounded by enemy eyes and ears. You will have a single room, of course. Clearly you will require privacy for your work. And you're a soloist now. You've earned a certain amount of freedom."

"You won't be coming?" I asked.

"As of today, no. You will be going solo."

"Solo?"

My voice tripped. Gerasova heard it. She cocked her head at me. I imagined what she saw: A soloist who feared going solo. A girl who flaunted her independence, but knew, deep down, that she was not her own master.

"What if I need . . ."

"There's an operation underway, Prima. It's top secret. If it goes well, you will know nothing about it. You will stay uninvolved. Believe it or not, we are very much hoping you will have to do nothing more than have tea with the First Lady and thank her daughter when she brings flowers to the dressing room. But we still need you ready. We need your remote viewing and your telepathic training. We expect you to report any and all significant disturbances in the psychosphere."

She handed me the logs and codebooks. I opened one and found basic biographical information on the Kennedys, a map of Washington, a list of attractions in New York, and a short phrase sheet: *Please turn down my bed. Do you have another color? More ketchup, please. Beg your pardon. This seat is taken.*

I laid one sheet over the other and saw the code revealed in their transparency.

"You will use the exercises. You will use the logs. You will hand over any observations to your contact, Igor, who will be introduced to you as your translator. And that's all. Unless, of course, things change. Then we jettison the universal mind. If that happens, you will likely find me at your side."

WE WERE FIGHTING AGAIN, Gosha and I. We'd been fighting lots since we had become . . . whatever we were. Usually our arguments ended in him rolling his eyes, rocking on his heels, and saying, "I think we've had enough for one evening, don't you Sveta?" But this time he wasn't backing down or walking away.

We were parked outside my building in his car. This one was a behemoth Moskvich with wood paneling. It was hardly a discreet vehicle, but it was the safest place to speak of secrets in the middle of the day, in the middle of Moscow, in mid-October, 1962.

"They are using you," he said. "The KGB is using you."

"Of course they are. I'm an asset. I'm useful."

"The Committee for State Security finds a use for everyone, Sveta. For anyone. You are letting them hold your career hostage."

I laughed. "My career has been taken hostage, has it? Are you talking about my promotion as the youngest principal in the history of the Bolshoi Ballet? Is that what you mean by my hostage career? The one that none other than Galina Ulanova has expressed a personal interest in? Maybe you should ask for your career to be held hostage—it just might do wonders for your prospects! Or is your little side business at the track flourishing?"

He gripped the wheel harder. I'd made him ridiculous.

"Not all hostages are unwilling, Sveta. Especially not here. Not in the Soviet Union. You know it as well as I do. There are no victims among us. Just like there are no criminals. There are only traitors. Traitors and spies. And if you don't want to be one . . . you have to be the other."

"I'm not a spy."

I had said it a million times. Usually because I didn't want to admit to him something that I didn't want to admit to myself. But this time I spat it through clenched teeth. A said it like a knife that would skewer him.

"A spy is a sneak," I added. "A spy is a snitch."

He heard me. He heard me tell him that as far as I was concerned, he had accused me of something far worse than being useful to the KGB.

"I didn't say that," he said softly. "I didn't say that you were spying. On me. Or on Vitya. Or on your colleagues or your neighbors or . . . I didn't say you were a rat, Sveta."

"You said I was their hostage. You said I owe them my career."

"I didn't." He shook his head. "I've seen you dance. I'm no expert, and I don't think that this woman, the one you say is an old friend of your mother's, is, either. She may be a high-ranking member of the Khrushchev clique and a KGB officer, but that alone is not enough to put you on the top of the Bolshoi billing."

He waited for me to ask how he knew about Gerasova. But I wouldn't give him the satisfaction. I thought of ancient grudges: *I bite my thumb at you.*

"I've seen you dance, Sveta," Gosha said. "You are exceptional. You are the best."

I looked him in the eye. Those unnatural eyes. They hid every trace of sincerity, but I knew he meant every word.

"I will never say that you don't deserve the artistic rank you have achieved. But in our country, Sveta, in our beloved *rodina*, you don't get what you deserve. You get what you grab. You get what you stand in line for. You get what you trade favors for. Everything you get, you get with difficulty."

An emergency vehicle flew past us, its siren warped.

Gosha turned away. "Look, I know it has not been easy for you to get where you are. Don't think I don't understand how hard it must be to balance your dreams against the thing that they have told you is more important—your duty."

I felt his words open an old wound. Gosha could speak the truth in ways that spilled blood without pain. I wanted to be done; I wanted to call a truce. I wanted to apologize for calling him a philistine, a delinquent, an ignoramus. Nothing could be more patently false. I was ready to wave the white flag with a sigh, a touch, a kiss.

"You're going to have to choose, you know," he said quietly. "You can't have it all."

So he had more blood to draw. I turned away, too. Now we were looking out the front window at two different futures. Two different disagreements.

"You can't have us both."

I laughed faintly. "Who's taking hostages?" I asked.

"I won't tell him. About Lubyanka. About the KGB and your Comrade Gerasova."

About us.

"Of course you won't," I said. "Just like I will never tell him. Just like I will never reveal to anyone the things I know about you. Because you and I, Gosha, are not snitches. We're survivors. And because you know that anyone who threatens to keep me from someone I love . . . will lose me forever."

I got out of the car and slammed the door behind me. As I walked away I asked myself for the hundredth time if I the truths I told Gosha were to protect him or to warn him. Did I want him to stop me or leave me? He'd do neither, of course. He'd win. He was a better survivor than I was.

NINETEEN
CRISIS

"*Blin*." It was all I could offer as I stood in the hotel room, with its enormous bed, custom-installed barre and mirror, and spectacular view of a sparkling river flanked with skyscrapers.

"*Blin*," I said again.

"We know how demanding a ballerina's schedule can be," oozed the man who claimed to be a hotel manager but whose dazzling white teeth and smartly tailored suit made me think he must be the rich capitalist who owned the joint. "So we've made it possible for you to do your warming up without even leaving your room." Or maybe he was undercover CIA. Maybe he was Jack Kennedy's personal spy. At any rate, he bore little resemblance to the toupeed manager of the hotel in East Berlin.

He whisked me through the suite, displaying all the amenities. My translator, Igor—an "understudy," but a decent fellow—was at a loss to explain them.

"For warming hot dogs," he ventured when the hotel manager held up a curling iron.

Igor was more useful in his role as a KGB shadow. Gerasova had told me to expect an indulgent minder, one who had been told to give me a long leash. What she had failed to mention was that Igor was as eager for that freedom as I was. He was a benign tail—one who was more interested in keeping his target in his sights than in filing reports about my unofficial activities that might require further responsibilities. Also, he wasn't above the occasional indulgence in Western materialism. He was practically addicted to chewing gum. When the hotel manager left us and I said I wanted to stretch my legs, Igor jumped up eagerly to fetch our coats.

Out on the street I walked briskly, enjoying the smooth asphalt beneath my feet and the rush of a hundred cars proclaiming rush hour in New York City. I kept myself open for disturbances in the psychosphere, but the sensory overload of the foreign city drowned out the ripples of weirdness. *Everything* here was strange.

We hadn't gone far when I learned the real reason for Igor's amenable character. We were standing on the corner, waiting for the light to change, and I saw his gaze locked on the window of a store that was already closed for the day. When the light changed he was still engrossed. I sidled up to him and suggested, "Maybe we will find time for some shopping tomorrow?"

"I certainly hope so," he replied. "My wife will have my head if I don't bring back an electric teakettle and a handbag from Bloomingdale's."

WE DANCED TO STANDING ovations at the Metropolitan Opera House and to rave reviews in the *Times* and the *Tribune*. Everywhere we went, we met fans, flashbulbs, waving flags, and placards of friendship. They interviewed me, along with Tatiana and Alexander, for a morning television show and called me "the fresh new face of the Bolshoi." I walked with a bounce in my step.

On the first Saturday of our New York engagement, an exotic man in a tuxedo and yellow bow tie appeared at my dressing room with a full entourage and an invitation.

"You haven't seen New York if you haven't seen it from the roof of the Saint Regis," he told me. His smile was beguiling but his eyes were hooded. He had a soft voice full of confidence, and the slimmest mustache on his upper lip. Igor, bless him, knew that my visitor was a famous singer as well as a "fellow traveler."

"He's one of us," he said in Russian. "A class warrior and a fighter for racial and social equality."

"And he wants to take me to a party?" I asked, my eyes still glued to the man's beautiful smile.

"Don't let the bourgeois suit fool you," whispered Igor. "He's a true proletariat—a banana hauler, you know."

"Lord, the whole world knows me as a damn banana-boat captain," groaned the handsome singer, who knew that a "banana" in Russian is a "banana" anywhere. Then, with the laugh and the patience of a man who had suffered worse humiliations than serenading a Russian ballerina with calypso tunes, Harry Belafonte introduced himself with his signature line. I felt my face break into a grin. He snapped his fingers and said, "Daylight's coming, but I don't want to go home." He held out his hand. "*Poshli,*" he said in lilting Russian, "let's have some fun."

And so I danced the night away on the roof of the St. Regis Hotel, while Igor snored sweetly in a corner. My date was right: the view of the city from on high was breathtaking. My head whirled at the limitless electrical grid that stretched below us on all sides; there was a pulse of connection, and I thought of Pavel's brightly networked monitor, scanning my mind like the red lights of traffic surging up and down Manhattan's avenues. Not even from the top of a Stalinscraper could Moscow compare with this busy, electrified world. I gazed upon the Chrysler and the Empire State buildings and thought that our skyscrapers, though newer than these, were ancient and hulking things: dinosaurs next to gazelles.

When daylight finally did arrive, I was cooling my feet in

the pool. Harry Belafonte talked as much as he danced and he listened as divinely as he spoke, so my English had grown wings in his company.

"Your man in the Kremlin's got too hot a temper," he was saying.

"Your man in the White House has too big an ego," I responded.

He hooted at that. "Doesn't seem to be hurting him much. My man Jack's a good man. Even if he is a stinking aristocrat. The American sort. The kind of aristocrat that makes revolutions, instead of running away from them."

"Oh. There will be revolution in America?" I asked. I was teasing, but his face was serious.

"No ma'am. There will be a long, slow fight for a better world. One where we all have the right to sit poolside. One where our politicians are as gifted as our artists."

A worn-out looking waiter arrived with two frosted glasses. Harry handed me a rum punch, light on the rum, and said, "To breakfast."

We clinked glasses and I took a sip. He leaned back on his hands and looked up at the lightening sky.

"Next time we drink punch in Havana, Svetlana. Is it a date?"

"Cuba?" I asked. "Maybe. But I think in Cuba you are not allowed?"

The singer turned and gave me his widest smile. "Oh, my dear. In Cuba I am always welcome. And the day I'm not is the day I take off the gloves."

I glanced at his hands. They were elegant indeed, but I hadn't recalled him wearing gloves.

When we arrived back at the hotel, Tatiana Bibikova was waiting in the lobby. "Let me come up to your suite, Sveta. I want to watch the television interview they taped, but my set is on the fritz." I invited her up, but inside the room we found a large potted plant where the set had been.

"Call the desk?" I asked Igor.

He did. When he hung up the phone he said "repairs."

Tatiana said, "How about the one in the bar? Can we watch it there?"

"Out of order," muttered Igor.

"*Chort*. It's like being at home," she grumbled and went back to bed.

"Come on, Igor," I wheedled, when we were alone. "I know you have your instructions. Just tell me—is it something I did? Or something one of the others did?"

"It's what the Americans did," he said simply.

"What, exactly, did they do?"

He pinched his lips with two fingers.

I controlled my exasperation. I knew better than to play my trump card: *I'm the one on call here, you piddling policeman. And if something serious is going on . . .*

"You know I will find out," I said. "You can't confiscate every newspaper, radio, and television in the city."

"No," he agreed. "But I can try."

When he had left, I paced the room, worried. I had been negligent in my "exercises." Now I'd have to make up for lost time. I set the metronome and closed the blinds, blocking out the city that had far too many minds to reveal the universal one. I tried to fathom something that might shed light on what the Americans did and whether it was something Gerasova and her intelligence colleagues had anticipated.

But instead, exhausted from a long night fending off daylight, I fell asleep.

WE WERE TOLD THE next evening. Igor's boss, the head of the KGB detail for the tour, gathered us into the lounge after the performance and briefed us.

The Americans had sent warships to blockade our allies in the Caribbean. Cuba, he said, the tiny bastion of Communist power in America's backyard, had done nothing to provoke this aggression. It was up to the Soviet Union to defend the Cuban people. At all cost.

"Make no mistake, comrades. The stakes are high. The Americans are arming for invasion. President Kennedy has escalated the military to DEFCON 3 and is broadcasting his warmongering to the American people on television as we speak. Comrade Khrushchev and the Soviet people want only peace. Our ambassador is working to talk sense into the Americans. He is now in the city, standing alongside our Cuban allies in the chambers of the United Nations. Your job, comrades, is to reinforce those diplomatic efforts."

"You want us to talk sense into the Americans?" asked Ilya.

The KGB-*shnik* was not amused.

"We want you, as always, to talk very little to the Americans. Now, more than ever, the civilian population must be regarded as enemy elements. Sign their programs. Smile for their cameras. But say nothing whatsoever about developments in Cuba."

We were dismissed.

Alone in my room, I considered what this meant. Had the top secret operation gone awry? Or was this development a surprise, unrelated to Gerasova's plans? Was I in New York to be close to Washington or to be close to the alleged rockets in Cuba? Or had I failed a very obvious test?

Next time in Havana.

Harry Belafonte had mentioned Cuba and I had giggled like a punch-drunk girl. I should have listened to my "fellow traveler" more closely. Because the gloves, it seemed, were clearly off.

I stood at the giant window. I looked out on the stillness of Manhattan's east side, which lacked the bright lights and neon signs of the bustling center. With my face pressed against the glass, I could just make out the silhouette of the United Nations headquarters. It soared upward over an empty stretch of river— a thin, white tower, lit up on every floor, even at this late hour. I stood for a long time, my forehead against the glass, trying to tap into some repository of the psychosphere. But I couldn't read the thoughts of a universal mind; I could only hear the confusion of the United Nations. I concentrated on the sympathetic vibrations of words untranslated: the cries of small nations trampled under the boots of rival superpowers; the collective objections of unheard voices, drowned out by the whine of missiles. I heard the muffled entreaty of strangers united only by duress.

I dutifully took out my notebooks and recorded what I heard. When I was done I reread my report. There was no clear message.

I dreamt that night of Harry Belafonte, and Cuban cigars the size of rockets.

AT NOON THE NEXT day I was standing at yet another hotel window looking out over yet another American river. The United Nations, scene of frantic negotiations to prevent a nuclear escalation in Cuba, was far away in New York. But the White House was just a mile down Pennsylvania Avenue.

We were scheduled to perform the next night. I would dance Juliet, the role I had dreamt of for as long as I could remember. They said the line for tickets stretched for blocks and blocks. I would have thrilled to hear it, but something told me that the public's curiosity had as much to do with the rising temperature of the Cold War as with my Juliet. The official word from management was sanguine: *Do not concern yourself with political propaganda. Focus on a performance that will demonstrate the Soviet Union's artistic and peace-loving values . . .*

But I knew that there was much more at stake than the Bolshoi's reputation.

There was a knock at the door.

Igor, looking grim, told me to get my coat.

I was being summoned to the Soviet Embassy.

The truth hit me harder than any psychic vision. *Unless things change*, Gerasova had said. Things had certainly changed. What good was mind reading when everyone's mind was on the same thing: Mutual assured destruction?

From the backseat of a car careening through the streets of a neighborhood called Foggy Bottom I struggled to dispel the fog in my brain. I plumbed the psychosphere, begging it for a sign that would show me how to protect the *rodina*. Or, at least, how to protect myself—from accusations that I had failed.

I was ushered into the Soviet Embassy without delay or fanfare. I followed Igor down busy corridors full of tension and cigarette smoke. We came to a small room where he left me alone with a pair of chairs, a heavy desk, and a portrait of Premier Nikita Khrushchev on the wall. Eventually the door opened and in walked Natalia Davydovna. I knew that her arrival was bad news, but I still wanted to throw my arms around her.

"Good evening, Comrade Gerasova," I said.

"Oh, but it isn't—is it, Prima?"

She sat in the chair opposite mine.

"So. We find ourselves at the center of an international crisis."

I hung my head. The weight of my failure was heavy. I had danced so well, but I had been asleep. The top secret operation, despite Gerasova's hopes, was no longer secret. Even my colleagues, blindfolded by their minders and made deaf and mute by their ignorance of English, could see and hear the truth: Khrushchev had placed live missiles in Cuba, aimed at Washington, D.C., and President Kennedy was prepared to retaliate. Nuclear war was imminent.

"So it's true?" I whispered. "We will annihilate each other? Over an island?"

"The politics are complicated. But the rules are simple. Like chess. Move and countermove." Gerasova sighed. "Do you play chess, Prima?"

"I'm Russian, Comrade Gerasova. Of course I play chess."

She frowned. "You weren't trained to be a chess master. I know that. You were trained to be a mind reader, a psychosoldier of the *rodina*. Right now the universal mind is about as clear as mud. I trust you have also come to that conclusion."

I thought of the static chatter coming from the United

Nations. A murky babble—neither universal nor united. Mud. I thought of my easy night with Harry Belafonte, who had not been afraid to speak his mind. It had felt wonderful—this sudden revelation of the obvious: It wasn't Americans who were our enemies. It was America.

Outside the window I heard children playing. I wondered how far we were from the White House. I wondered where the former ambassador, a man who knew Russians better than most and who chuckled diplomatically at Khrushchev's barbed comments, was now. Was he sitting poolside with a Soviet diplomat, a rum punch in one hand and a nuclear suitcase in the other?

I knew the answer. "Negotiations are not going well."

"That's just it," she said. "There are no negotiations. The clamor is too loud. There are too many intermediaries. Neither Kennedy nor Khrushchev can afford to look weak. Neither can be seen to be inviting reasonable talk. Because reasonable talk at DEFCON 2 has to include standing down."

I closed my eyes against the ticking in my head. I heard the whirl of a waltz and the ambassador's broad voice: *You must be prepared to be the butt in order to save face . . .*

Gerasova tapped the arm of her chair. "So. Tell me, Prima. What can you do for us in this predicament, I wonder?"

It was a sincere question, but I was at a loss. The KGB was asking me what I could do to prevent nuclear war. It was absurd. I had improvised once before, in Berlin. But to what end? I had saved no one's skin but my own that night, though it hurt to admit it. I shook my head.

"I can dance, Comrade Gerasova. That is what I do best."

"It is," she conceded. "But it's not enough, I fear."

I looked at the portrait of our leader on the wall—Nikita Sergeevich Khrushchev in a rare moment of silent statesmanship. He wore three stars on his chest and a civilian suit and tie. He looked . . . reasonable. Was Khrushchev a reasonable man? I thought so. Hadn't he denounced the Gulag? Hadn't he declared the end of tyranny and given us an explanation for why we had cowered under Stalin? Hadn't he agreed to visit America and consider the possibility that we might live in peace? We had all heard his toneless jokes and also his raging threats: *We will bury you!* But not with missiles, surely. Because didn't our leader also understand the basis of a great civilization? Didn't he know how to win by scoring easy, obvious points? Hadn't he stood among Hollywood's most glamorous stars and asked: *Now I have a question for you—which country has the best ballet?*

I rose and approached the portrait. *Our country has the best ballet.*

"What if it is?" I said. "What if it is enough?"

I clasped my hands together—Juliet's signature. Juliet clasps her hands in the crypt that has become her lover's tomb. She clasps them in prayer that her Romeo be returned, that fate intervene and undo the damage done by a quarrel made mortal, that the miscommunication be reversed. Now I stood in the Soviet Embassy in Washington, D.C., and clasped my hands in prayer—that the miscommunication between our countries would be reversed and that all the capitalist Capulets and all the Montagues of Moscow be saved.

By the best ballet.

"What if it were enough, just to dance?" I asked again.

Gerasova looked at me blankly.

"This chess game—isn't it better played when there are only two players? Face to face? Without onlookers and second-guessers and the muddy messages of . . ."

"The United Nations?" finished Gerasova.

"Politics," I suggested.

"The press," agreed Gerasova.

"And isn't it true that no single player can, in fact, win? Don't they both need to win this game? Aren't the stakes that high?" I thought of the maestro—both executioner and executed.

"A draw," nodded Gerasova. "A deliberate draw. A win-win, as opposed to a lose-lose. Yes, Prima. That's exactly it. Perhaps your diplomatic skills are sharper than your psychic gifts. But how does your dancing . . ."

I sat down, leaned forward; my answer was ready.

"When Juliet and Romeo, ostensible enemies, need a sanctuary, a place to promise an alliance, where do they go?"

Gerasova opened her mouth to speak, but nothing came out.

"If President Kennedy wants to talk peace, if our Nikita needs to make promises that no one in Moscow can hear . . . well, we need to find them a friar's crypt."

I saw it beginning to dawn on her, but I was in a hurry: "A private staging of *Romeo and Juliet* for the president of the United States," I said.

"Attended also by Khrushchev's personal emissary," said Gerasova, understanding. "With no press or secretaries or third parties."

"No ambassadors. No thoughts to saving face."

We considered the strange solution in silence.

Finally she stood. "I will propose it at once. Can you be ready in three hours?"

TWENTY
CRYPT

The media, entranced by the story of a Bolshoi star giving a private goodwill performance at the White House, made it easy. A mob of reporters awaited me as I emerged from the limousine, a stylish fur draped over Juliet's thin shift. Flashbulbs snapped wildly as I recited my prepared speech, with Igor translating:

"It is a great honor to be invited to dance for the first family of the United States. The Bolshoi Ballet speaks the language of the Soviet Union and of all classless societies, just as proudly as the Kremlin does. But dance is the universal language, understood by all peoples. Tonight, we are not enemies, whatever the political differences between our countries. Let me say no more about my proud Motherland, nor about the generosity of the American people who have welcomed us warmly in their great cities. Let me instead speak in the language of dance, which is better understood."

A swarm of secret servicemen swept me into the West Wing. Igor and one other inconspicuous KGB-*shnik* melted into our coterie. Once inside, the second agent stepped forward to shake my hand. He was no mere secret policeman. He removed his hat, his dark glasses, his false nose and mustache. He was First Deputy Premier Surykov, Khrushchev's right-hand man. His disguise was decent, but it was my choreographed distraction that had gotten him discreetly into the White House.

"I look forward to watching you dance," he said. And then he was hustled away.

I was led in the opposite direction, down a different hallway. My thoughts were on Juliet and the music Prokofiev wrote for her, so I was surprised to discover that I was picking up memories from the halls of the West Wing: *tears, treaties, scandals, shouts, feasts, and fires.* They came fast and furious. I was walking through the ghost history of our enemy. And suddenly, in the flesh, the first lady was walking with me as well.

I dropped into a quick curtsy. "Good evening, Mrs. Kennedy."

Jacqueline Kennedy was immaculate, from head to toe. Her hair was styled and her dress was stylish, just like in all the photographs and newsreels. But I couldn't help noticing the asymmetry of her famous face. The American president's wife was a beauty. But her face fought perfection. I liked that.

She took me by the arm and all the aides seemed to disappear. There was no one to translate her words, but I understood them. And I understood their subtext.

"I have been looking forward to the Bolshoi's visit for so long. I was simply devastated by the prospect that this . . . crisis . . . would interfere. I'm terribly pleased—no, I'm relieved—that a . . . solution has been found. It's a great honor to have a private viewing, Miss Kravshina."

And she was gone.

I was led down a staircase. Another phalanx of secret service waited. One of them, a woman, led me into a room to search me. I handed over a small bag holding my slippers and Juliet's "happy dagger."

"Not real," I assured her, but the woman confiscated it. Maybe tonight Juliet would live to see another day. I sat down and changed my shoes for the slippers.

Another corridor and another flight of stairs . . . and at last I emerged in the space where I was to perform a prelude to secret talks. It was a room three times longer than it was wide: Friar Lawrence's crypt was the presidential bowling alley. I made my way down the lanes to a small makeshift stage. Someone, a rare American who understood the needs of artists, had readied a small box of rosin. I rubbed the bottoms of my slippers in the sticky granules.

"When you are ready, Miss Kravshina," echoed a disembodied voice. A single light shone down on my stage. In the darkness I could see the shifting figures of a small audience.

"The music?" I asked tentatively. Then I remembered: I was facilitating world peace, for God's sake. "Act One, Scene Two—the Balcony," I directed in the voice of a true diva.

I took my position as the room filled with the music of Prokofiev: an organ introducing a girl lost in admiration of her own hand, which had recently been kissed by a masked man. I stepped onto my invisible balcony, beckoned by the sunrise and the strings. I was demure, a maiden seducing unseen admirers. I used every tender gesture in my *port de bras* to call out for my Romeo, though I knew he would not reveal himself. Not tonight. Tonight I would have to reject our families' animosity entirely on my own. I beckoned, I promised, my body was the bud of youth and passion. I danced the entire love scene solo, throwing myself into the same chase and embrace that I had rehearsed for weeks with Alexander, who was probably sitting at the hotel bar with the rest of the company, wondering if we would end our tour under a mushroom cloud.

As the music—Prokofiev's beautiful music—raced toward dawn, I lost myself in the prayer that I had only briefly considered in the Soviet Embassy. I knelt, hands clasped, knowing that even if I never danced Juliet again, she was now mine. I closed my eyes and prayed that my Motherland would protect all her wards. All her Oksanas and Alexanders and Sashas and Mishas and Vityas and Goshas. I felt a love for my *rodina* stronger than any Romeo could warrant.

When the clarinet promised undying love for the oboe, I stood. The sun, somewhere, was rising in the east, but I still had to mind the gutters of my unlikely stage. The love scene was over. I struck a final pose—Juliet's impossibly optimistic greeting of a new day, *a future brighter, more cheerful*.

Where there should have been the applause of a full house, there was only silence. In that silence I recognized a more personal emptiness. I understood that my future would never be bright enough to reveal the truth about my father. I would have to live without knowing where his innocence ended and his guilt began. But I would never succumb to the despair of Juliet. I would dance to the end. Without a happy dagger as an excuse.

Letting my arms fall, I took three steps toward my invisible audience. A single rose hurtled from the darkness and landed at my feet. I dropped to one knee and took the flower. I heard the first clap. Then another. I rose and a child emerged into the spotlight's edge. She was so like Oksana when we first met that tears sprung to my eyes. The girl gazed at me shyly and then looked over her shoulder to where her mother was walking serenely down the bowling lane. I bowed my head to the first lady. When I looked up, there was a third figure at the end of the alley. The president was approaching me, applauding.

He said, "That was mah-velous."

His smile was a struggle. His eyes were those of a boxer in his thirteenth round of a fight.

"I can't tell you how indebted we are for this diversion. But I must ask your forbearance." He stepped forward and took my hand in his. "You see we've only just begun. We need more time. Would you be so good as to indulge us?"

I nodded, unsure. A familiar voice clarified the situation.

"Negotiations take a long time, Svetlana," said Natalia Davydovna. "And you've taken up nine precious minutes. Mr. Kennedy and Comrade Surykov have agreed to continue talks as long as there is reasonable cover. So you will dance the ballet in its entirety. Then you will dress, exit, and wave to the pack of reporters so that they can go home with their story."

"Of course," I said, wondering how I was going to improvise an entire two-hour ballet on my own in the basement of the White House. Then I considered the much harder task of the two men who hoped to prevent a nuclear war in the span of Shakespeare's tragic love story. I curtsied to the president and his wife. I spoke the words that Lydia Timofeevna once taught the disgraced children of Orphanage #36 and that my own Oksana had quoted for weeks afterward:

"The two hours of our stage, if you with patient ears attend, our toil shall strive to mend."

Jack Kennedy turned to Comrade Gerasova for a translation.

"Not a problem, Mr. President. We wish you luck."

MY PRIVATE PERFORMANCE, CAREFULLY choreographed to distract a press corps intent on chronicling an apocalyptic standoff between Khrushchev and Kennedy over the nuclear missiles in Cuba, never made the paper. There was much bigger news: a US–Soviet accord to end the blockade of the island and remove all foreign missiles from Cuban soil.

Igor read the headlines aloud in my room.

"CRISIS OVER. ARMAGEDDON AVERTED. REASON PREVAILS AND WORLD SIGHS IN RELIEF."

"And the Moscow papers?" I asked.

"IMPERIALISTS COWER BEFORE SOVIET MIGHT," he said. "*Pravda* has a cartoon of Khrushchev as a ship captain, charting a course for peace."

"Or a hasty retreat from the Caribbean," I muttered.

Igor rebuked me. "Cuba remains ours, Svetlana Evgenievna, make no mistake. Havana is the Communist anchor in North America. It is a foothold the likes of which America will never have in Asia. Nikita took care of that—he booted them out of Turkey. They don't write that in the *Washington Post*, but you can be sure. This was a quid pro quo."

"I'm sure you are right," I said. "A win-win. An eye for an eye. Tit for tat. All's well that ends well. Unless 'tit for tat' means 'you kill my mate and I kill yours,' in which case all you've got is a dead Mercutio, a dead Tybalt, and a pair of dead star-crossed lovers."

I was still in bed, exhausted after a particularly emotional performance. There was another, more public, performance scheduled for tonight. One that was apt to be a huge celebration, given the news. I rose and pulled open the curtains, revealing the Potomac River sparkling and unbothered by politics.

"I have the whole day free till the performance this evening, Igor. Shall we go shopping?"

I DIDN'T SEE GERASOVA again until we were on the plane on our way back to Moscow. Ten days had passed since the resolution of the Cuban Missile Crisis. Each of those ten days had been a lovefest. All America, from Washington to Chicago to Pow-keepsie, had showered the Bolshoi Ballet with affection and posters and flowers. I had received a personal note from the White House.

We were over the Atlantic Ocean when I heard her voice.

"Olga dear, could I have this seat?"

Olga took her things and moved farther back so that Natalia Davydovna could sit by me.

"How are you feeling, Svetlana?"

"Never better, Comrade Gerasova. And you?"

She frowned. "I've been thinking about your Washington exposure."

I didn't like the sound of that. Exposure was bad. Like smallpox was bad. Like contagion was bad. Had I become contagious?

"I simply didn't anticipate it," continued Gerasova.

"Anticipate what?"

"The measure of your success," she said simply.

I wondered if she regretted it. I wondered if being a spymaster was like being a prima, and if new talent—even talent encouraged—was a threat.

"You are to be commended, Agent Prima," she said in a voice so casual it went under the radar more smoothly than a whisper. "Tell me what I can do to reward your service."

It was as unexpected as my success. As unbelievable as my spymaster's helplessness that day in the embassy when she asked how I could fix our very big problem. My mind swam with the possibilities, but there was only one answer. My heart was full of gratitude when I said: "Let me dance. Let me serve the *rodina* as a ballerina, not as a soldier. Let me be a prima, not Agent Prima."

INTERLUDE
VORKUTA 2015

"*What? You didn't know?*"

Svetlana Dukovskaya stops fiddling with the sugar bowl and addresses the young woman gaping at her from across the table. "You didn't know Khrushchev and Kennedy played chess with nuclear missiles? And I was nineteen. You didn't know about that . . . in Cuba?"

Lana shakes her head with a laugh. "No. No, it's not that. I mean yes, we were taught something of the sort."

She has gotten better at following her grandmother's story. She has learned, over the course of twelve hours, how to hear the thread of Svetlana's hidden history unwind. She's learned to listen. To hold her questions. To wait for the wandering words to settle down like a cat on a rug, sometimes for a short snooze. But they still surprise her—these moments when the old woman suddenly notices that she has been speaking aloud and that someone is listening. The moments when she addresses her granddaughter directly—to be sure she has understood.

"You didn't know that we almost went . . ." She makes a comical face of annihilation. Wide eyes, puckered lips, chipmunk cheeks. "Boom!"

"*Yes, I know about the eleventh-hour-in-the-nick-of-time resolution of the Cuban Missile Crisis,*" says Lana. "*But none of our history books mentioned* Romeo and Juliet *in the basement of the White House.*"

The old woman flaps her hand dismissively.

"*No. They took that chapter out. Or they took me out of that chapter. Just like my father . . .*"

Lana wants to go back to the plane. To Svetlana's request to be set free from the KGB. She wants to know if the spymaster agreed to let her Agent Prima go. But she is patient.

"*They kept it secret, that one,*" Svetlana continues. "*Even when they started dragging out . . . other things. When they started digging around. Digging up Camelot. Oh, they found drugs and . . . women. They found Marilyn Monroe and the mob. But they didn't find me. If they had, they would have said that the president of the United States was diddling dancers while the world nearly went . . . poof!*"

She makes the face again, this time with her fingers raining fallout.

"*But they didn't find me. Not me. No, not me—that* babushka *on the grassy knoll, yes. Not me.*"

"*How . . .*" begins Lana, looking around the cluttered room that she assumes marks the sum total square space of her grandmother's world since before the Cold War ended. "*How do you know about the grassy knoll? How do you know about all the Kennedy revelations?*"

"*The Internet, of course.*"

"*The Internet.*"

"*Da, dochka. We may be in Vorkuta, but there are computers in the library.*"

Lana leans back in her chair and tries to order her thoughts. There are so many questions. But her grandmother beats her to it:

"*Where's Marina?*"

Exactly, Lana thinks. Hours have passed, years have passed, since her grandmother began to talk about what she *remembers, and still there is no Marina Dukovskaya. Svetlana Kravshina's story was fascinating, but what about her daughter, Marina?*

"When did you marry Viktor Dukovsky?"

"When he agreed to be my husband."

"So—after Washington, after America—did you break with the KGB? Or did you tell Viktor about Lubyanka?"

Lana gets no answer.

"Is that why you married him? A fresh start? A new name? One not associated with Lubyanka 1717? A name with no Enemies of the People in its history?"

She sees something cross her grandmother's face. Something between confusion and alarm.

"Where is Marina? Where is my daughter?"

"I'll fetch her," Lana says quickly. "I will tell her to come. Would you like that, babushka?"

Svetlana Dukovskaya doesn't answer. She just stands and clears the coffee cups from the table. She is humming—Prokofiev's theme for Juliet.

Lana picks up her bag and finds her phone. She's missed several calls. She steps out onto the tiny balcony off the kitchen. Her grandmother lives in a shabby, mid-century construction, typical of the hundreds of thousands of residences that went up during the Khrushchev years, giving so many families their own four walls in which to keep secrets. Plus a balcony—usually used as a storeroom for marinated cabbage and pickled tomatoes.

Vorkuta's a long way from Verona, Lana thinks as she navigates the balcony full of provisions for a long Siberian winter.

She calls the hotel where her troupe is staying and leaves a message that she will be staying on in Vorkuta.

Next she sends her mother a message: Call me immediately.

Lana tucks her phone into her pocket and breathes the clean air of a dirty city trapped in a stunning wilderness. It's quiet in the kitchen behind her. She imagines her grandmother, sitting alone at that table, pickling cabbage on the balcony, navigating the streets of Vorkuta alone . . . for thirty years. Then she imagines Svetlana Dukovskaya, the library's most regular patron, exploring three decades' worth of secrets and lies on the Internet. Bookmarking the sites of KGB and CIA archives. Following the news of the Bolshoi Ballet. She would know, then, that her daughter Marina had joined the Bolshoi. And that Marina's daughter, a girl called Lana, had as well, before quitting it to start her own troupe, which had danced for the people of Vorkuta last night.

Lana imagines her grandmother clapping her hands in delight. Finally.

She steps back into the kitchen and finds the old woman slumped in the chair with her head tipped too far back.

"Babushka!" she cries in alarm.

But the old woman jerks upright and wipes her mouth with the back of her hand. "Where are we? Where were we?"

Lana breathes in relief. There is still time. Still time for her mother, Svetlana's daughter, to come and ask the most important question of all.

"Did you want to be a mother?"

ACT FOUR
PAWN
MOSCOW, 1964–1970

TWENTY-ONE
MARINA

It was the sort of winter that made you think nothing would ever grow again. The snow would never melt, the birds would never sing, and nothing would ever burst blooming from the cold, cold ground.

I looked out the window at the leaden sky and the evergreens whistling unheard beyond the thick glass pane. I knew it was hormones, all out of whack, that made me despondent. Hormones and the melancholy of midwinter. You couldn't ignore these things. Just like you couldn't ignore the fact that I was lying in the same hospital where I had watched my mother waste away and where I had first met Viktor.

"Five weeks," said the nurse. "Should I arrange for the specialist?"

My grief overflowed. I looked down at my belly covered in its hospital gown. It showed no sign of the child I couldn't ignore. I was pregnant. I had won half the solos of the season and now I had this tiny, helpless partner. Helpless and already wreaking havoc. A tear slid down my cheek and I brushed it away angrily.

"Svetlana Evgenievna," said the nurse. She was kind, deferential. She knew that she was dealing with a star ballerina. But that made the question all the more rhetorical. "When do you want to schedule the procedure? There is no need to wait."

"I want to wait."

The nurse began to speak but I cut her off.

"I want to wait."

She took her pen from her pocket and tapped my chart.

"You are still very young," she noted. "You have at least ten more years . . ."

"Please send in the young man outside."

The nurse nodded. She stepped out and beckoned Viktor into the room. She closed the door behind him. We were alone.

He thrust his hands into his pockets. "So?"

I burst into tears.

He crossed the room in a single step. He climbed onto the bed and took me in his arms. I wept. I soaked his shirt. I streaked my mascara. I sobbed into the crook of his neck. He spoke softly, repeating himself. I watched the evergreens swaying in time to his voice.

"I'm sorry it happened, Sveta. But you've been through much worse. It's a simple thing—in and out. Hell, my mother's had three and my cousin had her first last month. She'll come with you. With *us*. I'm sorry, Sveta. But it will be simple. You'll be back on your feet in a day. Back on your toes in a week. I'm sorry, Sveta."

He wiped my tear-stained face with his sleeve and kissed my forehead. He licked his lips, as though my sadness tasted good. He leaned in to kiss my mouth but I stopped him with a finger on his lips. So he kissed my finger.

"No."

"What no, Sveta?"

I traced his lips. I could feel the muscles in my neck quiver. There was too much sadness, too much emotion. Too many hormones. I frowned, trying to keep more tears away, but my face crumpled and they came. I needed to say what I had to say, so I said it—nearly unintelligible beneath my sobbing.

"My mother left me and they said it would be better if she had never, poor dear, but they were wrong and she was wrong and it would be wrong to leave and I won't because she didn't but she did . . . she did leave me and I won't. I will be a good mother, Viktor. A good mother, do you hear me? I won't wait. I won't give up and I never have and they can't tell me to wait. They can't tell me what to do with my body. This won't stop me. They won't stop me. I will have this baby and be a good mother and I will dance for ten more years, twenty more years. I won't do it, Vitya. I'm going to do it, Vitya."

And all the while he smoothed my hair like it was the flank of a wild horse and said, "Okay Sveta, okay."

I pulled away from him and he said it again.

"Okay Svetlana. You will be this child's mother. A good mother. And I will be . . . a good father."

I saw it in his face. The question of whether "I will be" was the same as "I am."

I hid against his chest and cried.

"It's okay, Sveta. It's okay, calm down."

"It's not okay," I said. "It's not okay, but I will make it okay." I stood and pulled off the hospital gown. I stood before him naked, vulnerable, and fierce. "I control my body," I said. "I'm in control of my body."

I saw him wince. He still didn't know that I had once let others try to control my mind. He was still thinking only about my body, over which he had no control.

How cruel I was.

"Sveta, am I . . . ?"

"Are you . . . ?" I prompted.

How cruel I was.

"Am I the father?"

I looked to the window and the bowed trees. The memory was sudden and staggering: *Viktor Dukovsky on a bench under a poplar tree, with all the time and love in the world.* A single howl slipped through the window and I slid into Vitya's arms. My mind cleared. My body relaxed. His embrace was my home.

"I want you to be my husband."

It was like the relief of spring. In midwinter.

MARINA VIKTOROVNA DUKOVSKAYA WAS born eight months later in the same hospital. She arrived right on time, weighing seven-and-a-half pounds. She had light eyes and dark hair. When they put her in my arms I traced the cowlick on the back of her head for hours. And I searched her eyes for flecks of gold.

At home on Cobbler's Lane, Viktor took dozens of pictures of the baby—Marina yawning, Marina sleeping, Marina nursing, baby Marya howling. When she finally slept, he snuggled up next to me with the photo album from our wedding.

I had worn a white minidress and high leather boots. The camera caught me midstride, as I climbed the stairs to the marriage office. My legs rippled muscle and my arms were taut. My face glowed. There was no trace of the freak-out my pregnancy had caused. There was also still no trace of the baby that we had not yet named Marina.

"I'm going to get that dress on within two weeks," I vowed now.

The next photo was of us standing in front of the registrar's desk: Oksana holding my flowers as I signed the marriage license; Gosha at Viktor's side, frozen in a joke. At the wedding banquet there was a laden table covered in a cloth declaring *Soviet Space Glory!* and a larger group—friends of Vitya's and my colleagues from the theater. There I was, held aloft by the Bolshoi's leading men and striking the pose of Kitri without her Spanish fan—a go-go gypsy. There was Vitya with his father, six inches shorter but almost as winsome as his son. Vitya's mother, a high-spirited woman with a smear of my lipstick on her cheek. Gosha with a ballerina on each arm. Oksana making a toast, her eyes intentionally crossed, silly and sweet. More snapshots, in and out of focus, of the best decision I had ever made.

"What was her name?"

Vitya was pointing to a guest, nearly out of the frame, but easily identifiable in the corner of our banquet table. I had nearly forgotten that I had invited her—even sought her out to ask her—to celebrate my marriage. Hormones, I had supposed then. A misplaced sense of maternal instinct. I hadn't seen her since.

"Natalia Davydovna," I answered carefully. "Natalia Davydovna Gerasova, a friend of my mother's."

He was silent for a moment. He nudged my hand to uncover her face, her half face. "Yes. Gerasova. She was in the news recently. 'Released of her duties.'"

He might have felt me stiffen. He might not have. But he asked, "What were her duties? Who was she?"

I sat up straighter in the bed. I covered the photo with my palm, casually, but instinctively.

"She was with the Ministry of Culture, I believe."

He grunted. "They usually don't bother reporting apparatchiks, is all. She must have been close to Khrushchev, and they only just now got rid of her. Or maybe Nikita has been making trouble out at the *dacha*. Maybe he's been rabble rousing from retirement."

I looked across the room at the crib with my daughter sleeping in it and felt calm. My baby was safe. Khrushchev had come and gone. His successor, a stiff old man named Brezhnev, would come and go. Let Natalia Davydovna, also, come . . . and let her go. They were insignificant. I had served the Motherland. Now I was a mother. And my baby was safe. My daughter was mine. Nothing would part us.

"She had ties to the KGB," I added. I wasn't sure why I said it. Except maybe because he lay there, long and lovely with the camera tucked under his arm, and I thought of all the photos Vitya would take of Marina, of us, of our family. We would fill this album and more. Natalia Davydovna Gerasova, who had allowed me to walk away from Lubyanka, got just one photo. I could allow her that.

Vitya said nothing for a long time. Finally he said, "Not any-more she doesn't."

And then he flipped the page.

We laughed at the next photo: Vitya on his knees, offering me a token of his undying affection—a Chaika vacuum cleaner, the first we had ever seen.

"Where is it, by the way?" he asked.

"Under the bed," I said.

We were still in a single room in the Bolshoi *kommunalka* with no carpets. Perhaps one day the odd bullet-shaped appara-tus would be something we could not live without, but for now we got much more use out of the wedding present Gosha had given us—a record player.

"Think maybe we could use the Chaika as a nursing pump?" he asked, squeezing my breast. I dropped the album on the floor and we wrestled, laughing, until we woke up the baby. I got her up and nursed her, swatting Viktor's hands away all the while. Then we wrapped Marya up warmly, popped her in the pram, and went for a long walk past the theater and out onto the bou-levard ring.

I felt free. I felt so free. I hoped that Natalia Davydovna, "relieved of her duties," felt the same exhilarating sense of lib-eration.

TWENTY-TWO
DYADYA GOSHA

Marina was already walking and talking when she met her Uncle Gosha for the first time.

"Dya-dya," I said, holding her in my arms. "Say, 'Dya-dya Go-sha.'"

She tucked her face into my neck.

"Shy," shrugged Gosha. He parted my hair where it fell over the baby's face and feigned surprise. The baby giggled. She sat up in my arms and grabbed Gosha's finger. I heard the sharp intake of his breath.

"Her eyes," he said.

"They usually turn after eighteen months," I said. I stage-whispered into Marina's ear, "Uncle Gosha. Say, Dyadya Gosha . . ." She did.

Gosha had been away for a long time, nearly two years. "The south," he had said during a rare telephone call. "Some work in Donetsk. Good work." I had just sucked my teeth, letting him hear what I thought of this "good work" in eastern Ukraine—a famous den of banditry and the home of a mafia that squeezed more money out of the soccer rackets than all the region's coal mines. Gosha had bragged of massive profits and luscious Party boss wives who had to be entertained while their husbands were at the football tournaments. But here he was, and I saw only threadbare jeans and the shiftiness of a man dissatisfied. I didn't know if I was repulsed or rueful, but when Marina grabbed onto her Uncle Gosha's finger, I hoped it hurt.

"You were gone a long time," I said.

"Couldn't be helped."

The memory of the last time I had seen him was still raw. I had relived it many times. It was a bitter night, still winter, though it was the premiere of a new ballet—*The Rite of Spring*. I had danced the role of the Chosen One, a sacrificial virgin. It was only a week after the wedding and it was no secret that I had not been typecast. In another week the costume would not hide what everyone in the theater already knew, and I would have to leave the stage until the baby was born. That night, after the premiere, I had done it again—fled my fans and left Viktor waiting in vain as I sped away with Gosha behind the wheel.

Georgi hadn't come to the performance, my debut as Svetlana Dukovskaya. He had said he had no interest in seeing me "danced to death" as the Chosen One. I had snapped at him, saying he was resentful of my success. He had assured me that he was in no way resentful. Only "curious, and yes—concerned," about my choices. He said he was sure I would be a wonderful mother and I thanked him. He said he was sure I would be an unhappy wife and I cried. He said he never wanted to see me unhappy; I said he was partly to blame; he asked me what that meant; I refused to say.

We had gone around and around in circles. Parked, the whole time, outside Kursky Station. Finally, close to midnight, Gosha handed me the keys to his car. He was boarding the 00:12 to Krasnodar, he said. I scoffed. I said he would be back in a week. I said I didn't drive, anyway.

"You've always been the driver, Svetlana," he had said.

Then he took a small bag from the backseat and crossed the street to the station. He didn't look back. I waited until the train's whistle was gone and then I drove very slowly back to Cobbler's Lane. In the morning Viktor ran down three flights of stairs in his pajamas to move the car, which I had left in the middle of the street, blocking traffic.

"I missed you," I said now, remembering the long, low whistle of Gosha leaving us. Leaving me.

Viktor came barreling into the room. We had moved into a two-room apartment just a week earlier and Vitya was still ferrying records from Cobbler's Lane and from the cellar at his parents' place.

"The prodigal uncle," he boomed. He dropped the load of records and spread his arms to embrace Gosha, nearly catching Marina's head with his elbow as he did. I moved to the window and watched them size each other up.

"Viktor, old man."

"Gosha, you goat."

"Congratulations, friend."

"What? On my double-weighted ball and chain?"

Viktor had his arm around Gosha's shoulders. He beamed at me and I smiled back. I cut my eyes at Gosha, whose expression was harder to read.

He was cleaned up. His hair was cropped close and his face was freshly shaven. But in this room, Georgi Levshik was the "old man." After years of affected world-weariness, he had finally grown into it. His maturity, like his worn leather jacket and twice-broken nose, became him. And it humbled me. I suddenly felt not young and beautiful—but silly and shallow. I wanted to know what he was thinking. What he thought of our new flat with its balcony and view of the river, of my happy home and healthy child. But I couldn't ask.

"Perfect," Gosha said . . . as though I had.

He pulled a pack of cigarettes from his pocket.

"Outside, you bum," said Viktor, leading him onto the balcony that overlooked the river. I watched them go and then took Marya into the bedroom. When I came back out, the men were in the kitchen. There was a bottle on the table. I joined them in a celebratory toast and sat wordlessly as Gosha spoke vaguely about "promising connections," "export deals," "serious players," and "seasonal business."

"Will you stay in Moscow now, Gosha?" I asked after a time.

He shrugged. "I've lost my resident pass. I can slum it for a bit, but you know—I've become accustomed to a certain lifestyle." He grinned and poured out another shot of vodka. "It includes soft beds and softer women. I'm not sure Moscow suits me anymore."

"Well, don't look to us to provide the ladies," said Viktor. "We never go out, on account of the baby. And Svet's girlfriends have more muscle than you and me both, brother. They only look like gossamer twigs. That said, consider our sofa your bed. It's new. We'll throw in a quilt as well, right Svet?"

Gosha turned his tawny eyes on me.

"Of course."

When the baby cried I sent Vitya to fetch her. I picked two cigarettes from Gosha's pack and jerked my head to the balcony. It was dark out. And cold. Gosha wrapped his jacket over my shoulders. I bent to his lighter, but after two puffs I flicked the cigarette out into the air. We watched the glow of its ember arc, an urban shooting star. Across the river the red star on top of the Stalinscraper held steady.

"Remember the night when you showed me the back entrance to that building?" I asked. "I had never been inside before. It seemed like the most impossible dream of luxury. We ran across the foyer and sent all the lifts to the top floor at once. You remember?"

Gosha nodded. "New Year's, 1959."

"They've promised me a flat there. On the eighth floor." I paused but he didn't react. "Five rooms. And a space in the garage."

"You'll be needing a driver, then," he said.

"I can drive myself."

I pulled my windblown hair back and tied it in a knot. We could hear Marya's muffled prattle inside. And Viktor, singing to his daughter. We didn't move.

"Where have you really been?" I whispered.

He took a long drag. "Krasnodar. Then Donetsk for a time. Kazan. I had a good spell that took me to Leningrad. I was living large. But I trusted the wrong sonofabitch and they put the screws on him, and the next thing I know I've got a situation with two possible outcomes, both of them bad."

I reached out and took the cigarette from his hand. I took one puff and then sent it, too, over the balcony. "Which did you choose?"

"Eight and a half months in Butyrskaya Prison."

I sighed. "You've been in Butyrskaya for eight months. You've been a half mile away for eight months."

He shot me an unreadable glance. "It was a hell of a lot better than the alternative."

I waited.

"Police informant," he explained. I couldn't help hearing the old accusation in his tone: that once upon a time I had chosen that route—cooperating with the authorities. It didn't matter that the information I had passed on had nothing to do with criminals, bootleggers, deviants, or "seasonal business." Georgi didn't know, he couldn't know, that I had never truly been a successful informant. That the thing I had hoped to find in the slippery psychosphere—the truth about my father—had remained elusive. Some pasts were secret, some were redacted; my father's was just a portal to other pasts—ones that I could only understand as shadows of my own.

Gosha didn't know that the only useful information I had ever disclosed was that the world is full of contradictory visions.

"Well. You're free now," I said. "Like me. You've paid, now you're free to do as you like."

He turned to face me. "We're never free, Svetlana. We live in the Soviet Union."

Through the glass doors of the balcony I could see my husband and my child dancing to music that was no longer dangerous. I so wanted to believe that we could do what we pleased.

"The Soviet Union is false and rotten," Gosha continued. "But Russia is not. Somewhere under the lies and the paranoia is our home. Our *rodina*."

I didn't know what to think of his uncharacteristic sentimentality. It was gone in a flash, replaced with sarcasm: "You've done your part protecting the Motherland, Sveta. I do my part sucking at her tit."

"It's not a joke, Gosha," I said. "Times have changed. The thaw is over and the hardliners are back. They tossed Nikita Khrushchev out on his ass and they won't suffer fools like you."

My voice was shrill, but I wasn't sure if it was anger or the surprise at finding myself scared for the first time in a long time. "You think it's a game? Even after Butyrskaya Prison? Do you? You know that Brezhnev has authorized the Supreme Court to give the death sentence for currency speculation? Currency speculation, Gosha! Child's play, I'm guessing, compared to the 'seasonal business' you specialize in."

"Don't talk to me about child's play, Sveta."

"Why are we already fighting?"

"Because you are making assumptions about my character that you know are not warranted."

"No," I said, shaking my head. "Because I worry about you."

Vitya opened the balcony door and blocked the cold with his body.

"Here's the plan, kids," he said, clapping his hands once for emphasis. "Sveta, darling, come in and take the baby and let poor Gosha escape from this hellish domestic bliss, would ya? Gosha—you and me are going to take the rest of that bottle to the bathhouse on Sandunovsky—the best *banya* in the city. You need a good shvitz to remind you that Moscow is where you are meant to be. Hurry up, now! Chop-chop!"

He did a two-step and closed the door. Gosha was laughing.

"What's funny?"

"He doesn't know that in fact, the finest *banya* in the city? It's in Butyrskaya Prison. Swear to God."

TWENTY-THREE
CHOICE

*A*rkady Danilov had been the artistic director of the Bolshoi Ballet for an entire season when I demanded a meeting with him. He had probably gone head-to-head with a number of headstrong ballerinas while I was on maternity leave, and won. But there was no way I was leaving his office without the thing I came for.

"Director Danilov. I was three months pregnant when I last danced this role. I drew wonderful reviews. I am still the youngest soloist in the company. The most convincing 'maiden' among us, even if I do have a child. You will have to come up with another excuse."

"Excuse," mumbled the artistic director, tugging on his trimly manicured beard. I saw his eyes on my legs, which were crossed and bare. I uncrossed and recrossed them, right over left, flashing a red spot where my knee had rested on my thigh. I felt Danilov react. A bull to a red flag. Then I felt him freeze. A bull facing a red flag . . . in a minefield.

"There was never any thought to depriving you of the role, Svetlana Evgenievna. I assure you, your wishes need only to be made known. You see, my understanding was that you favor the role of Juliet. And of course, with *Swan Lake* and *Coppélia* and *Giselle*, well, that's an awful lot of leads."

He continued to talk, offering excuses for his decision to cast Bibikova as the Chosen One in the upcoming run of *The Rite of Spring*.

I was listening, but I was not hearing. I was seeing. It had returned suddenly from a long dormancy—my ability to see memories. And what I saw now as Arkady Danilov explained to me his responsibility as the artistic director of the Bolshoi Ballet, was a boy in the throes of puberty visiting his grand-parents on a farm outside Voronezh. I saw little Arkady on the back of a tractor, exhilarated in equal parts by the machine between his legs, the magnificent bull snorting impatiently on the other side of the fence, and the pretty girl perched on that fence, midway between the tractor and the bull, watching.

The room was silent. I realized that he had stopped talking and that he, too, was distracted. I uncrossed my legs and coaxed the memory from my mind to his.

"I appreciate your concern for the troupe," I said. "And I agree that there must be fairness in the casting. But *The Rite* is the most modern ballet in our repertoire. I need it to estab-lish the versatility expected from a prima."

"Ah yes. The question of your promotion." He licked his lips. He took a sip from the glass of water on his desk.

"I am not in a hurry, Comrade Danilov," I assured him. "I am still young. But as you know, even before you arrived I was on the prima track. I have made two foreign tours, three premieres, countless command performances. It would be unseemly if, once the Ministry of Culture Committee on Resi-dential Assignments authorizes my spot in an apartment in the Stalinscraper on the embankment, I was not, in fact, a merited artist."

I could still feel the momentum of the tractor, the distraction of the girl, the menace of the bull.

"Arkady," I said, skipping the formal address.

"So you are saying . . ." he ventured, a man snapped from a trance.

"You are in charge, Comrade Danilov. I am sure you know what you are doing."

He nodded, stupidly. "You will dance the Chosen One again this spring, Svetlana Evgenievna."

He looked vaguely surprised at what had transpired. But he was not nearly as surprised as I was. I walked all the way home, telling myself that just because my long-dormant mental powers seemed to have awoken, I didn't necessarily have to do anything about them.

LESS THAN A MONTH later, I received an unexpected visitor. Unexpected, but somehow, given my experience in Danilov's office, not surprising.

I was in my dressing room at the end of a matinee performance of *The Rite of Spring*. I was wishing I hadn't demanded it back, the role of the girl sacrificed to protect the earth. To say that it hit a nerve—the tragedy implicit in the honor of being chosen for such a fate—would be simplistic. I simply felt that I had grown out of the role. I wished I had left it behind me, as I had left Juliet and the Sugar Plum Fairy.

I told myself to stop being so particular about my roles. Why should I care that Coppélia was a doll controlled by a puppet master? Six and a half years had passed since there had been strings attached to my career and I would soon be a prima. Ballets were all just stories, after all. *Skazki*. Fairy tales.

I wiped the red rouge circles from my cheeks. A warm front had moved in from the west, and all I was thinking of was the coming weekend, which I would spend with Viktor and Marina at the *dacha*. We would clean out the cobwebs and plant early bulbs. We would bring the stereo and listen to music and eat breakfast in the garden.

When in walked Comrade Gerasova.

I froze, a set of false eyelashes in my hand.

The former KGB boss placed a bouquet of roses on the table.

"You are surprised to see me," she said, sitting heavily in the chair next to me.

"I am, of course. But it's a pleasant surprise." I covered this lie with a thick layer of cold cream.

"You must have thought I was gone for good. Along with the rest of Khrushchev's closest officers."

"I heard that, yes." I watched her closely in the mirror. She had aged. Not badly, just inevitably. I wondered where she had been all this time. Surely nowhere worse than where she had met my mother so many years ago. Even if she had fallen afoul of the authorities, I thought, she would probably have been merely exiled to the countryside. Even felons under Brezhnev, I had learned from Gosha, had access to a good *banya*.

"It was a setback, the turnover," she said, referring to the change in the Kremlin four years earlier. "But I still serve the Security Apparatus. I was, in effect, demoted. But I still serve the Motherland. In a different capacity."

I was sincerely glad that she hadn't been subjected to further repression, I was—but I didn't like where the conversation was headed.

I said, "We are all obliged to change roles from time to time, Natalia Davydovna."

"Yes. Well. The fact is, I want my job back. You see, we made a great deal of progress in 1717 after your departure, Svetlana. Some very important projects with highly sensitive data were interrupted when Brezhnev took power. And frankly, he is jeopardizing state security by . . ."

I turned to cut her off decisively. "I don't wish to hear any more. Perhaps in the halls of Lubyanka it is acceptable, even appropriate, to question the policies and the personalities in the Kremlin. But this is the Bolshoi Theatre. And we do not discuss such things."

Her face was impassive. I had nearly forgotten how unflappable she was. It was not by giving up that Natalia Davydovna Gerasova had made it from the Gulag to Lubyanka.

"You're right," she said. "I didn't come to ensnare you in politics. I came to tell you this: your country still needs you. The enemy is no less determined and no less wily than when you left us. Moreover, your potential service to your Motherland is much greater now than it was when you were sixteen years old."

I leaned forward and lowered my voice. "I gave you three years. I won't give you more. I served my Motherland and now I am a mother. You, of all people, should understand how important it is for me to be my daughter's protector and a constant presence."

My voice choked, but I wasn't finished: "Do you remember when you agreed to let me go? Do you remember why you did? Because you saw as clearly as I did that I had served the *rodina* not by spying or meditating or whatever else it was that your team at 1717 thought they could train me to do—but by dancing. I owe the *rodina* nothing more than my unwavering loyalty to my art and to my unstinting performance onstage. *That* is what is greater now, Comrade Gerasova—not my potential, but my actual power. I am a star of the Bolshoi now. This is not a cover. Do you understand?"

"Of course I do. That is why I am here."

"I will not be part of your experiments."

"I don't want you as a subject, Svetlana Evgenievna."

"Then why are you here?"

"Because I need my job. I need to continue my work. To protect the state. To do so, I must be validated. And you, Svetlana, have validity. Like it or not, you are the kind of person who confers . . . importance."

"You came to ask me to recommend you," I clarified.

"If you were to make an appearance, even a symbolic one, at 1717 . . ."

"You told me I would never return."

"That was true at the time. The truth changes, Svetlana; I don't need to tell you that. Today the truth is different. If you were to cross the threshold, just to confirm that you once straddled that line . . ." She didn't finish the thought. "We all operate in our separate arenas, Svetlana Evgenievna. But only some arenas have room for queens. Queens can make generals. Queens can raise the fallen and bestow them with medals. You are a queen. A queen on the Bolshoi stage."

I shook my head. I considered accusing her of counterrevolutionary thought, but that was as absurd as what she was suggesting herself: that I might feel obliged to raise a fallen general.

"I have your father's file. Come back to Lubyanka and I will give it to you."

I closed my eyes and cursed the memories: Of generals and maestros, arms raised in surrender or in command. Of queens who have lost their minds. Of queens who have lost their heads. I allowed myself to become Prima, but I would not be used as a pawn. I had accepted the obscurity of the past to do so, and I did not need to challenge that now.

I wiped the cold cream from my face and said, "I will never set foot in Lubyanka 1717 again."

Gerasova left without another word. When the door closed behind her, I realized two things: even as a prima, I would still be Prima. Even as a queen, I might never be free.

Because a queen can be captured, just like a pawn.

I WAS STILL RATTLED when I arrived at the entrance of the majestic Stalinscraper on the embankment. I was no longer a teenager. I was quite capable of balancing my roles as wife, mother, and star of the stage. But my encounter with Gerasova had reprised a bitter role that had been stolen from me: that of a loving and beloved daughter.

I turned the key in the ignition and, in the hermetic quiet of the car, I allowed myself to remember. Not my father, the secrets of whose death may or may not have been in Gerasova's possession. It was my mother I was remembering. In particular, the day that my mother stepped aside and let the Motherland take over. The day I had fled from a frightening hallucination on the Bolshoi stage and my mother had sent a chief of intelligence to find me.

What sort of mother gives her daughter to the Motherland?

What sort of Motherland depends on orphaned children for its protection?

I rolled down the window and breathed the first warm shoots of spring. I imagined the delight on my little Marina's face when, tomorrow morning, we would wake to birdsong and run barefoot through the thin layer of mud that was Russia, thawed. I stepped out of the car and gathered my bags from the backseat. I climbed the stairs to the elegant marble foyer. I hadn't yet gotten used to its luxury.

"Good day, Svetlana Evgenievna," said the eagle-eyed lady whose job was to notice everyone and everything that passed the threshold.

"I've left my car in the drive," I said. "We will be leaving for the *dacha* tonight."

"Very good, Svetlana Evgenievna."

I stepped into the elevator and pushed the button for the eighth floor. My spirits rose with the lift. By the time I slid open the gleaming door of the cage and stepped onto the private landing, I was again focused on the present.

"I'm home," I called.

Viktor called from the kitchen: "Gosha dropped off fresh lamb kebabs and a brand-new icebox for the *dacha*. We can make ice cream!"

"Mama, look at me," came a tinkling voice in response.

I turned and saw my daughter balanced on the tiptoes of the cleaning woman's clogs. She was miming the steps of the dance of the little swans.

TWENTY-FOUR
NEW YEAR'S, 1970

It was a quarter to nine and Viktor was only half dressed. I was in the hallway, untangling my long, looping earrings. The gala began in fifteen minutes, which meant I should make my entrance in an hour. Prima ballerinas must have perfect timing, especially when they are late.

"Vitya, darling, please," I said, finding him lying on the sofa in the big room.

"Almost. We're almost done."

Marya was straddling her father. She had completely unbuttoned his tuxedo shirt and was putting the finishing touches on his naked chest with a fistful of markers.

"Dear God, Vitya—what have you . . ."

"Fireworks, Mama," Marya answered for him.

"In case it's overcast," explained Viktor. "I'll flash my own personal New Year's salute." He addressed our daughter seriously. "Should we draw some on my tush?"

Marina dissolved in giggles. I pulled her from her perch and marched her into her room.

"You're gonna get it worse, Papa," she sulked from the doorway.

She was right. She knew a kettle about to blow.

I yelled at him. I yelled "Infantile!" and "Jackass!" and "On my most important night!"

Dyadya Gosha arrived in the nick of time.

"You better wear a thick undershirt, old man," he said when he saw Marina's work. Viktor headed for the bathroom. Marya came running out of her exile and jumped into Gosha's arms. She picked his pockets clean and when he sat her down on the sofa, her mouth was full of chocolate creams. He took off his cap and handed me the small packet wrapped in tissue paper he had hidden underneath it.

"Happy New Year, Sveta."

I wrapped my arms around his neck. "Tonight they make me a prima, Gosha."

"Huge," he whispered. "Colossal. A dream come true."

"I wish you could come," I said as I pulled away from him and adjusted the silk wrap over my arms.

"No, you don't." He was smiling. There was no bitterness or cynicism on this, my most important night. "You might wish I could take Viktor's place because I don't have fireworks on my belly. But you know I'd cause you more shame than even his technicolor torso."

"Not shame," I said softly.

"Problems."

I looked down at my daughter, who had stopped chewing to listen to the heaviness of our silence.

"Should I open it?" I asked, holding up the packet.

"Yes!" she shouted.

I looked at Gosha.

"Makes no difference. I'm not one for ceremony, Sveta. That's your territory." He bent down and tickled Marina's chin. "Who's going to eat fried potatoes and stay up till midnight with her Uncle Gosha, huh?"

A HALF HOUR LATER, Svetlana and Viktor Dukovsky were announced in the grand ballroom of the Hotel Metropol, across Teatralnaya Square from the Bolshoi Theatre.

I dazzled the room. Vitya charmed his tablemates. Through-out the gala dinner in honor of the new decade and the newest prima ballerina of the Bolshoi Ballet, a golden tiara glittered in my hair.

And no one noticed the tiny slip of tissue paper caught in its clasp.

INTERLUDE
VORKUTA 2015

*M*arina Dukovskaya lands in Siberia six hours after boarding the plane in Moscow. In those six hours, Lana had been reliving the first six years of her mother's life. Now they embrace each other in Vorkuta's airport.

"I don't remember what she looks like," Marina says as she waits with her daughter at the bus stop.

"She looks like the babushka in a skazka," says Lana. "Small, magical . . . an old soul in a modern-day fairy tale."

"How is it that she hid for so long?"

"That's how skazki begin: Long, long ago in a kingdom far, far away . . ."

"Russian fairy tales are horrible. They never have happy endings."

Lana takes her mother's hand and squeezes it. "This one's not over yet."

She sits on the bench and pulls Marina down, too.

"Do you remember drawing on your father's belly with markers?"

Marina smiles, shakes her head no.

"Do you remember a golden tiara?"

Marina nods. *"Her prized possession."*

"And the first time you went to the Bolshoi?"

"Swan Lake. Sveta was the White Swan."

"And your first class as a student at the Academy?"

"I was nine. Mama was already an Artist of the People."

"And did you know that she had once been an Enemy of the People?"

Marina frowns. *"Once. Once upon a time . . . what do you mean 'once'? She was arrested on November 10, 1982, the same day Brezhnev died. I remember it clearly. I had to walk home alone from the theater. But before I did, I had a vision, a premonition. I thought I saw her, aged and disgraced. Two days later it came true. They found her wandering the grounds of a secret laboratory. She was out of her head, saying she had proof of a terrible state secret. Human trials. Biological weapons. She was institutionalized. She was branded an enemy. Overnight from Artist of the People to Enemy of the People. Pop and I had no choice but to flee."*

Lana turns to face her mother. *"Ma,"* she says. *"Before that— long before you and your father had to defect—Svetlana was already branded. Her parents were Enemies of the People under Stalin, three decades earlier. She was a ward of the state, Ma—the daughter of Enemies of the People. Her fate went full circle."*

For a moment the only response comes from the grasshoppers in the fields around them.

"She told you that?"

"She did."

"She never told me that."

"She wouldn't have."

Lana steps out into the street and sees the dust of an approaching bus.

"I'm not sure what chapter we are on, Ma. Fairy tales aren't big on foreshadowing. Skazki sometimes have surprises."

The bus pulls to a stop. Marina and Lana climb on board, take a seat, and head back into town for the last chapter of the *Dukovskaya skazka.*

FINALE
MOSCOW TO VORKUTA, 1982–2015

November dusk crept into Moscow like a spy. I didn't even notice it until it had stolen the day and vanished into the night. By then, I, too, was gone.

Svetlana Dukovskaya was in a cell in Lubyanka. It had held thousands of innocent prisoners, but she was guilty as charged: She had trespassed. She had agitated. She had revealed state secrets. She was unstable.

The secrets were ones that the state had taught her to reveal. Here—in this very building. Twenty years ago. She had stumbled, unescorted, into the psychosphere of Lubyanka. She had penetrated a whitewashed wall of memories and seen horrible truths about what the state did to its people.

Worse than torture, worse than terror—the Motherland had been conducting human experiments. Not efforts to make psychically-empowered operatives like Agent Prima more powerful; experiments that brutalized and disposed of ordinary, unknowing comrades.

I held my head in my hands and whispered: "I remember your crimes. I remember what you did to us."

A quarter century after it was first created, the Psychological Intelligence Unit was a much larger apparatus. It had moved out of the shadows and out of the limited quarters of 1717 to occupy three wings of the fourth floor of Lubyanka. It was run now by Colonel Maksim Naryshkin, who had steered the Unit's work into new waters: Maksim had turned psychological intelligence into psychiatric experimentation. He was finding ways to create psychosis in order to treat it. In order to punish it.

When Svetlana Dukovskaya contacted Natalia Davydovna just before New Year's to say that she was willing to support the unit's work for a limited time and under specific conditions, Colonel Naryshkin demanded that he have access to his former test subject.

I knew, from the moment I walked into his laboratory, that he was the wolf. Maksim was the wolf at the door that I had feared since I was a ward of the state.

Svetlana was bound by a contract, but not by her conscience. When Gerasova said she would insulate her from Maksim, Svetlana said, "Just live up to your part of the deal." But when the older woman handed her the thin file marked Kravshin, Evgeny, Svetlana said, "Aren't you ashamed, Natalia Davydovna. You know as well as I do that these are nothing but papers. Falsified, erased, fabricated. These are papers. Not my father."

My mother, Vera Kravshina, used to tell a story about a pianist she knew in the camps. A marvelous musician, she said, who had lost her whole family in Stalin's terror but endured on the comfort of her music. One day, the guards told the woman she would give a camp-wide music recital. The pianist stood before her fellow inmates—proud and happy. Her eyes, I am sure, saw footlights and ladies in evening wear, instead of prisoners in quilted coats. She approached the old instrument in the drafty hall as if it were a grand piano in the Conservatory. She seated herself at the bench, stretched her hands wide, and lifted the cover. But you see, someone had decided to repair the piano ahead of the recital. And that someone had removed the clavichord and had not replaced it in time, and when that pianist, already fragile and damaged, saw nothing but a void, well—her soul and her sanity disappeared with those eighty-eight keys.

No. Of course I didn't dare open the file. Did I want to see the erased person that was my father? Did I want to see the empty place where his soul should have been? Did I want to throw my sanity into that void, too?

Svetlana had seen Maksim's work. She had seen it askance and she had seen it directly and she had seen what it had done to men and women, who were not called "comrades" but "subjects" and "patients." And even though Svetlana Dukovskaya was an Artist of the People and the Queen of the Bolshoi, she knew she had to pretend not to see . . . or she would be captured. A queen, become a pawn. So for months, Maksim and the agent once called Prima cooperated formally, while battling silently.

"Pictures, Svetlana Evgenievna. Pictures of my enemies in compromised positions. Perhaps with a lovely member of the corps looking for advancement?"

Because Colonel Naryshkin worried that someone would interfere with his work. And the only way to be sure that no one interfered with his work was to make sure that there was no one who could interfere with his work. He would topple everyone who stood in his way. He had an Artist of the People as a weapon.

"*Give me names.*"
She gave him initials.
"*Give me photos.*"
She gave him programs, playbills, autographs.
He ordered that the Agent once known as Prima undergo psychiatric evaluation. She balked. She faltered. She barged into Gerasova's office to protest and learned that Natalia Davydovna had been sent to a sanatorium after an episode of nervous psychosis. Svetlana panicked.
"*Let me out,*" *she begged.*

And the wolf said, "I'll huff and I'll puff" . . . and I said, "oh no you don't, you are the gray wolf of the *skazka* and I will ride you to the cage of the phoenix, and I will deliver the golden egg and you will let me go."

"*Give me something on Lukino. You give me something on Lukino and you will have fulfilled the terms of your agreement.*"
Svetlana stood. She reached across the desk and shook his hand. Lukino was the laboratory where her husband Viktor worked. Vitya knew no secrets, of this she was sure. Vitya was not even entirely sure what the laboratory, located in an off-limits zapretnaya zona and classified as top secret, produced to warrant its status. He rode the suburban train to a forbidden zone, flashed a pass, and crunched numbers daily. He did it with the same habit that his wife flashed her pass at the Bolshoi Theatre. But he was a nobody. She was a somebody.
She was a queen who had been captured and could only escape by trespassing a zapretnaya zona—a forbidden zone.
That night she lay next to her husband and tapped into his psychosphere.

On a spring night in 1978, the village of Lukino was poisoned. The whole village—deliberately—poisoned. Because they wanted to know: What would happen? What would happen if the whole village of Lukino took a deep breath of something that kept them from breathing again? Because that's what the Motherland needs. Something to keep our enemies from breathing. And we might just have it, in that little laboratory. Something called anthrax. Yes. And so the wolf huffed and he puffed and he blew aerosolized anthrax down everyone's house.

That night Svetlana Dukovskaya remembered something that happened three years earlier, and not to her. She remembered an experiment authorized not by Maksim, head of treatment at the Committee for State Security's Psychological Intelligence Unit, but by one of his political rivals—a man who ran a biological weapons lab on the outskirts of Moscow in a place called Lukino. During this experiment, hundreds of people who lived and worked in the shadow of a secret laboratory they knew nothing about had died agonizing deaths. Agonizing, but not pointless. They had proven the effectiveness of a new biological weapon called anthrax.

There were orphans among the dead. There were dancers among the dead.

Perhaps that was why Svetlana Dukovskaya, an orphaned ballerina, on a November night three years later, had no difficulty remembering their deaths. She remembered something that had not happened to her, but now—it was. It was happening to her.

The memory tripped a wire. With the force of an electric shock, Svetlana experienced the dreadful breadth and disregard with which the Soviet Union had always treated its people, pawns in the pursuit of superior nuclear, chemical, biological, and, yes, psychological weapons. Victims of a constant pursuit of a brighter future.

She sat up, slick with sweat, and hurried to the bed of her sleeping daughter, Marina. She did not wake her. Just sat by her side, despairing. Because if she didn't cry wolf, there could be no bright future . . . for anyone.

I went to Vitya. I shook him and hissed in his ear: *Vitya, Vitya, Vitya.* But he stroked my hair like the flanks of a horse and I couldn't tell who was more nervous. *It's okay Sveta, ni slova Sveta.* So I went to Natalia and she was in a hospital bed and her face was not impassive and for the first time I read all her fears and she said *ni slova* and all eighty-eight keys were gone when she opened her mouth, empty of teeth and advice and promises and sanity.

Not a word. *Ni slova.* Cue the maestro. Ready the guns.

Desperate, Svetlana wondered if she should tell Maksim, but when she stood outside his door she was overwhelmed by more memories. Deliberate exposures from just behind the door—electric shock, experimental drugs, hallucino-genic injections, mental torture. Her own.

I was a victim? I was a pawn. I was the maestro, holding a baton. I looked at my hands, covered in blood. I refused to wash them. I went to Lukino and rattled the gate with my bloody *port de bras.*

On November 10, 1982, Svetlana Dukovskaya paraded her knowledge through the corridors of Lubyanka and then fled to Lukino, where she was detained and arrested and informed that she had committed a crime against the state. She knew it. As well as she knew that the state had committed a crime against her and every-one she had ever loved. She knew her mind was not her

*own. It had been removed for repairs, like the keyboard
in a ghostly hall.*

They tampered with my memories. They messed with my
mind. They weaponized me in a war against my people. I was in
a cell in Lubyanka. It had held thousands of innocent prisoners,
but I was guilty as charged: I had trespassed. I had agitated. I
had revealed state secrets. I was unstable.

*That same night, the Kremlin bells tolled in mourning for
Leonid Brezhnev, the General Secretary of the Communist
Party and leader of the Soviet Union for eighteen years.
Only three people knew that the bells marked the end of
another era—the one in which eighteen-year-old Marina
Dukovskaya had lived a happy life of privilege, anticipat-
ing a bright future.*

*Svetlana Dukovskaya was en route to a psychiatric hos-
pital in Siberia—a facility that Colonel Maksim Naryshkin
administered from his large office in Lubyanka. He authorized the clinicians to use "all means" to extract Svetlana's
secrets and then silence her. Then he turned his attention
to Svetlana's daughter, Marina, and her husband, Viktor.
But it was too late—they were already in flight to the West,
facilitated by a known parasite named Georgi Levshik.*

The wolf had blown down my house. No. I blew down my
house. I huffed and I puffed . . . and where is the phoenix in this
endless *skazka*?

* * *

"BUT YOU DIDN'T HAVE to do it! No one made you do it.
That's what you are telling us."

"Ma. Mama." It is Lana who puts a hand on Marina's shoulder. "You must listen."

But Marina, a woman who had refused to believe that her mother was dead, is finally surrendering to decades of bereavement. Svetlana Dukovskaya has just confessed that she allowed herself—even volunteered herself, a queen—to be made into a pawn.

"Why did you do it?" she pleads, tears spilling down her cheeks. "Why did you go back? Why did you agree? You threw it all away—not just your career, but our lives. You put Pop and me in danger. You made us run from our home, our lives. You did that! You forced us to leave our *rodina*, abandon the Motherland! What were you thinking?"

Svetlana blinks under the onslaught. Lana wavers in the doorway.

"Not what I was thinking," says the old woman. "What I was seeing."

"But that's just it," Marina insists. "I saw things, too. Maybe not what you saw, but I had nightmares, too. I saw your fate. I saw it—just as clearly as I saw Pop's death. I saw both those things before they happened. And I want to know why you let . . ."

"You blame me."

Marina is sobbing. Svetlana is cowering. Lana is frozen in the doorway, wondering what she has done.

"Of course I do!"

"Mama. Don't. She's not strong enough . . ."

"The hell I'm not," says Svetlana. But she has already staggered to the floor.

SVETLANA SLEEPS THROUGH THE night and much of the next morning. Marina paces the small apartment and takes long walks through the weedy lanes of Vorkuta. Lana rummages through the ephemera of her grandmother's long exile. She is looking for the answer to her mother's first question: *How did she stay hidden for so long?*

When she finally wakes, Svetlana shuffles into the kitchen

and sees the two younger women at her table. She clasps her hands—Juliet in prayer—and says, "I dreamt you left me."

Marina rises and wraps her mother in her arms. She doesn't say anything about anyone leaving anyone else. She is hoping that her mother's enslaved memories have forgotten the things she said last night.

But Svetlana has not forgotten.

"I know how it feels, *dochka*." She sits at the table and folds her hands. "I never forgave my mother. They let her come back to me; I didn't trust her. She tried to make it right; I didn't thank her. I buried her in the ground, and I still didn't forgive her. They killed my father, too. He might not have been as innocent as Viktor. Vitya, my lovely Vitya. He was harmless. And gentle. But my father . . . I don't know."

She crushes a grain of sugar under her thumb.

"Pop loved you very much," Marina says. "He never accepted that you were gone."

Now Lana speaks. "You didn't either, Ma. Tell her. You never believed that Svetlana was dead."

There was more about that, she thought. But how could she explain to this old woman that Viktor's obsession with Svetlana had driven him to an early death? Or that Marina's determination to find her mother had made her leave Lana's father? There's no room for those stories. There is no room for those men. There is only room in this kitchen for the women—the three of them, the daughters, the survivors of their family tragedy.

"Marina never gave up, *babushka*," Lana says. "As soon as it was possible, she came back and looked for you. We both wish that you had made it easier to find you."

The old woman doesn't answer. Marina looks uncomfortable, like she wants to flee the small kitchen and escape to the Siberian steppe, where the vastness hides more than a single old woman. Lana has seen her mother destroyed by loss. Now she wants a truth that might heal her.

"I know that you knew, *babushka*. You told me. You could

use a computer. You could find out. You knew that your daughter was alive and living in Moscow. I've seen the binders under your bed. The printed pages from the Internet . . ."

Marina's eyes fill with tears. "It doesn't matter. We're together now, *dochka*."

"It does matter," Lana insists. "Grandmother," she says gently but firmly. "Why didn't you come back to your daughter? Why didn't you leave this place when they finally released you and find Marina?"

Now it is Svetlana who weeps.

"I told you. Because I never forgave my mother. I thought Marya would never forgive me."

Truth fills the room like a summer breeze. Like the internal music of a certain *Doctor Zhivago*. Three generations of Dukovskayas. Three women robbed of their fathers, hobbled by their mothers, left on their own. Three injured dancers—prisoners, pawns, and devoted acolytes of the Bolshoi Ballet.

Lana stretches her arms along the edge of the circular table. The three women join hands. They are still not round, they are still not whole. They are a tight triangle—stable and supported. They are, all of them, forgiven. They sit for a long time as the insects outside sing songs older than fairy tales.

* * *

SVETLANA DUKOVSKAYA IS LAID to rest two months later. She is buried in the same Moscow cemetery as her mother, though Vera Konstantinovna's grave is an anonymous plot, while Svetlana Evgenievna's has an engraved stone in a parcel reserved for prestige.

Lana kneels and traces the epitaph for her grandmother, who has risen from a fall from grace for the last time.

SVETLANA DUKOVSKAYA, 1944–2015
ARTIST OF THE PEOPLE

Only the second date is fresh. The grave was erected long ago by someone who had believed that the ballerina was already gone. Or wanted to believe it.

"Was it Gosha who put up the headstone?" asks Lana.

"Who knows. Gosha did many things, I think, in those days after we fled," says Marina.

"He was trying to protect you."

"Yes. He probably saved my life. And perhaps . . . perhaps he saved my mother's, such as it was."

Lana had met this "Uncle Gosha" briefly in New York a year ago, on the same trip that had finally revealed her own father and the black spot that was Marina's childhood. Now she wondered what Georgi Levshik might say if he could be here. If he had not died in the spring, having made his peace with Marina, the girl he loved as much as he'd loved her mother.

"Do you still blame Dyadya Gosha for your father's death?" she asks.

"Lana, darling. If we've learned nothing at all, we have learned that there is no blame worth nursing in our family."

A small, muddy backhoe rattles through the arch in the ancient brick wall. "Dukovskaya?" calls the driver.

Marina nods and the man maneuvers the machine into position. The coffin is already in place, waiting for its cover of earth.

"Wait!"

Lana hurries up to the backhoe.

"Could you give us just a moment?" The man shrugs and pulls a packet of cigarettes from his shirt.

Lana returns to her mother and asks: "Is there anything else?"

Marina knits her brows. "What do you mean?"

"Is there anything . . . that still bothers you? Is there anything you wish you knew? Anything that would comfort you? And her?"

One minute passes. Another begins.

"I wish I knew why she went back," Marina says finally. "I'm not like her. If you gave me the KGB file on Svetlana Dukovskaya,

I would read it. I want to know what she did and why. Why she let herself be a pawn when she had already been granted her freedom. I wish I knew what would make her do that."

The man with the backhoe stumps out his cigarette, coughs.

Lana is still uncertain, after all these weeks, if she is doing the right thing: she pulls a folded piece of paper from her purse and hands it to Marina.

"I found it in the binder, under the bed. She must have done a better job plumbing the KGB archives than any of us. But I guess she also knew where to look."

Marina unfolds the document. Another minute passes as she reads it. Lana watches her mother grapple with another unarmed truth.

Finally Marina hands the paper back.

"For Gosha. She did it for Gosha."

Lana breathes. "Is that okay?"

Like sunrise in the desert, the truth transforms the landscape. Marina's acceptance is full of grace.

"Yes. It's okay. He's the only one. The only who knew all her secrets. The only one who knew her. It's okay."

Marina Dukovskaya walks to the open grave and drops the folded piece of paper onto the coffin below. She nods to the waiting workman, who climbs into his cab and shovels dirt into the grave.

Marina takes Lana's hand as they watch the burial of a true Russian: a body, a soul, and a single paper.

Affidavit

I, Svetlana Dukovskaya, Prima Ballerina of the Bolshoi Ballet
and Artist of the People, hereby agree to serve the Psychological
Intelligence Unit of the Committee for State Security under the
directorate of Major Maksim Vladimirovich Naryshkin.

It is understood that my services are voluntary and subject to
strict State control. I agree to abide by protocols of top secret
classified intelligence gathering. My services will terminate with
the discretion of the Directorate's Governing Committee upon
completion of the Directorate's determined information quota.

It is further understood that the prisoner Georgi Ivanovich
Levshik, sentenced to death by shooting under Article 154 of
the Soviet Criminal Code for engaging in large-scale profiteering,
speculation, and economic crimes against the state, will be freed
on signature of this document.

Signed on this day, 31 December 1981,
by Svetlana Evgenievna Dukovskaya

GLOSSARY OF RUSSIAN WORDS

Baba Yaga—the witch in many Russian fairy tales

babushka, (babushki, pl.)—grandmother, old woman

banya—bath, sauna

chort/k chortu—devil/to the devil; an expletive or rude dismissal

dacha—country house

devushka, (devushki, pl.)—girl, girls

dochka—daughter

dyadya—uncle

grazhdanka—citizen

Gulag—the Soviet prison camp network

kommunalka—Communal apartment, common in the Soviet Union

Komsomol—Communist Youth organization

krisa—rat

milaya—adj. sweet, term of affection

muzhik (muzhiki, pl.)—a peasant, colloquially a good guy with simple tastes

nepriyatnosti—unpleasantness

ni slova—not a word

nyetu/nyet—none/no

ochi chornye—"Dark Eyes"; a popular Russian song

platzkart—lowest class of travel on a passenger train

Pobeda—victory, also the brand of Soviet manufactured automobile

poshi—let's go

rodina—Motherland, homeland, birthplace

skazka, (skazki, pl.)—fairy tale

stilyaga (stilyagi, pl.)—"style seeker," hipster, a counterculture group of Soviet youth

svoloch—swine, bastard

vor v zakone—literally, "thief of the code," part of a crime family

zapretnaya zona—forbidden zone

zdravstvuy/zdrastvuyte—hello (formal and informal)

AUTHOR'S NOTE

ORPHAN, AGENT, PRIMA, PAWN is a work of fiction.

When I began writing this prequel—book one in the Bolshoi Saga—it didn't occur to me that I might have to make such an overt disclaimer. I thought, in fact, that I would end the book with a note revealing that some of the more far-out elements of Svetlana Dukovskaya's story—rock and roll bootlegs recorded on x-ray film; the daughter of an Enemy of the People becoming a medaled Artist of the People; a poet treated as an ideological weapon of the Cold War; spies trained to tap into the psychosphere—are actually based on true events.

But then Donald Trump invited Russian hackers to launch a cyber-war against his opponent. And then President-elect Trump made it clear that he thinks more of Russia's intelligence agencies than his own. When, in the midst of a disorienting and bizarre reversal of traditional beliefs on geopolitical strategy, the President of the United States proudly called his relationship with our historic foe an "asset" (a term with a very specific meaning in espionage parlance), I just about fell out of my chair. My once fantastical storyline about Russian mind-hackers had been Trumped!

So now I can only remind my readers that long before "Cozy Bear" and "Fancy Bear" (Google them! And while you are at it Google "psychosphere" and "Putin" or "Gerasimov Doctrine" and you might understand where Sveta's spymaster got her name), before Donald Trump and Vladimir Putin together rewrote the rule book on misinformation, disinformation and FAKE NEWS!, before all this outrageousness that is either the dawn of a wonderful Russian/American détente or the beginning of Cold War 2.0, there was the first Cold War and the period that Sveta would have known as the Thaw.

That era, the decade following the death of Soviet dictator Joseph Stalin, was a time of cultural and social relaxation, but also of increased paranoia about the intentions of the West. It was a period when Russians became less terrified of their government, but also less certain of their faith in their Motherland. It is a fascinating time in Russian history and a fine backdrop for a story about family secrets.

So for those readers who would like to spend a bit more time in Svetlana's Cold War or explore Moscow during the Thaw, I recommend the following books:

I, Maya Plisetskaya by Maya Plisetskaya
Hustling on Gorky Street by Yuri Brokhin
Symphony for the City of the Dead by M.T. Anderson
Doctor Zhivago by Boris Pasternak
Twilight of the Eastern Gods by Ismail Kadare
Red Plenty by Francis Spufford

These titles are evenly divided between the fiction and nonfiction shelves. But I am confident that each of the authors took liberties with history. Because sometimes fact is not just stranger than fiction, it is also harder to pin down.

Elizabeth Kiem
London, March 2017